**Praise for Heather Blake's
Wishcraft Mystery Series**

A Witch Before Dying

"*A Witch Before Dying* by Heather Blake is quite simply a fantastic read from cover to cover. It's a magical tale, but it's also a very human one, and it's a perfect companion for the lazy, magical, seemingly endless days of summer." —The Season for Romance (top pick)

"*A Witch Before Dying* is a fun twist on typical witchy mysteries . . . with a delightful cast of characters magical, human, and animal." —The Mystery Reader

"Four magic wands for *A Witch Before Dying*—get your copy today!" —MyShelf.com

It Takes a Witch

"Blending magic, romance, and mystery, this is a charming story."
 —*New York Times* bestselling author Denise Swanson

"Magic and murder . . . what could be better? It's exactly the book you've been wishing for!"
 —Casey Daniels, author of *Supernatural Born Killers*

"Blake successfully blends crime, magic, romance, and self-discovery in her lively debut. . . . Fans of paranormal cozies will look forward to the sequel."
 —*Publishers Weekly*

continued . . .

Also by Heather Blake

A Witch Before Dying
It Takes a Witch

The Good, the Bad, and the Witchy

A WISHCRAFT MYSTERY

HEATHER BLAKE

AN OBSIDIAN MYSTERY

OBSIDIAN
Published by the Penguin Group
Penguin Group (USA) Inc., 375 Hudson Street,
New York, New York 10014, USA

USA | Canada | UK | Ireland | Australia | New Zealand | India | South Africa | China

Penguin Books Ltd., Registered Offices: 80 Strand, London WC2R 0RL, England
For more information about the Penguin Group visit penguin.com.

First published by Obsidian, an imprint of New American Library,
a division of Penguin Group (USA) Inc.

First Printing, April 2013
10 9 8 7 6 5 4 3 2 1

OBSIDIAN and logo are trademarks of Penguin Group (USA) Inc.

ISBN 978-0-451-23969-3

Printed in the United States of America

ALWAYS LEARNING   PEARSON

ACKNOWLEDGMENTS

I've said it before, and I'll say it again: I have the best readers ever, whose creativity never ceases to amaze me. So it's no wonder that when I asked for help on social media with certain names for this book, there were so many suggestions that it was hard to choose which to use.

I ended up picking Jennifer W.'s suggestion, via Twitter, of "Stiffington" for Hot Rod's surname and Zuzana U.'s recommendation, via my Facebook page, of "Boo Manor" for the name of the festival's family-friendly haunted house. A big thank-you to both!

If you'd like to follow me (and perhaps help me with another book!) I can be found on Facebook at www.facebook.com/heatherblakebooks and @booksbyheather on Twitter.

Tis the witching hour of night,
Orbed is the moon and bright,
And the stars they glisten, glisten,
Seeming with bright eyes to listen
For what listen they?

John Keats

Chapter One

The longer I lived in the Enchanted Village, the more I realized that not only did magic live here, but also the truly eccentric.

There were some strange, strange people in this neighborhood.

Including eighty-year-old gothic maven Harriette Harkette, who was throwing herself a girls-only birthday party to celebrate the big day. She had hired As You Wish, my aunt Ve's personal concierge service, to plan the black-and-white-themed party—which was taking place tonight.

Ve shouted to be heard above the thumping music. "Are you sure you hired a stripper, Darcy?" She adjusted the black rose floral arrangement on the refreshments table.

The flowers, named Witching Hour roses, were quite stunning. They were midnight black—Harriette's favorite color—and had recently won international awards and acclaim from elite rose societies for being the first naturally black flower ever cultivated. However, the roses still seemed a little morbid to me, the dark color reminding me more of a funeral than a celebration.

Trying to ignore Ve's question, I checked the food

platters. There were plenty of hors d'oeuvres, but the birthday cake, the centerpiece, hadn't yet arrived. I'd give it ten more minutes, then make a call to Evan Sullivan, owner of the local bakery, to see what was holding up the delivery.

A handful of fine lines around Ve's eyes crinkled as she tipped her head and assessed me shrewdly, complete with a narrowed squint and raised coppery eyebrows. The look was softened only by a few long strands of hair that had escaped her ever-present hair clip and framed her round face. "Darcy? The stripper?"

The open bar, across the room, was stacked three to four deep with women waiting for refills. Suddenly, I wanted to join them but instead gave Ve a saucy look. "Don't you trust me?"

Appearance-wise, the only thing my aunt and I had in common was our eye color—blue with gold flecks. I was taller, slimmer, with long dark hair and an oval face. But as for personality? Our stubbornness, evasiveness, and sassiness were a perfect match.

"No," Ve said drily.

She was a smart witch.

The stripper had been a source of contention between us, and I hadn't exactly followed orders as I should have. There was going to be a stripper, yes, but perhaps not the kind of stripper everyone was expecting. . . .

Ve and I were two of the very many women in the party room of the Cauldron, the village's pub. I wasn't sure which was rowdier—the Friday night crowd at the long mahogany bar top or Harriette's group of nearest and dearest girlfriends.

The floor vibrated beneath my feet, a result of the bass being emitted from the deejay's enormous speakers. He looked a little scared as he played "I Will Survive" and women sang along at the top of their lungs while giving him dirty looks, he being the sole man in the room. He tried not to make eye contact as he shouldered the anger of every woman-done-wrong on the dance floor. I noticed Harriette's three best friends (the four women were collectively known as the Wicked Widows–or the Wickeds for short) were singing the loudest, and I suddenly wondered if it was no mistake that they were widowed and not divorced.

But no. That was probably just paranoia whispering in my ear. It had been doing that a lot since the recent murder investigations. Happily, it had been months since I'd been mixed up in a homicide, and personally, I wanted to keep that trend going.

Why this was a girls-only party, I had no idea. Not even Harriette's mysterious new fiancé had been invited. But that may have been because Harriette had insisted we hire a stripper for the party and not—as everyone in the village suspected—that the fiancé was a figment of Harriette's eccentric imagination.

The event definitely had more the feel of a bachelorette party than a birthday bash, which made me question whether Harriette had a surprise wedding planned in the near future. Was this birthday celebration only a ruse to throw herself a bachelorette party without coming out and saying so?

The recent announcement of her engagement had set town tongues wagging. At my sister, Harper's, bookstore, Spellbound Bookshop, a betting pool placed the odds that Harriette had fabricated the existence of the man at three to one. Exactly *why* she would do such a thing remained a mystery, except she was eccentric, but that seemed to be reason enough.

Dressed head to toe in black, one of Harriette's two daughters, Lydia, glowered in the corner, her arms crossed tightly. She didn't appear to be having a good time, but that might have had more to do with the bachelorette-party vibe than anything. Lydia Harkette Wentworth had been quite vocal in her displeasure of her mother's remarriage—and it showed in every deep-set frown line on her face.

I wondered why she'd even come tonight if she was just going to be a sourpuss. It probably wasn't to see the stripper.

Adjusting the belt on a black wrap dress that hugged her many curves, Aunt Ve said, "What are you up to, Darcy Merriweather?"

I fussed with the napkins and checked on my dog, Missy, who was watching the dance floor with anxious eyes, carefully guarding her puppy paws from drunken stilettos. "I don't know what you mean, Ve. I hired a stripper. He'll be here soon."

I hadn't wanted to hire him at all, considering Harriette's age. A twenty-something gyrating exotic dancer might send her right over the hill and into an early grave.

Ve heartily disagreed, and dare I say it? There had been a gleam in her eye that made me suspect she'd been storing up wads of one-dollar bills for tonight's big event.

My aunt also qualified as one of the village's eccentrics.

I set a small dish of water on the floor for Missy. This probably wasn't the best place for her, but with the crowds in the village for the opening night of the Harvest Festival taking place on the public green, I didn't dare leave her home alone. She, a small gray and white Schnoodle (she was a mix of a miniature schnauzer and toy poodle), was the Harry Houdini of dogs, able to shed her collar and escape any enclosure, tether, or cage I put her in. I had yet to figure out how she did it. Tonight, she was better off here, with me, where I could keep an eye on her. The last thing I wanted was for some tourist to think she was a stray and wander off with her.

"How soon?" Ve adjusted her fringed purple scarf and looked around as if she hoped the stripper would stroll through the door at that very minute, thrusting this way and that.

I checked my watch. "Soon."

"Doesn't he need time to oil himself up?" She patted her head, noticed the escaped tresses, and tucked them back into her fancy clip. "I could help with that."

"There's oil involved?" I shuddered. "Wouldn't that make a big mess? Leave stains?"

"This is not the time to be worrying about laundry." Ve laughed. "You've led a sheltered life, Darcy dear."

"You say that like it's a bad thing." But I couldn't argue that it was true. Up until I moved to the village in June, I *had* lived a sheltered life—an unhappy divorcée and the office manager for my father's dental practice in Ohio, I had spent most of my free time keeping tabs on my slightly felonious sister, Harper, and had absolutely no idea I was a *witch*. And that Harper was, too.

All that changed with a visit from Aunt Ve after my father died. And before you could say, "Bippity boppity boo," Harper and I had moved almost a thousand miles to the tourist hot spot of the Enchanted Village, a themed neighborhood of Salem, Massachusetts. A place where magic lived.

Magic, in the form of witches. Or "Crafters" as we're called around these parts (not that mortals knew we existed). Ve, Harper, and I were Wishcrafters—witches with the ability to grant wishes using a special spell. However, there were limitations to our magic, including dozens of rules and regulations we had to follow—the Wishcraft Laws—which were governed by the Craft's secret Elder.

I'd been called before the Elder several times in the past few months for violations. I was really hoping to make it through to New Year's without having to visit with her again. A witch could hope.

I played with long black strands of my dark ponytail as I glanced around at everyone gathered. There was no way to tell mortal from Crafter at first glance—just a telltale eye twitch and village word of mouth. Even after five months of living here, I was still learning who was who, but I knew a good many women in this room had Crafting abilities.

Birthday girl Harriette, a Floracrafter (she'd grown the amazing black roses herself), had yet to arrive.

"It's not necessarily a good thing," Ve said, grabbing my hands. "Especially when you don't know how to throw a party. Alcohol, cake, and a stripper. Done." She twirled me around in a dizzying move. "Oh, and dancing."

Missy barked as if in agreement. The traitor.

I smiled. "You brought a wad of one-dollar bills, didn't you?"

Ve winked. "Of course."

"What would Terry say?"

Terry Goodwin was her new (and old) love interest. They'd once been married; now they dated casually. Terry was pushing for exclusivity, but Ve was in no rush to be tied down again.

My aunt had monogamy issues.

Ve made a scrunched-up face. "Probably to enjoy my-self."

I rolled my eyes. "Since when are strippers part of a birthday party, anyway?"

"Since Harriette requested one, and we always grant our clients' wishes. What time is he supposed to arrive?"

"Nine." It was only eight thirty. I glanced around. The room looked amazing. Black fabric with white rosettes draped the walls, and high pub tables were cloaked with black-and-white floral-printed cloths. White candles decorated with delicate hand-drawn flowers flickered in the dimly lit room. It all looked amazing. Modern. Elegant. And very much like Harriette.

Ve narrowed her eyes. "You're up to something. I can tell."

The pulsing music vibrated my vertebrae. "Harriette Harkette is eighty years old. Don't you think a stripper might send her into cardiac arrest? I really don't want that on my conscience, do you?"

Ve tipped her head side to side. "Depends on how hot the stripper is."

"Ve!"

"What?" she asked innocently. "Eighty? Harriette's lived a good, long life."

"You're horrible," I said with a smile.

Ve wagged a finger. Her nails had been painted black tonight in honor of the party girl.

The—heaven help me—stripper would be arriving soon. The cake, however, was starting to worry me. It should have been here more than an hour ago. I pulled out my cell phone and sent a quick text message to my good friend Evan Sullivan, owner of the Gingerbread Shack, asking how soon till delivery of the beautiful three-tiered cake he'd made.

As I did so, the deejay played a dramatic drumroll, and I looked up as the door to the party room slowly opened.

All smiles, Harriette slinked in. The women, except for Lydia, went wild.

I'd never seen anyone who slinked before, but Harriette did. One long stride after another—she looked ready to launch into a tango at any moment. She threw her arms in the air. "Let the party begin!"

"Staying Alive" started playing, which I thought was the deejay's form of retribution for all the glares he received during "I Will Survive," and Harriette speared him with a glowering look.

He pretended to ignore her. Wise man.

In my opinion, Harriette possessed a Dr. Jekyll and Mr. Hyde complex. One minute, she was happy as could be, the life of the party, and the next minute . . . viper. I hoped tonight her fangs would stay sheathed.

"Velma! The place looks glorious!" Harriette kissed both of Ve's cheeks and then mine.

She cast a dubious glance at Missy, who growled low in her throat.

Harriette leaned down and growled right back.

Missy bared her teeth, and I scooped her up before she could take a nip out of Harriette's bony ankle.

Harriette screamed money. Tall, lithe, gaunt cheeks, long nose, pointed chin. Razor-sharp blue eyes, crisp white hair pulled back into a fancy hairdo. Diamonds dripped from her earlobes and neck. A long black gown hugged her thin frame, and its cuffs and hem were edged in white feathers. A diamond-crusted belt cinched her tiny waist. Sparkling silver peep-toed heels showed off crimson toenails, completing the outrageous outfit.

An enormous yellow diamond glittered on her ring finger, and for the millionth time since learning she was engaged, I wondered about her supposed fiancé.

Louis.

Harriette never revealed his surname, so unless he was of the Cher or Prince mind-set, she was probably keeping it mum on purpose. Which made me instantly suspicious—it was no secret that my bet at Spellbound was definitely in favor of the man being make-believe.

As far as anyone knew, Louis wasn't from the village, and Harriette revealed frustratingly little about the relationship.

My cell phone buzzed.

"Excuse me," I said, stepping aside to check the message. I shifted Missy to the crook of my left arm and opened my phone. The display revealed: *Michael left an hour and a half ago.*

The message was from Evan, responding to the text I had sent him a few minutes ago. I frowned. Where was Michael Healey, the bakery's deliveryman, then? The Gingerbread Shack was just across the square—it shouldn't have taken him but five minutes to drop off the cake.

I texted back (not easy when holding an irritated Schnoodle): *No sign of him. Or the cake.*

"The Wickeds have packed their five-dollar bills, Velma," Harriette said loudly, eyebrows high, "so I hope the stripper is outstanding. Young, hot, sexy." She wiggled her hips.

Ve shot me an "I told you so" look.

Which had me extremely worried, and I wondered what constituted "young" to an eighty-year-old. Because it was true I'd hired a stripper, but according to his bio, he was pushing seventy. I suddenly had the feeling the joke wouldn't go over as well as I hoped. If I didn't fix this soon, I was sure to see Harriette's fangs tonight.

I bit my lip and shuddered at the thought.

"Is your fiancé young, Harriette?" Ve asked oh-so casually.

I had to give it to my aunt—she had no qualms about prying into other people's affairs.

Harriette pursed fire-engine red lips. "Louis is a bit younger than I am, it's true."

"How much so?" Ve pressed.

My phone buzzed. EVAN: *I can see van in lot.*

ME: *How? Superhuman vision?*

EVAN: *Binoculars.*

I didn't even want to know why Evan had binoculars at the bakery.

"Enough to make me feel young again," Harriette said with a long, drawn-out sigh. She glanced around, and her snake eyes narrowed on the empty spot on the dessert table reserved for the cake. "Has the cake not yet arrived?"

I smelled venom in the air and said quickly, "I'm going to go check on it. I'll be right back."

Stepping out would also give me time to walk Missy and figure out how to get a replacement stripper here as quickly as possible.

I pushed my way through the pubgoers and out onto the sidewalk. I clipped on Missy's leash, set her down, and looked around. The village looked nothing short of incredible. The Harvest Festival was in full swing. A huge bonfire lit one end of the green, and a Ferris wheel anchored the other. In between were booths and carnival rides and even a mock haunted house—all attractions to lure in tourists. But underneath it all, below the surface, something crackled in the air. Magic.

It made me smile. This time of year was special to Crafters. Halloween, which was next weekend, was our biggest holiday celebration.

The square was packed with tourists and villagers alike. The moon, a waxing crescent, hung high in the sky; the night was mild, the fall foliage glorious, and I wished I could enjoy it fully.

Unfortunately, I couldn't grant my own wishes (one of the Wishcraft Laws), which meant I had to find a young, hot, sexy stripper ASAP.

I nibbled a fingernail and thought about the "entertainment" Web site that had been recommended to me by Evan. I didn't remember seeing a phone number, but as it was the only local place to hire strippers, once I was done out here, I would borrow Ve's smartphone (I still had an older model flip phone) to access the site and see if I could reach someone in charge to change my order.

Missy and I dodged a gaggle of window-shoppers as we made our way toward the public parking lot adjacent to the pub. Along the walk, I couldn't help thinking about single dad Nick Sawyer, and how young (okay, he was thirty-five, but still), hot and sexy he was. Alas, he wasn't a stripper (I could dream), but the village's police chief. We'd been dating since the end of summer.

I turned the corner, and sure enough, the Ginger-bread Shack's delivery van was parked at the back of the lot, near the path leading to the Enchanted Trail, a paved walkway that looped behind the square.

As I trotted toward it, I listened as the calliope of the Ghoulousel (a ghost-themed carousel) piped a happy, perky tune to the backdrop of all the other sounds. Bells, whistles. Murmured voices. Squeals from small children. Laughter.

I was enjoying the ambiance until Missy suddenly stopped short.

"What?" I asked her, looking around for anyone hiding in the shadows along the pub's stone exterior.

She growled.

Not a warning growl, but something primal. Almost fearful.

Goose bumps rose on my arms. I picked her up. "You're freaking me out, Missy."

It didn't help that she was trembling.

The calliope suddenly sounded ominous as I doubled my pace and made it across the parking lot to the van in record time. Cupping my eyes, I peered into the delivery van's window. On the driver's seat were a cell phone and sunglasses. An empty lemon-lime sports drink sat in the cup holder, and a fast-food bag rested on the passenger seat. There was no sign of Michael.

Try as I might—I couldn't see into the back of the van. The wind kicked up, rustling leaves and bringing a

chill to the air. Pinpricks of fear poked my spine as I
walked around the van to the rear doors, and Missy
started growling again. I held her more tightly and told
myself I was being silly, that Michael was just fine, the
cake was fine, that everything was fine, fine, fine.

But . . . lately, the village hadn't been so idyllic. There
had been murders here—cases that I'd helped solve.

Maybe that was why I was being so paranoid. I had
murder on my mind—never a good thing when creeping
around in the dark.

Michael probably just went over to the festival—it *was*
hard to resist its lure. There were caramel apples over
there, after all. Lots of them. They certainly tempted me.

In fact, after the stripper arrived, I planned to cut out
of Harriette's party early to meet Nick for a late date
that involved one of those apples. We planned to ride the
silly rides and play the outrageously priced games until
the festival closed up shop for the night.

Swallowing hard, I wrapped my hand around the cold
door handle and pulled. Hinges creaked eerily, and I jumped
out of the way as if I expected the bogeyman to leap out.

Fortunately, for my sanity, he didn't.

Inside the back of the van, Harriette's cake sat proudly,
looking beautiful with its black-and-white motif.

There was still no sign of Michael.

My ponytail slashed against my face from a sudden
gust of wind. I tucked my hair into the collar of my turtleneck as I tried to figure out how to carry the cake into
the pub myself. Missy continued to shake, and I startled
when I heard voices on the Enchanted Trail. Old-
fashioned gaslights and white twinkle lights strung in the
trees illuminated the shortcut path that led from the
parking lot to the paved trail as a couple emerged, holding hands and snuggling against each other.

I relaxed a little, trying not to let my anxiety get the

better of me, but as the couple passed by, Missy growled and wriggled. I set her down, and she took off toward the trampled dirt path, stretching her leash to its limits.

She beelined for something lying in the brush. Something that suddenly brought back those pinpricks.

A shoe.

A large sneaker.

So out of place that it made me nervous.

Glancing around, I walked slowly toward it. Wind whistled through the trees, echoing eerily above my head. "W-what did you find, Missy?"

Missy half growled, half cried.

My heart beat so hard I could feel it in my throat.

Fine, fine, fine, I sang in my head.

The shoe lay on the edge of the path, upside down in the long grass. I held up my cell phone, using its glow as a flashlight as I looked around the shrubby area.

Missy pulled me deeper into the tall brush, her nose to the ground. Suddenly, she let out a loud yap and started whimpering.

My hand shook as I aimed my cell phone her way. The wind stopped, and the night was deafeningly quiet as the light fell upon my worst nightmare.

A bloody sock-covered foot stuck out from beneath a mound of branches.

Chapter Two

You would think death would put a damper on a party. Not so when Harriette was the guest of honor.

She refused to let a little thing like murder get in her way of a good time. And woe to anyone who tried to stop her.

Like Ve. Like her daughter Lydia. Like the police.

There would be no postponement. The party would go on.

Without me, fortunately, since I didn't want to be around when the stripper showed up. I never did cancel my original order. He was going to have to do.

I leaned against the pub's stone wall, watching several police officers cordon off the parking lot and trailhead. I shifted uncomfortably—ever since I found Michael Healey's body, I'd felt strange. As if there were added weight to my shoulders. Almost as if someone were leaning on me.

Of course there was no added weight and no one was leaning on me, so I adjusted my denim jacket and rolled my shoulders a few times to try and ease the tension. It helped a bit.

A large crowd had gathered along with several emergency vehicles. Crime-scene techs combed the delivery van. They were carefully placing Michael's belongings into clear plastic bags.

Missy sat at my feet. Evan Sullivan stood next to me, his blue eyes watery. His twin sister, Starla, stood on my other side. The two had become best friends to me over the past few months. We had a lot in common—mostly our Wishcrafting abilities, though technically they were Cross-Crafters (witches who'd inherited two sets of abilities, one from each parent). Crossers (as I'd recently nicknamed them) almost always favored one trait over the other. Though Evan and Starla were both half Wishcrafter and half Bakecrafter, Starla could grant wishes like no one's business (but couldn't bake her way out of an Easy Bake Oven), and Evan was the opposite.

Starla and I were both divorcées, and all three of us were all currently single (though they were both single and still looking for Mr. Right whereas I hoped I had found mine), had a fondness for our dogs (Evan lovingly called Starla's bichon frise "the Beast"), and we all had a low tolerance level for jogging—but we did it anyway.

"This is just horrible," Starla said. Blond and perpetually perky, she looked decidedly gloomy as she slumped against the wall. Tears pooled in her eyes. It broke my heart.

Truth be told, I wasn't used to having friends, never mind *best* friends. Growing up, I'd been too busy raising Harper to hang out with kids my own age. My father may have tried to push me to go out once or twice, but I'd never had a good time, and Harper had driven him crazy with her endless rounds of tedious questions (Why do people get hiccups? Why are yawns contagious? How come fish don't die when a pond freezes? Can animals commit suicide?). Dad stopped trying after that. Which was pretty much the story of his life after my mother died. In my heart, I knew I'd lost my father that day as well. He drank too much and kept to himself. He'd never stopped grieving her death, even at the expense of his own daughters. I hoped now, ten months after he'd passed, that he was finally at peace.

Since moving to the Enchanted Village, both Harper and I had more friends than we could count. It was a curious feeling to say the least, but one I was grateful for. I took hold of Starla's hand, and she clasped mine tightly in return.

I tried to hold in my own grief at Michael's passing so I could stay strong for my friends. I hadn't known him nearly as well as they did, but Michael and I had become friends over the past four months with my frequent visits to the bakery.

I swallowed hard, easily picturing his wide, warm smile, his twinkly blue eyes, and long surfer-type blond hair—and thinking about how I'd never see those things again. Letting out a breath, I blinked to keep tears in check. He had an air of maturity about him that belied his true age. When I first met him, I thought he was in his late twenties, but really he was barely twenty-one. Too young to die.

Evan's voice cracked as he said, "Who could have done this?"

Hunched over, Starla drew imaginary circles on the sidewalk with the toe of her knee-high leather boot. "Was it a robbery gone wrong?" she asked me, her eyes dull and cloudy.

"I don't know." After I'd discovered Michael's body, I scooped up Missy and ran for the hills before I passed out at the sight of the blood. I didn't do well with blood. I'd called the police as soon as I reached the relative safety (there were lots of handsy men getting their drink on tonight) of the pub. It hadn't taken the police long to arrive. "It's possible, I guess."

There were a lot of people in the village tonight. Crime happened—it was a sad fact of life. But a robbery gone wrong? I wasn't sure. It seemed so random. "Did Michael carry any cash on him from the shop?" I asked Evan.

"No." He raked his fingers through his perfectly styled hair, raising ginger-blond tufts. "Bakery goods are paid for in advance of delivery. He might have had some tip money. Not much, though."

Maybe someone didn't know that, however.

"It doesn't make any sense," Starla said. "Michael was an Illumicrafter. Everyone loves Illumicrafters."

"Michael was a Crafter?" I hadn't known. Illumicrafters were witches who had the ability to provide light. They glowed—their personalities and sometimes literally. They were people-persons. Friendly, outgoing, charming.

"He kept it to himself, mostly," Evan said. "Though he didn't say so, I felt he resented his Craft a bit because it didn't provide a career like some other Crafts. Unless he wanted to be a human Gloworm at a carnival, he was kind of out of luck. He was always mentioning how fortunate I was to have the bakery."

Wishcrafting wasn't the easiest Craft to turn into a career, either, but my aunt Ve had made it work by opening As You Wish. However, I couldn't even begin to imagine what Michael could do as an Illumicrafter—except perhaps a job as a politician since Illumis were so well liked.

And he had been liked.

His murder had to have been random. Otherwise Starla was right—it just didn't make sense.

Like something out of a TV crime show, portable spotlights lit the whole area. I could see Police Chief

Nick Sawyer moving around, talking with techs and with
his officers. His eyes squinted in concentration, and I
wondered if he'd found any clues yet. Any leads as to
who would do such a thing and why.

"Poor Amy," Evan said, staring dully into the lights. "I
wonder if she knows yet."

Amy. Michael's younger sister. A Sally Field look-
alike (from her *Gidget* years), she was a cute little thing
with bright inquisitive green eyes. She was one of Harper's favorite customers at Spellbound, where Amy often
studied. A sophomore at Tufts, she was hoping to become a veterinarian.

The siblings' father walked out when they were little,
never to be seen again, and their mom died about two
years ago. Michael had been working a couple of jobs to
take care of Amy ever since.

Which was a lot to shoulder for a young man—and
explained why he seemed so mature.

"Do they have any other siblings?" I asked. "Or family we can call?"

Evan stuck his hands into the pockets of dark-wash
jeans. "It was just the two of them."

Just like Harper and me before Aunt Ve came into
our lives. I tried to imagine what life would be like if
something horrible happened to Harper, and the thought
alone made me so sad that tears welled.

I shook my head, thanking my lucky stars that Harper
was just fine. I was fine. Ve was fine. We were all fine, fine,
fine.

Missy shifted, moving closer to my legs. My throat had
tightened, and I wondered what the protocol was for no-
tifying next of kin. If I were in Amy's shoes, I wouldn't
want to see my brother lying in the bushes. I wouldn't
want that to be my last memory of him. I hoped Nick
kept her away and would go instead to the apartment

above the bakery that Evan rented to Michael and Amy. Evan had cut the rent a bit so they could afford it. Most likely, he'd cut the rent *a lot*, not a *bit*. He had a soft heart.

The mother hen in me immediately started worrying about this girl I barely knew. What would she do now? Where would she go? How would she even be able to afford the pittance of rent Evan charged? What about school? Colleges were crazy expensive.

The strange weight had returned to my shoulders, and I felt myself deflate from the stress of it all. I couldn't believe there'd been another murder in the village. And certainly not one of someone so young.

A police officer, Glinda Hansel, worked at pushing back the crowd. We had a history, Glinda and I. An interesting one, as I once thought her mother a baby-booming-bimbo homewrecker, and Glinda once thought she had a chance with my boyfriend.

I still thought her mother a bimbo, and she still thought she had a chance with Nick.

We kept our interactions civil, and except for the whole she-wants-my-boyfriend thing, I kind of liked her. She was sweet and funny. (I hated to admit that.)

However, I didn't believe the feeling was mutual. She kept glancing my way, probably hoping I'd disappear magically.

Vaporcrafting, however, was not my specialty, and Nick had specifically told me to stick around until he could talk with me more formally.

Along the fringe of the crowd, I spotted a man hurrying toward the pub. He carried a garment bag, and his bald head gleamed under the gaslights.

I recognized his face from the entertainment Web site Evan had recommended to me. I'd hired him at first sight.

Hot Rod Stiffington.

And by the photos on the site, the prized "six-pack" Hot Rod advertised referred to his beer belly, not to any kind of ab muscles.

He headed for the Cauldron's front door, and I counted my blessings that I wasn't going to be inside for his arrival at Harriette's party.

"We should go see if we can find Amy," Evan said to Starla. "She shouldn't be alone right now."

Starla nodded, gave my hand a squeeze before she released it, and fussed with the decorative toggles on her sweater dress. "We should, but I'm sure she's not alone."

Evan groaned. "I forgot about him."

"Him who?" I asked.

"Fisk Khoury," Starla answered, tucking a stray blond hair behind her ear. "You've probably seen him around town."

"Or on wanted posters," Evan added darkly.

"Not true," Starla said to me as she elbowed her brother. "He only looks scary and isn't actually a criminal."

Evan countered with "That we know of." He glanced at me. "Medium height, olive skin tone, wiry, with long curly hair, beady little brown eyes, and puffy lips. Wears a lot of black and lets his pants hang down to his knees."

I recognized the description. "Is he the one who strums funeral songs on his guitar at talent night at the Witch's Brew?"

Missy growled again and shimmied closer to my ankles.

"He's the one," Starla said.

I didn't like to judge books by covers—I mean, look at me. I looked like your average girl next door but was actually a witch. However, Fisk's appearance certainly gave me pause. "Is he any relation to Dash Khoury?" He had to be. It wasn't a common surname.

Tall, handsome, regal-looking, and of Indian descent,

Dash Khoury was a botanical genius, a Terracrafter with impeccable gardening skills who was the local landscaper in charge of the village's green spaces, an immense job. I recalled with a start that he was also married to Trista Harkette, Harriette's younger daughter. The black sheep of the family.

According to the best gossip in the village (Aunt Ve), Floracrafter Trista had been disowned by her mother when she married a Terracrafter, who was deemed "beneath" her.

Floracrafters were well-known for their snobbery and superiority complexes, which I never quite understood. Although no Crafter was truly created equal, each of us had magical abilities, and none of those talents was singled out as being better than another. Floras were especially biased against Terras for some reason I still hadn't learned.

Despite threats of being disowned, Trista had married Dash without a second thought. Instead of slinking out of town ashamed (as Harriette had hoped), Trista stayed put, kept her maiden name to irritate her mother, and staked her claim in the village by opening an upscale lingerie shop, Something Wicked, in the square. About ten years ago, she developed one of the hottest selling bras on the market—the AbracadaBra. The bra that worked magic. Probably literally, but I wasn't positive about that. That bra had made Trista a multimillionaire, but no matter how big a success she was, she still remained in the small shop in the square, and she had yet to receive the approval of her mother.

In fact, mother and daughter hadn't spoken in more than twenty years.

"Fisk is Dash and Trista's son," Evan said.

"He looks a lot like his mom," Starla said, then added unnecessarily, "You know, without the droopy pants."

Now that I knew the relation, I could see the resemblance to his grandmother as well. They had the same eyes. My nosy side wanted to know if Harriette had any kind of relationship with Fisk. She had disowned Trista for marrying a Terracrafter, so how did Harriette feel about her grandson, who had to be a Terra-Flora Cross-Crafter? Had she cut him out of her life, too?

I pushed my nosiness aside for now and tried to focus on the conversation. "What does Fisk have to do with Amy?"

"They've been dating for a couple of months now," Starla said.

How hadn't I known this?

"They're glued at the hip. It's appalling," Evan said, rolling his eyes. He shoved away from the wall and adjusted the spiffy tie beneath his argyle sweater vest. It wasn't often he was seen looking anything other than impeccable, and tonight was no different. "I'll see you later, Darcy." He walked away, head hung low.

"I think they're kind of sweet," Starla said loudly to his back.

"Starla needs a date," Evan called over his shoulder.

Sticking her tongue out at his retreating form, she said softly, "I hope Fisk didn't have anything to do with what happened to Michael."

It was a startling statement. "Why would you think so?"

"Starla!" Evan called impatiently. He stood at the edge of the crowd, waiting for her. "Are you coming?"

"I'll be right there!" she yelled back to him. To me, she said, "Fisk and Michael have been best friends since they were teenagers and worked together at Dash's landscaping company. But lately, they've been at each other's throats."

That tidbit really caught my attention. "Why? Because Fisk was dating Michael's little sister?"

Slim shoulders lifted in a shrug. "I'm not sure, but you might want to let Nick know." She bent and petted Missy's head before walking off.

The curiosity-seeking horde grew by the minute. On the village green, hundreds more people had stopped what they were doing and stared as word of a murder caught on the wind and spread like dandelion fluff in a strong breeze. Rides had come to a halt; the bonfire had nearly fizzled out. It was eerie.

Out of the corner of my eye, I saw Ve wending through the crowd, a determined look in her eyes as she searched faces—probably looking for me.

Uh-oh.

I guessed Hot Rod's body wasn't the one she'd dreamed of oiling.

Shimmying my way along the wall, I scooted around the back corner of the pub and into the service alley behind the building. Safely out of sight.

I hoped Ve wouldn't be so mad by the time I went home.

Or put a hex on me or something.

But no. She couldn't . . . well, at least not without consequences. The Craft motto was Do No Harm.

I was pretty sure Ve wouldn't cross that line.

Fairly sure.

Okay, I was worried.

Hot Rod had quite the beer belly. In fact, he looked four months pregnant.

"Hiding?" someone asked.

Surprised, I jumped, and then looked accusingly at Missy. A little warning would have been nice. She really wasn't the best watchdog.

She, however, was too busy to notice my glare as she jumped on Nick's leg and bathed his hand in doggy kisses.

"Don't let her find me," I whispered, sparing glances around the building.

"Her who?" Nick asked, tiny frown lines feathering out from the corners of his dark eyes.

"Ve."

"Why is Ve after you?"

"It might have something to do with Hot Rod Stiffington."

Amusement flickered in his eyes as he leaned in. "Who?"

"The aging, overweight, balding stripper I hired."

He dragged a hand down his face, but his smile remained. "For Harriette's party?"

I nodded.

His smile widened.

I loved his smile.

But then I suddenly remembered why he was here.

Why I was here.

I nodded to the woods. "Any idea what happened there? Robbery? Something like that?"

"Don't know yet," he said, his eyes hooded. He wore a black fleece coat over his police-issued long-sleeve black polo shirt. Flat-front khaki pants fit him perfectly. I had to admit, I loved the village's casual police uniforms.

"Will the medical examiner's team be here soon?" I asked, figuring the quicker the body was removed, the sooner the crowd would dissipate, the sooner answers could be found.

"The crew will be here in five minutes or so. It's going to be a late night." Long after the crowd left, Nick would still be searching the woods, scouring for clues.

"Do you want me to pick up Mimi? She can spend the night with Ve and me."

He smirked, the corner of his mouth twitching. "Are

you planning to use my daughter as a buffer between you and Ve?"

"Yes, yes, I am."

He grinned. "I'm sure Mimi would love to stay with you, and you'd be doing me a huge favor."

It wasn't often that Nick, a single dad, had to put work before his twelve-year-old daughter, but on those rare occasions, I was glad I could help. Mimi had become like another little sister to me. In a way, I guess she was. Mimi was also a Wishcrafter—her late mother, Melina, had been one, and Mimi inherited the ability. Nick, on the other hand, was a Halfcrafter, a mortal who knowingly married into the Craft family and was allowed to know all our secrets so Mimi could learn her Craft properly. And though he was technically now half Wishcrafter (through marriage), he didn't have any powers of his own. But because he was a Halfcrafter, other Crafters could discuss their abilities with him. Which came in handy for me, especially as I helped Mimi learn her Craft and at those times when I was mixed up in crimes involving Crafters.

"As soon as I'm done here, I'll hop over and pick up Mimi at Spellbound." She was there helping out Harper tonight.

"I'll call her and let her know you're coming, but first I need to ask you some questions."

Unfortunately, I was becoming a pro at answering these kinds of inquiries since this was the third body I'd found since moving to the village. I had no doubt I was going to get a reputation soon as a death magnet—if I didn't have one already.

As the team from the medical examiner's office arrived and pushed a stretcher across the parking lot, I told Nick about how I'd come to find Michael's body—and about what Starla had said about Fisk Khoury. Nick took notes, nodding but not interrupting my story. By the time I was done, my chest hurt.

"You okay?" he asked. Over the last few months his dark hair had grown out a little bit, becoming wavier with the length. It softened the hard edges of his face. I liked the look. A lot. So much so that at random times—like now—I had to curl my hands into fists to keep from reaching out and running my hands through his hair.

I was pretty sure he wouldn't mind the gesture—but now wasn't exactly the right place or time. "My heart aches. It makes no sense—I didn't know him all that well. We weren't close friends—just friendly."

Nick stepped in closer and wrapped his arms around me. I felt the stubble of his five-o'clock shadow brush my temple as he dropped a kiss on top of my head. He held me close, and I really just wanted to stay in his arms for the rest of the night. I loved the feel of his heart beating against mine, and the way he held me as if he'd shoulder all my troubles if he could. And for a brief second I didn't feel that ominous weight on my shoulders anymore. I sighed in relief. In contentment.

He rested his forehead on mine and said, "You feel that way because you're a good person, Darcy Merriweather. Loving and caring." His eyes glistened with mischief. "All very attractive qualities."

"There goes my theory that you're just dating me for my body," I teased.

He grinned. "Well, there's that, too."

I gave him a playful shove, and he gave me a quick kiss on the lips.

This also wasn't the time or place to be more affectionate. Not that we'd been all that intimate so far. We'd been taking our relationship slowly. Ice age slow. And now . . . well, I thought it might be time for a little heat wave. Especially if the heady look in his eyes was any indication.

"Chief?" a voice said from nearby. Glinda Hansel stood a few feet away, looking decidedly uncomfortable as twin spots of color reddened her cheeks. "Sorry to interrupt," she said, not sounding apologetic at all. "The medical examiner's team wants to talk to you."

Nick didn't release me as he said, "I'll be right there."

She gave a quick nod and spun around.

He held me just a little tighter before letting me go. "I have to get back."

I felt the immediate loss of his warmth and buttoned my jacket to chase away the sudden chill. "What happened to Michael exactly?" I asked, not sure I really wanted to know.

His voice was hoarse as he said, "Looks like he was stabbed to death."

There was something in his tone, a hesitancy. He wasn't telling me everything. "What else?"

He rested his hands on my shoulders and gave them a squeeze. "Not for me to say at this point."

I could tell by the steely set of his jaw that I wasn't going to get more out of him tonight.

We set a time to meet up tomorrow morning, and as I watched him walk away, I saw Glinda giving me the stink eye. I smiled and gave her a finger wave. She turned her back on me.

So much for civility.

I scooped up Missy and was ready to battle my way across the square to Harper's shop when a bony hand shot out of the darkness and grabbed my shoulder.

Chapter Three

I let out a little *"Eee"* and spun around.

Lydia Harkette Wentworth's face glowed in the ambient light. Bright and shiny close-set eyes searched my face. "I need to talk to you, Darcy."

Placing my hand on my pounding heart, I said, "It was supposed to be a joke."

Deep wrinkles creased her forehead. "What was?"

"Hot Rod?"

"Who?"

I rocked on my heels. "The entertainer? The, ah, stripper?"

Her thin face softened. "Oh! He was a hoot and a half. A big hit."

"He was?"

"My mother adored him. Fawned all over him."

My jaw dropped. "She did?"

Now Lydia really studied me. "You seem surprised."

I pulled myself together. I'd convinced myself the debacle of Hot Rod was why Lydia had sought me out. "I'm just relieved," I stammered. "He's not exactly young, hot, and sexy—as your mother requested."

"Ah," she said. "I understand. Mother is a tough critic. Willard still cringes every time she speaks to him, and we've been married twenty-five years."

Floracrafter Willard Wentworth, Lydia's husband, ran one of the Harkette family businesses—the Black Thorn, the local florist shop. He was the fussy, prickly type anyway ("thorn" was so appropriate for him), so I could only imagine how Harriette's scrutiny affected him, especially since they were always in such close proximity. Lydia and Willard had lived in a carriage house on Harriette's property since they were married, so they were mere yards away from Harriette at all times. I didn't know how Willard put up with it. I wouldn't have lasted a week under Harriette's watchful viper eyes.

I placed Lydia somewhere in her early fifties and noted she hadn't aged well. She was thin like her mother, but with her sun-damaged skin, wrinkles, and near-constant frown, she looked more like Harriette's slightly younger sister.

A harsh assessment, maybe, but sadly true.

"Trust me," she said. "Sexy is in the eye of the beholder. Have no fear, Darcy. Mother adores Hot Rod. I believe she's making plans with him to attend her New Year's Eve bash." Lydia smiled, her lips forming a tight thin line. "Mother certainly has her elitist moments, but not when it comes to throwing a memorable party."

Trista Harkette had been cast out of the family for marrying a Terracrafter—yet a balding paunchy stripper was just fine with her mother?

What kind of family was this? They went beyond eccentric and straight into weird. Or maybe Harriette truly did have a Jekyll and Hyde personality.

I put Missy down and she trotted around the alley, stretching as far as her leash would allow, soaking up all the smells. I heard a noise above me and looked up to see my neighbor, Archie, land on the eave of the pub's roof. He was a gorgeous macaw familiar, mostly red with flashes of blue and yellow. Spotting me, he flapped a wing in my direction—his version of waving.

A "familiar" was a Crafter spirit who took on an animal form after death in order to extend his or her life (sometimes for centuries). There were several familiars (that I knew of) in the village, including one of my closest friends, a mouse named Pepe.

Archie was exceedingly chatty, a former nineteenth-century theater actor and a current movie buff. He was also the Elder's right-hand man, her eyes and ears. No doubt he would report what was going on directly back to her.

I didn't want to call attention to him, so I gave him a subtle finger wave and turned my attention back to Lydia.

She hadn't noticed Archie's arrival. Her focus was solely on the commotion in the parking lot. She *tsk*ed, shaking her head sympathetically. As she frowned, deep creases wrinkled her forehead. "Do we know yet who was killed? Was it someone local?"

When I first reported finding the body, I didn't tell anyone I thought it was Michael. Since I'd seen only a foot, I wanted to be sure before I started a possible rumor. But now his identity had been confirmed, and I didn't think it was a secret, so I said, "Michael Healey. Did you know him?"

Lydia gasped. Her hand flew to her mouth, and tears filled her eyes.

I took that as a yes.

"You're sure?"

I nodded, feeling strange again. The weight was back. It felt as if someone were standing behind me, invading my space. An invisible person.

A ghost? Michael's ghost? I pushed the crazy thought aside.

"That poor boy. He was such a good kid." She shook her head. "He used to work as a part-time handyman at the Elysian Fields. Such a big help. He had many talents."

Harriette owned property neighboring her estate on the outskirts of the village, a compound of four gorgeous state-of-the-art greenhouses and dozens of acres she'd named the Elysian Fields. The greenhouses were divided among the four Wicked Widows, each controlling her own greenhouse and what was grown within. Lydia worked primarily for her mother, helping to cultivate those beautiful black roses, but she also oversaw the whole operation.

I shook my head. "Used to work there? When?"

"He quit two months ago after working for us for nearly a year. He had an amazing talent with the plants. They thrived under his care, even the ones not cultivated by magic."

I realized with a start that gardening was a perfect career for an Illumicrafter. His glow would help the plants grow. "Why did he quit?" I asked. From what I'd heard, he needed the money.

Missy sniffed along the building's foundation. Archie, I noticed, had moved to the upper branches of a tree closer to the crime scene.

Lydia's lips pursed. "I'm not sure."

By the way she fidgeted, I had the feeling she wasn't telling me the truth.

She attempted to elaborate. "About a month after Michael left, I went to see him and tried to talk him into coming back, but he flat-out refused. Wouldn't even consider it, even though I offered him a big raise. He told me money was of no concern to him."

Considering what Evan and Starla had just told me

about his working several jobs, money had to be a huge concern for him. Had he spoken out of pride? Or had he found another source of income?

She wrung her hands and stared at the crime-scene techs. "Such a loss. He had a sister, didn't he?"

"Amy."

"I'll have to see what I can do about helping her out. Mother will want to help, too—she adored Michael and is going to be heartbroken to hear about his death. To think we were inside having a party while he was . . ."

I was grateful she didn't finish that thought.

Missy wandered back to me, and I picked her up. "I should probably get going." The longer I stayed out here, the more likely it was Ve would find me.

"But wait," Lydia said, grabbing my arm again. "I have something I want to run past you." She glanced over my shoulder, at an officer directing a tow truck toward the Gingerbread Shack delivery van. "Maybe we should go somewhere quieter?"

The words were on my tongue to turn her down, but there was something in her eyes that intrigued me. I wanted to hear what she had to say. However, between the police, the crowd, and the festival, there wasn't a quiet spot within a mile. The lesser evil was obvious. "The trail?"

She nodded.

We walked the alley behind the shops and used the cut-through behind the Furry Toadstool, the local pet store, to reach the trail.

The Enchanted Trail was well lit and, like everywhere else in the village, crowded. We headed away from the pub, away from the crime scene. In this case, the phrase "out of sight, out of mind" wasn't working. There was definitely a presence around me. I could feel it pulsing like a heartbeat. *Whump, whump.* It was a completely nutty thought, except for one little fact.

It was a known phenomenon that after death, the spirit of an Illumicrafter was often mistaken for a ghost. It was the whole glowing thing—which apparently didn't go away after the Illumicrafter died. Around me, however, there was just darkness. And that heartbeat. *Whump, whump. Whump, whump.*

I was fuzzy on the whole death process for Crafters and needed to ask Ve for a little more clarification. I knew some spirits chose to take on animal forms (familiars), and some spirits passed immediately on to whatever afterworld awaited them, but what about the ones who weren't so keen to do either? The ones in limbo? In the mortal world, those people *would* be ghosts. But what about the Crafter spirits? Would they become ghosts as well?

Holding in a sigh, I set Missy on the trail, and she trotted ahead, her nose to the ground. If she felt the presence, she wasn't letting on.

Whump, whump.

The disturbance wasn't frightening, but it felt just plain strange, almost making me feel claustrophobic. I had to wonder why it was following me. And how I could get rid of it.

We walked for a few minutes in silence before Lydia said, "I'm just going to say it."

Thank goodness, because my curiosity was killing me.

Tree branches creaked as the wind picked up again. A few crickets chirped a sweet melody, and when I drew in a deep breath, I savored the crisp fall air.

Lydia said, "I want to hire As You Wish."

"To do what?" I asked, veering out of the way of a woman speed-walking.

"To prove that my mother's so-called fiancé, Louis, is a gold-digging money-grubber. If that's even his real name. I have to stop this wedding, Darcy, before it's too late. My mother is making a huge mistake, and she won't listen to reason."

I knew Lydia hadn't been happy about her mother's remarriage, but to openly want to stop the wedding? Wow. "Do you have reason to think Louis is a phony?"

I had to confess that I was already mentally spending my bookshop betting pool winnings. I desperately needed new running shoes.

"For one, he's always full of excuses as to why he can never join us for dinner."

"Wait. Have you ever met him face-to-face?" I asked.

A small family passed by us, the little toddlers dressed as Thing One and Thing Two running ahead of their parents on stubby little legs. People often wore costumes to the festival.

"No," Lydia said. "No one has. Only Mother."

I thought it strange no *villager* had, but for Harriette's own family not to have met him? Odd. Very odd.

"And recently, I've discovered that she's given him money."

Warning bells went off in my head. "How much money?"

She glanced at me. "Five thousand."

Those warning bells turned into loud whoops. "Why?"

"Mother wouldn't say. She said it didn't matter. Well, it certainly matters to me if he's taking her for a ride."

I could see why Lydia was concerned, and I said so.

"You haven't heard the worst of it. This past Tuesday at an emergency meeting of the Wickeds at Mother's house, I was in the garden—"

I cut her off. "Why was there an emergency meeting?"

Her lips pursed. "I wish I knew. Mother kept me out of that loop."

"Is that normal?"

"Unfortunately, yes. Anyhow, I was cutting herbs for dinner when Mother stepped out onto the deck to take a cell phone call. She didn't see me, but I could hear parts of her conversation. She was speaking to Marcus Debrowski and asking him about changing her will."

"To include Louis?"

"I assume so. Mother has an appointment with Marcus on Monday morning." Lydia wrung her hands. "None of us knows this man, but suddenly he's worming his way into a fortune? I don't like it. Not one bit."

Lawcrafter Marcus Debrowski was the village's best lawyer. He was also my sister Harper's current sweetheart. Maybe I could squirrel some information out of him—or get Harper to do it for me. She'd probably have better luck.

Nosy to my core, I asked, "Are you currently the sole beneficiary of your mother's estate?"

Lydia's spine straightened. "I assume. Well, other than the Wickeds who will inherit their greenhouses, that is," she added. "And don't get me started on that."

Well, if there was a way to pique my curiosity, that was it. "You don't think the greenhouses should go to them?"

Wind ruffled her hair. "Not really. I'd like the Elysian Fields to revert back to a family-only business." She glanced at me, a guilty flush in her cheeks. "Even if they do inherit, Imogene is talking about retiring soon to somewhere warm and sunny all year long—I'm sure I can buy her out. Though I can't imagine her not being at her greenhouse every day. She never had kids, and she treats her orchids like her babies. I know I couldn't just up and walk away from it all. I'll believe her retirement when I see it."

Seventy-something Imogene Millikan was an interesting lady. At first glance, she seemed to have bucked the pretentious Floracrafter stereotype since she looked more hippie drippy than high society, but on closer inspection, one could recognize her prim upbringing in her mannerisms and in her speech.

I quickly ran through what I knew about the other two Wickeds, Bertie Braun and her former daughter-in-law, Ophelia Braun-Wickham, which was surprisingly little. Bertie specialized in lilies, while Ophelia worked with saffron crocuses. "And Bertie and Ophelia? Would you try to buy them out as well?"

Lydia said lightly, "They should never have had greenhouses at the Elysian Fields to begin with. My father lost the two greenhouses in a poker game to Bertie's husband years and years ago. Mother nearly killed him, let me tell you, seeing as how Bertie and Ophelia are Terracrafters. Mr. Braun gave one greenhouse to his wife, and one to his son, Ophelia's first husband. After Ophelia's husband died, Ophelia took over that greenhouse."

I was so shocked, I stopped dead in my tracks. "Bertie and Ophelia are Terracrafters?" I hadn't known—I'd always assumed they were Floras like Harriette. I did recall Aunt Ve's telling me that father and son had died in a tragic plane crash almost three years ago.

Lydia smiled at my shock. "Yes. Good ones, too, despite their hostility toward each other, but that doesn't mean I want them to stay."

"They don't get along?" This was news to me.

"Not since Ophelia remarried last year. Bertie doesn't care for Hammond Wickham at all, and she doesn't like her four-year-old grandson being raised by a man other than her son. It's caused much dissension in the family."

It had to be hard for Bertie to see Ophelia moving on, but she was a young woman. Surely Bertie could understand that Ophelia had a whole life to live ahead of her.

I glanced at Lydia. I had to ask, "Do you feel the same way as your mother toward Terracrafters?"

"Not at all. It's a stupid discrimination that has torn our family apart. I like them just fine. The only reason I want them to go is that I want the Elysian Fields to stay in the family. As nice as they are, they aren't family."

Maybe Lydia could finally explain to me why there was a rift between the Terras and Floras in the first place. "Where did the discrimination originate?"

Wind sent leaves skittering across the path. "Some Floracrafter generations ago deemed himself better than a Terra because a Terra had to work so hard to cultivate a flower, whereas a Flora simply had to touch a stem. It caught on. It's the age-old theme of white collar versus blue collar. Upper crust versus wrong side of the tracks. Silver spoon versus hard work. Gilded lilies versus dirty fingernails. It's an embarrassment to our Craft, and I'm doing everything I can to get my mother to see my way of things. I think she finally might be listening, too, as she's been much friendlier to Bertie and Ophelia in the past few months. Mother holds a lot of clout—other Floras will follow her lead."

Friendly toward them only in the past few months? I kept a firm hand on Missy's leash as a squirrel scampered across the path and she tried to chase after it. "I thought the Wicked Widows were best friends?"

"I wouldn't say best friends. Friends. Friendly acquaintances." She made a sour face. "Acquaintances at best. Except for Mother and Imogene, who've been best friends since their twenties. The Wickeds tolerate one another well enough to keep the Elysian Fields running smoothly. Even though each greenhouse is run individually, the Wickeds understand that people are judged by the company they keep. They hold one another to the highest standards. Mother and Imogene have worked diligently to make sure Ophelia's and Bertie's products are up to snuff. But as I said, things have been much better lately. I truly think they're all actually becoming friends. For real."

I'd never witnessed them being anything but amiable to one another, but then I supposed Glinda and I appeared to be friends as well. "I'm glad to hear that, but I'm surprised Bertie, Ophelia, and Imogene don't have their own greenhouses on their own land by now." I certainly wouldn't want to work under Harriette's viper eyes. "Aren't they all successful wealthy women?"

"Rolling in it," Lydia said with a bit of wonder. "Certain flowers are a hot commodity, and the Wickeds grow the rarest varieties. Except for Ophelia—she's happy sticking with the tried and true. 'If it ain't broke,' she always says. I can't blame her. She's the richest of them all, thanks to her expensive little red saffron threads. Do you know it takes seventy thousand flowers to make one pound of saffron?"

"That's a lot of plants."

"No, Darcy, that's a lot of *money*. Saffron sells for hundreds of dollars an *ounce*. More than gold."

"Where is all the saffron grown?" Surely not in her greenhouse—it was big but not seventy thousand flowers big.

"She has a plantation in Spain, but she keeps a crop in her greenhouse for local markets."

"All that money but they still use your mother's greenhouses?" It didn't make sense.

In the shadows of the path, Lydia looked more her age. "It's not the greenhouses, Darcy. It's the *land*. The name Elysian Fields comes from Greek mythology, the place where heroes and those chosen by the gods were buried."

"I'm not sure I understand," I said.

"The land under the greenhouses is rumored to be where the very first Crafters in this region were buried, long before cemeteries and grave markers. Simply put, the Elysian Fields are magical."

"Wow," I said, wrapping my brain around that. "Is that how you can produce naturally black flowers?"

Whump-whump-whump-whump.

I glanced around, but saw nothing unusual. I could only feel the weight and the increased heart rate from my tagalong's agitation.

She hesitated before saying, "It's part of it. I can't tell you more," she said. "It's top secret."

I smiled at her serious tone. "Really?"

"Darcy, you wouldn't believe the lengths people would go to replicate our flowers."

It was all so fascinating, but I set the Wickeds aside for now and tried to focus on what had led us down this conversational path. Harriette's will. "What about your sister?"

"What about her?" she snapped.

Whoa. Okay. Even though Lydia didn't share her mother's prejudices, I sensed some bad blood with her sister and wondered where it came from. "Is she in your mother's will?" Trista Harkette had been disowned. . . . I presumed that meant from Harriette's will, too, but I wanted to know for sure because I was nosy like that.

"She hardly needs the money."

It was true, thanks to the AbracadaBra, but since she was a Floracrafter, the Elysian Fields were her legacy, too. "And you do?"

"It's not the point, Darcy," she said dismissively. "Trista does her own thing, always has. She doesn't deserve any part of the Elysian Fields. She hasn't earned it."

"Like you?" I asked softly, suddenly realizing why Lydia had snapped at her sister's name.

"Damn right, like me. I've done everything ever asked of me. I married another Flora to please my mother, I work sixteen-hour days, I love that place—I've done everything right. The Elysian Fields are my reward. Mine alone. Well, mine and Willard's."

So much for her statement about reverting the Elysian Fields to a *family* business. Lydia wanted the place to herself—and by the way she'd absently tacked on Willard's name, I had a feeling he'd be lucky to get a twelve-by-twelve plot of land to garden.

Lydia drew in a deep breath and let it out. "I'm sorry. I get a little worked up thinking about people taking things that they haven't earned, which brings me back to this shyster Louis. He shouldn't get anything from my mother." Kicking a stone across the path, she added, "It makes me sick to think that someone may be preying on her and her fortune."

Chirping crickets suddenly silenced as Missy approached a clump of grass. As soon as she walked past, the sound started back up.

"Unfortunately, Darcy, I don't have much information on Louis at all. That's why I need your help." She stopped walking and faced me. "I have to stop Mother from making a huge mistake. If Louis doesn't exist, I need to protect her from making a complete fool of herself. If he does exist, then what is he hiding? Why won't he meet us? Why is he borrowing money? Not only is Mother risking her fortune, but I'm worried what a man of compromised morals would do if he learned about the Craft. He could ruin everything."

It was an angle I hadn't thought about. There were, of course, safety precautions in place to deal with nosy mortals. And to deal with Crafters who stepped out of line. Hopefully, it wouldn't come down to turning Louis into a frog.

"Will you take the job, Darcy? Will you locate Louis and find out what he's all about?"

"As You Wish's motto is No Job Is Too Big or Too Small," I said. For some reason, however, I had a feeling this job was going to be quite the challenge. "I'll certainly do my best to find out as much as I can about Louis, but, Lydia, what if I prove that he's a perfectly nice man?"

Her face tightened. "Then I'll just have to find another way to stop them from getting married, won't I?"

Chapter Four

The village green was ablaze in flashy festival lights—bright autumnal colors—and the usual delicate white fairy lights, twinkling prettily in the darkness as Missy and I crossed the village green, headed toward Spellbound Bookshop, Harper's store, to pick up Mimi. The scent of fried dough hung in the air, along with the crispness of the season. There was still a huge crowd gathered in front of the public parking lot, so activity amid the festival booths was limited. The caramel apple stand had no line at all, but I no longer had an appetite. Even for caramel apples. Which was saying something.

Lydia and I had set up a time for her to stop by As You Wish in the morning to fill out the necessary paperwork for me to start working on finding Louis. I didn't have much to go on, which made me nervous, but one way or another I'd track the man down.

If he existed.

It was a big if.

My boots clicked on the paved path as I considered the impact of another murder on village tourism. Experience led me to believe it would only increase the number of visitors, as it had in the past. People were just plain morbid. And a murder in the village around Halloween? The media was going to have a field day with that. If they ever found out that Michael was a witch ... I couldn't even imagine the fallout. Fortunately, that wasn't likely to happen. Crafters guarded our secret closely—and there were magical ways to keep mortals in check if they stumbled on the truth. There was the whole frog thing (used only in the most extreme cases), and I'd recently learned about a spell for a mind cleanse that could erase short-term memories.

I smiled, thinking a spell like that would have come in handy when I was going through my divorce. I'd have loved to get rid of memories of my ex-husband.

Then I shook my head. No, I *wouldn't* want that. I had to remember those mistakes so I didn't make them again. My marriage had been one big painful lesson, but from it I'd become much wiser.

I hoped.

The twining paths of the village green were littered with fallen leaves, rustling with each step Missy and I took. I stopped to admire a decorative urn full of flowers and plants, all dark in color, including pitch-black pansies and petunias, that helped set the spooky Halloween mood. The black petals reminded me of Harriette's roses, which reminded me of her party, which reminded me of her cake, which reminded me of Michael, and just like that, I felt the weight of grief on my chest again.

It didn't help that a presence was still following me.

Whump, whump.

I glanced down at Missy. "Do you feel that?"

Her dark eyes blinked at me, and her white eyebrows lifted as if she hadn't a clue what I was talking about.

If she sensed the presence, she wasn't the least bit bothered.

Great. A friendly ghost.

Michael?

I could easily picture his smile, and just like that, my heart ached again.

Missy put her front paws on my knees and bounced. I picked her up, and as she licked my chin, I smiled. The little dog had come into my life almost a year ago after Harper shoplifted her from a puppy-mill-affiliated pet shop in an attempt to bring light to the horrible situation going on in the store. There had been an arrest (Harper's), additional charges filed (against the shop and the puppy mill), and restitution made (which was why I now owned a Schnoodle). Harper had been sentenced to community service, and Missy (aka Miss Demeanor) had become part of our family.

The move here to the Enchanted Village from Ohio hadn't been smooth for Missy, but the longer we were here, the more she settled in. All three of us, actually.

Truthfully, the minute I arrived, I'd felt at home, at peace. I *belonged* here. Harper had a harder adjustment, but after she took over Spellbound and moved out of Ve's house and into an apartment above the bookshop, she seemed much happier.

Her relationship with village Lawcrafter Marcus Debrowski might have something to do with her current state of mind as well.

As I set Missy back on the ground, I heard a disturbance from the crowd and turned to see the medical examiner's van pulling away. Shuddering, I suddenly felt a little weak and grabbed onto the flower urn for balance. My fingertips grazed the velvety petals of a petunia, and I found myself fascinated with the little plant.

"Pedestrian but very pretty," a voice said from behind me.

I jumped, grabbing my heart. Turning slowly, I was
fully prepared to see some sort of glowing apparition.
Instead, I found Dash Khoury, Trista Harkette's husband, kneeling on the path. Missy was giving him a fond
hello.

"Sorry. Didn't mean to scare you," he said to me as he
scratched her back. His dark eyes held none of their
usual warmth.

Archie, my movie-buff friend, had once waxed on
about how Dash looked like an older Oded Fehr, an Is-
raeli actor I knew only from *The Mummy* (Archie was a
huge fan). Although Dash had darker skin and longer
hair, the resemblance was uncanny, and Archie always
swooned when Dash was around. He had quite the crush
on the Terracrafter.

"It's okay." My heartbeat *might* settle into a normal
rhythm by tomorrow. "What were you saying? 'Pedestrian'?"

As he stood, easily towering over me, Missy went
about sniffing his shoes. "The flowers. Petunias. Pansies.
But they're beautiful."

"I'm amazed they're still alive this far into the season." The village had already seen a few frosty nights.

He waggled long mocha fingers. "Magic, Darcy."

"Ah." Right. He was a Terracrafter, a Crafter with a
power to grow just about anything, anytime, anywhere. I
examined the petunia. "The color is stunning. You don't
see too many black flowers."

Long dark hair fell about his shoulders in thick—but
tamed—waves. I didn't know his age for certain but
placed him somewhere in his late forties. Crow's-feet
stretched from the corner of his eyes as he spoke in mea-
sured tones. "Black flowers are an illusion, if you will.
They're really plants with highly saturated colors. Reds,

purples, blues. These petunias are actually a deep purple that gives the appearance of black."

Now that he said it, I could see the blush of purple on the blooms. I suddenly thought about the Witching Hour roses and all the awards and accolades they'd received for being *naturally* black. I wanted to ask Dash about that, but I also recognized that talking to him about his estranged mother-in-law's flowers might be a bit inappropriate.

"Are you sure you're okay?" Dash asked. "You still look a little pale."

"Long day," I said, "and not enough to eat."

"I can get you something from one of the booths . . . ," he offered.

"No, no. Thank you." I tried for a smile but failed. "I don't have much of an appetite." I glanced over my shoulder at the crowd and swallowed hard. "I was there when the body was found." He didn't need to know all the gory details.

Dash's eyes filled with a sheen of tears, and his face turned stony, stoic. He drew in a deep breath. "I warned that boy," he said under his breath, more to himself than to me.

Whump-whump-whump-whump. The pulsing around me had kicked up a notch, and I felt a wash of anxiety come over me.

"Warned who? Michael?"

He nodded, giving one short quick jerk of his head.

"Warned him about what?"

Suddenly, a ringing filled the air. He held up a shaky finger, pulled a phone out of his pocket, and looked at the display. "I'm sorry," he said. "I have to take it. It's Trista."

He stepped to the side while my imagination ran wild. *What* had he warned Michael about?

A few seconds later Dash snapped his phone shut and turned toward me. His face had drained of color. "I have to go."

And just like that, he sprinted away.

I stared after him.

Looking down at Missy, I said, "What was that all about?"

She barked.

Sometimes I wished she could talk, that she was a familiar. But if she was, she wasn't letting it be known to me.

My curiosity made me edgy. I made a mental note to tell Nick what Dash had said about warning Michael. Maybe the Terracrafter knew something important about Michael's death.

In fact, I hoped it would lead to whoever had killed him, because I hated the thought of a killer on the loose in the village.

Whump-whump-whump-whump. The anxiety-laced pulsing made me even more light-headed.

"Calm down," I said aloud to the presence. "You have to calm down."

Whump-whump-whump.

"Better," I murmured. Then I realized what I was doing.

I was talking to a ghost.

Looking down at Missy, I said, "I've lost my mind. Let's go see Harper."

Missy's tail swung back and forth. Apparently, she agreed with me about my sanity.

We walked slowly, and as we approached the shop, I saw Harper standing on the other side of the big display window, binoculars pressed to her eyes.

Was I the only one in the village without binoculars?

Harper was tiny, just a smidge over five feet tall. With

her cute short haircut, big elfish eyes, and feisty personality, she fit perfectly into this eccentric village.

A bell jingled as I pushed into the shop. Harper lowered the binoculars and narrowed her eyes on me. "You
had something to do with what's happening across the
square, didn't you?"

Harper had a strange affinity for anything criminally
forensic and was forever envious that I kept finding dead
bodies.

Personally, it was a talent I could do without.

"I plead the fifth." I dropped into a cozy armchair and
unclipped Missy's leash so she could wander around the
shop in search of Pie, Harper's kitten.

"I knew it," Harper said.

The store was empty. I assumed all the customers
were across the square, gawking at the crime scene. I
loved what Harper had done with the shop over the last
couple of months. Using Van Gogh's *Starry Night* as in-
spiration, she'd painted the walls a deep blue with swirls
of golds and creams. Glass stars hung from the ceiling.
One long wall housed what looked to be a haunted forest. A dozen tall black spooky Tim Burton–type trees
with hollowed-out trunks held narrow shelves full of
books. Above, curlicue branches stretched and intertwined with one another, some touching and spreading
across the ceiling. For the middle of the store, Harper
had hired Nick, who was a woodcrafter in his spare time,
to build shelving made of birch branches. The back wall
was covered in three-dimensional iron vines that twisted
and turned, holding books at odd angles. The children's
nook had been sectioned off with another set of spooky
trees, and I had painted a mural of a forest alight with
fairies and elves. The area was filled with miniature pad-
ded toadstools of varying shapes, sizes, and colors to be
used as chairs or tables. It should have been too much.

Too gaudy. But it wasn't. It was a feast for the senses. All in all, Harper had brought the Enchanted Forest inside the shop, and customers had rightly been enchanted.

Harper relinquished her spot at the window and sat in the cushy armchair across from me. "Was that a medical examiner's van I saw?"

Ignoring her question, I glanced around. "Where's Mimi?" Nick's daughter was why I was here, after all.

"Reconnaissance. She'll be back soon."

I rolled my eyes. Of course Harper had sent Mimi to see what was going on. . . . Her nosiness knew no bounds. I stretched out my legs and settled in to wait for Mimi. After she returned, we'd run to her place, pack an overnight bag, and pick up Higgins, Nick and Mimi's massive dog, as well. I couldn't very well leave the St. Bernard home alone all night.

"What?" Harper said. "*I* couldn't leave the shop."

Harper had hired a few part-time employees, including Angela Curtis, a woman we'd shared an ill-fated cooking class with a few months ago, but apparently Harper was manning the shop alone tonight.

"What happened over there?" she asked. "Did a tourist have a heart attack or something? I saw that haunted house. That thing's terrifying. I almost had a heart attack just walking past it."

"The haunted house is called Boo Manor, for heaven's sake. It's as scary as a rubber ducky." It was harmless—designed to be family friendly—but Harper had always been terrified of haunted houses. Honestly, Halloween was her least favorite holiday, which was kind of ironic considering she was a *witch*.

"Mark my words," she said. "It's a big ol' den of bad juju."

Harper had a knack for sensing bad juju—and death, too. I was surprised she hadn't sensed the murder.

"Now tell me what happened!" she said, jiggling her feet.

Sometimes she was like a four-year-old. "There was a murder," I said. She was bound to find out anyway. "On the path behind the pub leading to the Enchanted Trail."

Harper's brown eyes widened, and her jaw dropped. "A murder? Who was killed? When did this happen?"

I fidgeted in my seat.

"You found the body, didn't you?" she accused, folding her arms. A pout tugged at the corners of her lips.

I was never going to hear the end of this. I tried to downplay my involvement. "It wasn't *me*. It was Missy who found him." I pointed at the dog.

Missy was, at that moment, trying her best to convince Pie to come down from a bookshelf and play with her. So far, the tail wagging wasn't working on the orange tabby.

Poor Missy. She received much the same reaction from Tilda, Aunt Ve's persnickety Himalayan, at home. Maybe she needed a playmate. It was something to think about.

Harper threw her hands in the air, and her big despairing elfin eyes looked pained. "Why can't I ever find a dead body?"

"This from the girl who is scared of Boo Manor?"

Pointedly, she said, "A dead body isn't going to jump out at me, is it, Darcy?"

"You never know."

"You're not making me feel better." She shifted, trying to get comfortable.

I couldn't help but smile. Only my sister would need consoling over not finding a dead body.

Suddenly, she leaned forward, her brown eyes alight with morbid curiosity. "Who was it? Anyone we know?"

The lump was back in my throat. "Michael Healey."

Harper gasped. "No way!"

I watched as Pie slowly made his way down the bookshelves to bat a paw at Missy's head—toying with the dog. Missy was apparently thrilled to be accosted in such a way and bounced happily, much like a pogo stick.

"He was supposed to have delivered a cake to Harriette Harkette's party," I explained to Harper, "but he never showed up. Long story short, the van was in the pub's lot, with the cake in it, and Missy found the body in the shrubbery. . . ."

Harper held up a hand, palm out. "Whoa now! What do you mean 'long story short'? I want details! Lots of them."

Of course she did. "I don't really have any. I saw a bloody sock; then I ran and called the police. Nick said Michael had been stabbed."

Harper blinked, then winced as if picturing the injury. "Stabbed?"

I nodded.

"Gruesome."

I nodded again.

"Why would someone want to hurt him? He was one of the most personable people I knew."

"That's because he is—was—an Illumicrafter. Amy, too, I guess. Did you know that?"

She shook her head and smoothed the golden brown hair over her ears. She had an adorable long-layered pixie cut—one I envied. I'd tried the style once years ago and couldn't pull it off. So I'd grown out my dark hair, and out it remained. The long length suited me—it was perfect for an easy ponytail, and I'd recently added bangs, so it felt like an updated look, even though it really wasn't.

I wasn't all that fond of change, but after the upheaval

of moving to the village, I was getting much better at adapting.

"Really?" Harper said. "I guess it makes sense. Amy is just as bright and bubbly as he is. Was." She bit her thumbnail. "Does she know yet?"

I leaned back in the cozy chair, letting some of my nervous energy seep away. The bookshop had that effect on me. It was a soothing place, despite there having been a murder just outside its back door a few months previously. "She should by now. The police sent someone to her place, and Evan and Starla went to make sure she's okay."

"I just can't believe it. Amy was here earlier, studying for midterms." Harper continued to chew on her nail; then she tipped her head and bit her lip.

"What?" I asked.

"What, what?" she countered.

Giving up on Pie, Missy came over and hopped up on my lap. I rubbed her ears. "You tell me."

"Maybe it's nothing, but earlier, when Amy was in here, she got a phone call, packed up in a hurry, and rushed off. She dropped some of her notes on the way out, but when I yelled after her, she didn't even turn around. Just kept running down the sidewalk, papers scattering behind her. I did my best to pick them all up."

I sat straighter. "What time was this?"

"A little after seven."

Right around the time Evan Sullivan said Michael had left the bakery.

Whump-whump-whump-whump.

Not this again. I tried to ignore it. "Do you have any idea who called?"

She shifted and shook her head. "I'd assumed it was that boyfriend of hers. When he says jump, she asks how high."

Fisk Khoury, Dash and Trista's son. "Really?"

"It certainly feels that way. I haven't decided yet if he's controlling or if she's just desperate to please him. Little by little I've seen a change in her. Gone are her colorful sweaters replaced by black tees. Her once-blond hair is now black with dark pink streaks. That lightness and brightness in her is slowly fading. Even her grades have been dropping. I've tried to talk to her about it, but I think he's her first real boyfriend, and she's too head over heels to see the dysfunction. I think Michael tried to talk to her about it, too."

"I heard he and Fisk weren't getting along. Is that true?"

"It might be," she said slyly. "Where are you getting your information?"

I rolled my eyes at her lack of subtlety. "Starla."

"Ooh, she's good." Harper tucked her legs beneath her. "It's true. I've seen Michael and Fisk arguing more than once lately."

"About?"

Whump-whump-whump-whump.

"I wish I knew. It's always out of earshot." She glanced around, her gaze darting here, there, everywhere, finally landing on me. "Do you feel that?"

My nerves jumped at the word "wish," but I quickly relaxed. Wishcraft Law prohibited Wishcrafters from granting their own wishes—or granting the wishes of other Wishcrafters. We were plain out of luck when it came to wishing, except when it came to the tried and true methods of wishbones, eyelashes, dandelions, and falling stars. Oh, and magical amulets, which, as I learned, could be dangerous in the wrong hands. "Feel what?"

"I don't know. It's . . . I don't know." Shimmying as if she had the heebie-jeebies, she looked around suspiciously.

I had a pretty good idea what she was talking about, but I didn't want to tell her there was probably a ghost in the room. She had trouble with kiddie haunted houses—I didn't even want to think about what the knowledge of a real ghost would do to her.

I tried to distract her. "I just ran into Dash Khoury on the green, and he said he'd tried to warn Michael about something." If Fisk was a controlling force on Amy, it might explain why he and Michael had been at odds lately. I had to assume Michael would do anything to protect his sister—even if it meant turning against his best friend.

"Really? About what?"

"I don't know. He got a call from Trista and took off before he could tell me."

"Sounds intriguing."

She was right; it did.

She said, "I know that Michael and Amy are both very close to Dash and Trista. They think of them almost like family."

Almost but not quite. After all, Amy was dating Fisk.

Harper tapped her chin and gave me a half smile. "My curiosity is killing me. Dash was very much a father figure to Michael, so Michael most likely would have gone to him with any problems he was having lately. But what exactly would he have been warning Michael against?"

Whump-whump-whump-whump.

Harper snapped her head left and right. "Seriously, you don't feel that?"

Trying to look innocent, I shook my head. "I know that Fisk looks a little scary, but do you think he's dangerous?"

She arched an eyebrow. "If you're asking if I think he could have killed Michael . . . I don't know. I tend to think he's all talk and no action. But if you're asking if he's dangerous to Amy . . . that answer is yes. If he *is* controlling, he holds the potential to destroy her. Her hopes, her dreams, her *light*. Everything."

Which left me wondering exactly how far Fisk would go to protect that hold over her.

Chapter Five

An hour later, I followed my motley crew into the mudroom at As You Wish. Mimi and I kicked off our shoes as Higgins charged past us.

"Well, me-oh-my! Look who decided to come home," Ve sang loudly from the kitchen. "Is there something you forgot to tell me about the stripper, Dar—" Suddenly, she stopped talking, gasped, then let out an ear-splitting scream. *"Eeeee!"*

I, too, would have screamed if a huge St. Bernard had come galloping toward me at full speed.

She stopped screaming long enough to yell at the dog. "Down, Higgins! Down!"

Unfortunately for Ve, Higgins wasn't listening.

"You'd better go rescue her," I said to Mimi, nudging her forward. "Higgins might slobber her to death."

I hung up my coat, my bag, and Missy's leash. The little dog trotted ahead of me into the kitchen as if there were nothing out of the ordinary about Ve's being molested by a massive mutt. As I stepped over the threshold, I really wished I'd had a camera to capture the scene.

Ve was sitting on the counter, and Higgins was doing

his best to join her up there. Drool pooled at the corners of his mouth, and Mimi, who was maybe one hundred pounds soaking wet, was trying her best to tug Higgins backward. It was an image that I would have liked to frame, but that was impossible.

Even if I'd had a camera with me, the shot wouldn't have turned out. Wishcrafters, in photos and videos, emitted a blinding white light, like a starburst. It might have been a cute shot of Higgins, however.

"Down, down!" Ve yelled as a giant pink tongue lapped at her chin and her cheeks.

"He loves you, Aunt Ve," Mimi said, pulling with all her might.

Ve's hair (which I'd never once seen down) was coming loose from its clip. Coppery strands framed her face. "The feeling, my dear, is not mutual. Down, Higgins! Darcy, a little help?"

"But I'm enjoying the show," I said, heading for a specific cabinet.

Whump, whump. The ghost (Michael?) had finally calmed down after my talk with Harper. I hoped it stayed that way for a while.

Ve threw me a dark I-will-get-back-at-you look. Laughing, I pulled a giant rawhide bone that we kept for Higgins's visits from the cabinet, and tossed it down the hallway and into the family room. The floor vibrated as he took off after it.

Ve, still sitting on the counter, shuddered as she assessed the drool damage. "I need a shower. And maybe a cigarette."

Mimi giggled, and it reminded me that she wasn't a little kid who didn't understand innuendos. She was almost thirteen—her birthday was in a couple of months, and she was wise beyond her years. This was maybe because she was naturally bright, or maybe because she hadn't had the easiest of childhoods. It wasn't until after her mother died and Nick had moved them here that Mimi discovered that she, too, was a witch.

We'd pretty much adopted the girl into the family. She was like a little sister to Harper and me, and Ve insisted Mimi call her "Aunt," too. I wasn't sure Ve felt as loving toward Mimi and Nick's massive St. Bernard, however. Especially at the moment, while she was covered in Higgins's drool.

I heard slurping in the living room. Higgins was in doggy heaven with his treat. Missy had zero interest in what Higgins was up to, and instead focused all her attention on Mimi. The dog looked to be in her own form of nirvana as Mimi picked her up and cuddled her.

I glanced around, looking for Tilda, Ve's prissy cat, but she was nowhere to be found. Smart kitty—she probably saw Higgins and took off for one of her favorite hiding spots.

"What were you saying about a stripper, Aunt Ve?"

Ve shot me an exasperated look. "Stripper?"

Ah, playing dumb. It was a reasonable avoidance technique, but Mimi was much too smart to fall for it.

Mimi nodded. "When we were coming in, you were saying something about a stripper to Darcy." Her brown eyes grew even wider. "Was there was a stripper at Harriette's party tonight?"

Personally, I'd rather be talking to Mimi about the stripper than the murder. She'd peppered me with questions for the past hour, ever since she returned to the bookstore, while we stopped by her house to pick up clothes and Higgins, and during the walk back here.

Stripping was a nice change of topic.

Ve smiled sweetly. "Are you staying the night, Mimi?"

Mimi nodded. Her curly black hair had been pulled back into one long braid. She'd grown since I first met her—by a good two inches. A few more inches and we'd be seeing eye to eye. At the rate she was going, she would be supermodel tall by her freshman year of high school. "My dad has to work late because of the murder. Did you hear about that? Poor Michael, right? I just saw him at the bakery yesterday." She frowned. "He gave me an extra cake pop. He was so nice."

I slid my arm around her. We'd already discussed—at length—the extra cake pop and how kind Michael had always been to her.

"Who do you think killed him?" she asked. Her eyes widened again. "Do you think there's a serial killer in the village?"

I didn't like the note of excitement in her voice. She'd been hanging around with Harper a bit too much.

Ve carefully slid off the counter. "Yes, Michael was a very kind soul; yes, I heard about the murder; and no, I don't think there's a serial killer in the village."

"How can you be so sure?" Mimi asked.

Ve tapped Mimi's nose playfully. "For one thing, only one person has died. Nothing serial about that."

Mimi frowned as though she hadn't thought the definition of serial killer all the way through. After a long second, she said, "So, the stripper?"

I had to laugh at her tenacity.

Ve eyed the liquor cabinet as she crossed to the sink to clean off the drool. "Stripper?" she tittered. "What stripper?"

Someone knocked once, then opened the back door. "Hello?"

I turned as the man stepped into the kitchen. My jaw dropped.

"Sorry to interrupt," he said. "I forgot my duffel bag in the bathroom. . . ."

"*That* stripper," I said to Mimi, elbowing her.

Higgins, I noticed, hadn't budged at the entrance of a stranger. I had the feeling a parade of poodles could march through the family room and his attention wouldn't waver from that rawhide.

Missy's ears twitched, but she didn't seem to be eager to leave Mimi's arms to assess the man, either.

"I prefer 'revealing entertainer,'" Hot Rod Stiffington said, shoving a hand in my direction. "Nice to meet you."

"Darcy Merriweather," I said, shaking his hand. "And this is Mimi Sawyer." My gaze slid to my aunt. "I assume you know Ve?"

"We met earlier," he said.

Ve's cheeks were a rosy red, and she wouldn't meet my eye. "I'll, ah, get your bag." She scurried down the hallway toward the guest bath.

Mimi shook Rod's hand, and kept staring. "Are you a Chippendale? You seem a little—"

I cut her off before she said something we might all regret. "Mimi, how do you even know about Chippendales?"

"YouTube."

Ah. Had to love the Internet.

"No, I'm not a Chippendale," Hot Rod said with a self-deprecating smile as he swiped a hand over his bald head.

As if it needed to be said aloud.

Fortunately, Hot Rod was fully covered. He wore dark sweatpants and a zippered sweatshirt, its fabric stretched over his belly. Up close, he looked a little bit like my favorite high school teacher, Mr. Rickman, a wonderful man whose death during my senior year had left me heartbroken.

I immediately softened toward Hot Rod.

Wrinkles multiplied as a smile spread on Hot Rod's

face. "My work is more . . . a comedy routine than a dance routine."

And just like that, I liked him even more.

Mimi eyed him appraisingly. "I can see that."

"What are you doing here again?" I asked, wishing Mr. Rickman was still around to teach Mimi tact. "You said you forgot a bag?" It was then that I noticed two wineglasses in the sink.

Hmm. What had Ve been up to while I was gone?

Ve came rushing back into the kitchen. She thrust a large bag at Hot Rod, and her hands went to her blotchy throat. "There you go, Rodney! I know you have to be getting back, so don't let us keep you."

His eyes twinkled. "Right. Thanks again for your hospitality, Ve."

I wondered if "hospitality" was a euphemism in this case. I studied Ve carefully, but other than her full body blush, she wasn't giving much away.

"It was lovely of you to invite me over in the first place." He turned to me. "I didn't know what to do since my car was blocked in by emergency vehicles, and then, like an angel dropped from the sky, Ve was there, inviting me back here so I could change and wait for the traffic to clear out."

An angel, my foot. More like a little devil.

"It was nice to have a slight respite before heading home," he said.

I also wondered if "respite" was a euphemism. What had Ve been thinking? I fished for information. "I heard Harriette really enjoyed your show tonight."

"Oh, she did," Ve said, practically pushing Hot Rod toward the back door by the sheer force of her glare. "Rodney was a big hit, but he really must be going."

She was as subtle as a sledgehammer.

"Yes," he said. "I must. It's been a pleasure, ladies." He doffed an imaginary cap and headed out the back door.

As soon as the latch clicked into place, Mimi and I turned to face Ve.

She tried to head us off at the pass. "Have there been any developments in the murder case?" She placed an emphasis on the word "murder" in an attempt to distract.

Mimi fell for it. "Dad says Michael— Ow!"

I'd stomped on her foot. "Ve? Is there something you forgot to tell us about the stripper?"

Pursing her lips, she said, "Touché. Now, about poor Michael . . ."

Mimi opened her mouth, looked at me, then snapped it closed again. Missy, still tucked cozily in Mimi's arms, blinked at Ve. Apparently, she wanted answers, too.

"Hot Rod?" I pressed.

Ve folded her arms. "He's adorable."

He was, in an older-guy kind of way.

"And Terry?" I asked of her boyfriend.

"It was just one drink," Ve said, trying to justify herself.

"Uh-huh." My aunt had issues with monogamy. She'd already been married four times (once to Terry), and she had almost walked down the aisle again this past summer but canceled the wedding at the last minute. "Are you sure it was just a drink?"

Ve cast a look at Mimi, rolled her eyes, pouted and said, "It's not like I didn't try for something a bit *more*, but he wasn't interested. Turned me down flat. My ego is crushed. I'm going to take a bath, then go to bed." She headed toward the back staircase, then turned around. "We'll never see Hot Rod again."

I swear there was wistfulness in her voice.

"So," she continued, "we'll just keep his visit to ourselves, right, girls?"

It wasn't so much a request as an order.

"Right," Mimi and I said in unison.

Ve nodded and trundled up the steps.

When she was out of earshot, Mimi said, "That was nice of Ve to invite Rod back here."

"Yeah, nice." I pulled two mugs from the cabinet along with the container of hot chocolate mix.

Mimi smiled—she had Nick's smile. "She's going to see him again, isn't she?"

"She's probably calling him right now."

"Do you think he'll let us call him 'Uncle Hot Rod'?"

I was laughing when Ve appeared at the top of the steps, a curious look on her face. "Has either of you seen Tilda?"

Mimi shook her head, and I said, "Not tonight."

Ve came down the steps. "She's not upstairs."

"She's probably lying low because of Higgins," I said, abandoning the cocoa mix. "Let's split up and search the house."

By midnight, we'd looked high, low, and even under a now-snoozing Higgins (just in case). There was no sign of her.

Tilda was missing.

Chapter Six

"*A stem blooms devoid of light, at the darkest time of night.*"

I came awake with a start and looked around.

Missy lifted her chin and blinked drowsily at me, as if wondering why I had disturbed her sleep. I patted her head, and she settled back down as Higgins snored from his spot on the floor. The bed shifted as Mimi rolled over in her sleep. Usually when she stayed the night, she slept in Harper's old room down the hall, but at some point in the wee hours, she'd climbed in with me.

As much as Michael Healey's murder fascinated her, it had also clearly freaked her out—she'd been too scared to sleep alone.

A stem blooms devoid of light, at the darkest time of night.

Had I dreamed the voice whispering to me? It was just the four of us here. Two of us couldn't talk, one was still sound asleep, and then there was me. I glanced around. Maybe Archie or Pepe, my mouse familiar friend, had snuck in?

But no—there was no one else.

Well. Except for the ghost.

Whump-whump.

"Michael?" I whispered. "Is that you?"

Before I moved to the village, I never in a million years would have guessed I'd try talking to a ghost. Of course, back then I never dreamed I was a witch. That familiars existed. That magic was real.

My life had come a long way.

At the sound of my voice, Missy cracked open an eye.

"Sorry," I said to her. "Go back to sleep."

An owl hooted somewhere in the distance, sounding sad and lonely. It was almost five in the morning, and I knew there'd be no going back to sleep for me. I wiggled my way out from under the covers without further disturbing Mimi, Missy, or Higgins. There was a time when I lamented sleeping alone—the recovery from my divorce had taken me a while—but now I was rather missing my empty bed. Especially if a ghost shared it as well.

It wasn't something I really wanted to think about, so I slipped on my glasses and my robe and went downstairs. I glanced at Tilda's bowls and immediately felt a pang. Where could she be? She wasn't much of an outdoor cat—she wandered around the yard from time to time, but she'd never strayed beyond the fence before.

We'd already started the phone chain, asking neighbors to keep an eye out for her. Later today, I'd hand out Lost flyers. Someone had to have seen her. White and gray puffballs with attitude didn't just disappear.

Or did they?

There was a familiar that was here at the house a lot. I'd heard her voice a dozen times, but Ve would never tell me who it was. I'd questioned both Missy and Tilda, but neither had responded to me. . . . If either was a familiar, they didn't want me to know.

If Tilda *was* a familiar, she might have other business

to attend to beyond the house . . . but wouldn't Ve know
that and say so before an all-out search party was formed?

It was all so confusing, this magic stuff. I hoped one
day I'd get used to it. One day soon.

The automatic coffeepot had already brewed the first
pot of coffee, and I poured myself a big mug. I unlocked
the back door and hoped that I'd find Tilda curled up on
the back step, but I immediately knew that was a silly
notion. If she'd found her way home, she would have
come in through the doggy door we'd left open.

I sighed as I tightened my sash and sat on the porch
swing. Frost had settled overnight, and the grass was
crisp with shards of frozen dew. Cascading ivy vines covered the fence and trailed up and over the arched iron
gate. During the warmer months, showy clematis blooms
intertwined with the ivy, the bright flowers a beautiful
contrast against deep green leaves.

My eye wandered next door, to Terry Goodwin's house.
As usual, all the shades and drapes were drawn. He was
a private man—mostly because he bore such an uncanny
resemblance to an older Elvis that I had started wondering if he could possibly be the singer. Maybe all those
rumors about his being alive were true. . . .

Only after realizing Elvis would be in his late seventies
did I stop speculating. Terry wasn't that old—more likely
in his early sixties as far as I could tell. Archie's ornate
iron cage, I noticed, was empty, which wasn't unusual this
time of day. Terry often took the macaw in at night to
protect him from the elements—and brazen tourists. Archie, of course, also had his own version of a doggy door.
As the Elder's right-hand bird, he had to be at her beck
and call. All hours. Day or night. Inside or out.

The porch swing squeaked slightly as I swayed back
and forth. In the quiet of the moment, I realized with a
start that I was alone. No presence. I breathed in the

sharp chilly air, feeling the sting in my nostrils, and I felt myself relax.

I was alone. It was blissful.

The feeling, however, didn't last long, as the silence was broken by the sound of flapping wings.

Archie flew toward me, looking as bright as a polished gem under the soft glow of the porch light and the backdrop of frosted landscape behind him. His hood was a vibrant red, and the blues, greens, and yellows in his tail reminded me of the tropics. Of warm sand, fruity drinks with little umbrellas, and lazy days without a care in the world.

Oh, if only it were true.

Unfortunately, I had many cares. Including a murder, a ghost, and a missing pet.

For a second, I thought Archie might be here under orders from the Elder, but then he called out a cheerful, "Tally ho, Darcy!" as he swooped downward. With a dramatic flourish he landed on the porch railing.

I breathed in soothing coffee steam and said, "'It takes an early bird to get the best of a worm like me.'"

He tipped his feathered head and considered me with a dark eye. "*Pillow Talk.*"

"You're good," I said.

"I know." He fluffed his plumage.

We often tried to stump each other with movie quotes. It had become quite the competition.

I sipped my coffee, loving the slow burn down my throat. "You're up early."

"Haven't been to bed yet."

He had a deep yet playful voice. Well, playful when he was being himself. When he was acting as a representative of the Elder, he sounded formal and intimidating. "Working?"

"Intelligence gathering for the Elder."

"Which means?"

"Spying on village residents, of course."

I smiled. "Of course."

"This murder has the Elder on edge." He leaned in and whispered, "She's scary when she's on edge."

"I think she's scary all the time." Talk about intimidating. She had inconceivable powers—and as the Craft's judge and jury, she had the ability to revoke any Crafter's magic if she found a Crafter in violation of a Craft law. She met with violators in a clearing in the Enchanted Forest—she was always hidden within a magical tree, so her true identity wasn't revealed. I often wondered who she really was, and whether I'd met her yet in and around the village.

"That's because you don't know her well yet," Archie said with an amused lilt to his voice. "She's quite personable."

Yet? I had no plans to meet with her ever again. Meeting with her usually meant I'd screwed up. Again. "Did you learn anything about the murder?" I asked, changing the subject before he suggested a getting-to-know-you tea with the Elder.

"Dreadful business," he said, shaking out his feathers. "No suspects as of yet, though I did learn one interesting piece of news. Fisk Khoury has a black eye. Apparently he'd been involved in an altercation early last evening."

"With Michael?"

"Indeed. They were seen going at it in the alley behind the bakery. Vince Paxton broke it up and sent them on their way."

Vince Paxton owned Lotions and Potions, the village bath and body shop, and he was also a Seeker—a mortal who sought to become a Crafter. Which was nearly impossible, save for a few exceptions. Crafting was hereditary—a mortal could never obtain any Crafting powers. Vince knew that, but it didn't stop him from trying. I had to admire his persistence.

"Around seven?" I asked.

"How did you know?"

"Evan said Michael had left to deliver Harriette Harkette's cake around then, and Harper said that Amy Healey received a disturbing phone call at seven and left in a hurry." I took another sip of my coffee and dribbled on my robe. I thumbed the droplet away and asked, "Do you know what they were fighting about?"

"Negative. Vince, however, might know." Archie tipped his head and blinked at me.

Subtle, he wasn't. "You want me to talk to him."

"What a brilliant idea!"

I rolled my eyes.

Starting to feel a chill, I pulled my robe up closer to my chin. Archie obviously couldn't question Vince.

I slowly rocked in the swing. My good friend Mrs. Pennywhistle worked for Vince part-time at Lotions and Potions, and I wished she wasn't out of town—she would have already wheedled any information about the fight out of Vince. He was going to become suspicious if I started asking him questions—so I was going to have to be sneaky about it.

"What are you thinking about? You've a most curious look on your face," Archie said. His claws curled around the railing, and his colorful tail feathers looked startlingly vibrant against the pale purple paint.

"Manipulation."

"Ah, very good."

I studied him, his dark eyes. "Does the Elder think a Crafter is involved in Michael's murder?"

His wing twitched. "Unknown at this time."

He'd paused just a second too long before answering. If a Crafter had somehow used his or her power to hurt

Michael, the Elder would know immediately as the Craft motto was Do No Harm. But if a Crafter had killed Michael—but hadn't used magic to do it, the Elder wouldn't have any way of knowing.

Archie's hesitation, however, had me suspicious that he knew more than he let on. "What aren't you telling me, Archibald?"

He blinked innocently. "I don't know what you mean."

"You're the one who needs my help to get information from Vince. Don't you think you should share what you know with me?"

"Negative."

"That doesn't seem fair."

" 'Ah, but nobody said life was fair.' "

"*Mommie Dearest*," I said grudgingly.

"Faye Dunaway at her finest," Archie said with reverence.

"You're not going to tell me anything else, are you?"

"About?" he asked innocently.

Undoubtedly he was under orders to keep quiet. "All right. We'll play by your rules for now." I finished off my coffee and finally noticed how cold I was. I set my mug on the floorboards, and as I straightened, the doggy door opening caught my eye. I was reminded again about poor Tilda, and a fresh wave of tension came over me. "You didn't happen to see Tilda during your travels last night, did you?"

He brightened. "Is she missing?"

"You don't have to sound so happy about it."

"But, Darcy, she looks at me like I'm a snack."

It was true. She did. "Be that as it may, have you seen her?"

"No." He shook his head, his neck feathers shimmering in the light.

"If you had seen her, would you tell me?"

"Doubtful. Did I mention the snack thing?"

I really couldn't blame him. After a long second, I said, "Do you know if Tilda's a familiar?"

He waved a wing at me. "Oh, no you don't, Darcy Merriweather. Familiars are for you to discover on your own."

"Why?"

"Why what?"

"Why do I have to discover them on my own? I learn about most Crafters in the village through word of mouth. Why not familiars, too?"

"It's not for me to decide," he said with a strange tone.

I set my foot on the floorboards to stop rocking. "Whose decision is it?"

"My beak is sealed."

"The Elder's?"

He made a humming noise, as if talking with his beak closed. I couldn't help but wonder why the Elder would make such an edict.

While I pondered, I saw a flash on the village green. A bright light that was extinguished as suddenly as it had appeared. I blinked, wondering if I'd imagined it. That was twice this morning that I questioned my imagination. It was becoming something of a common occurrence.

The hinges on the swing creaked softly. *A stem blooms devoid of light, at the darkest time of night.* The verse kept playing in my head. I would bet my last Peppermint Pattie that I hadn't imagined—or dreamed—those words. So, who had spoken them? And why?

"Archie, can Crafters become ghosts?"

Archie tipped his head side to side. "I don't rightly know. They can become spirits, of course. But ghosts? Not certain."

"What's the difference between the two?"

He thought for a second, then said, "I don't know, but the Elder would, Darcy."

I was afraid he was going to say that. I didn't particularly want to meet with her.

"Shall I set up a time?"

"Not yet," I said.

He mimicked a chicken's squawking.

"You're not funny," I said, standing.

"I am so."

Smiling, I turned to go inside. As I did so, I saw another flash on the green. I glanced at Archie. "Did you see that?"

"What?" he asked.

"A light on the green. It keeps turning on and off."

"Probably one of the vendors setting up early."

Maybe. But my instincts told me otherwise.

Chapter Seven

I laced up my running shoes and hit the path along the green at a good clip. A few months ago I couldn't even jog half a mile, and now I was regularly running several miles a day. Most of the time I ran with Starla, Evan, or Nick. Today, I had the ghost with me.

Whump, whump.

I assumed the ghost was Michael and wondered if there was a way I could find out for sure.

I had to admit, it was rather comforting knowing I wasn't alone on these trails. It was still dark, and the festival—especially the harmless haunted house—looked a little spooky in shadow.

I kept an eye out for that strange flash of light I'd seen earlier—and for a flash of Tilda's white fur. She didn't much like me. In fact, she kept spitting up hairballs in my bed. But I'd become rather attached to her, and I hoped she was all right, that someone had taken her in last night and was just waiting till morning to call the phone number on her collar tag. My heart broke at the thought of her out in the cold.

A light was on in the Gingerbread Shack—Evan was already there prepping the day's treats. I wondered how he and Starla had fared with Amy last night, and I decided to stop in and ask. I was zigzagging across the green when I spotted the glow.

I slowed to a stop near the Ghoulousel and stared at the public parking lot. The Gingerbread Shack van had been towed, and yellow police tape had been strung around the entire lot. But right at the spot where Michael's body had been found, something was emitting a dazzling bright light.

Whump-whump-whump.

The ghost was getting worked up about something.

As I watched, the light flickered and died out, then came back on a moment later, full blaze.

What on earth?

I was debating what to do when a force pushed me from behind, shoving me forward, toward the glow.

Enough was enough. "Now listen here," I said in a sharp whisper. "I don't mind you hanging around, but no shoving me around! It's freaky. Understand?"

A tiny light flickered. It could have been mistaken for a firefly, but I knew. I smiled. "Good."

I turned back toward the glow in the parking lot. I could have sworn it was bigger, brighter, like a giant beacon.

"I take it," I said, "by your pushing that you want me to go over there. Flash once for yes, twice for no."

The tiny light flashed once.

I was afraid of that. I swallowed hard and asked for confirmation of what I already suspected. "Are you Michael?"

Another single flash. *Yes.*

My throat tightened with emotion as I let that sink in. I had been assuming the presence was him, but to have it confirmed was unsettling. After all, he'd been murdered not twelve hours ago. My heart ached with grief for what he'd gone through.

"Why are you following me?" I asked, my words tight with emotion.

Nothing flashed, and there was no *whump*ing, either. After a long moment, I felt another nudge and realized that a searing heat accompanied the contact, as if a hot poker were, well, poking me.

"All right," I finally said, pulling myself together. "I get the message. Let's go. There will be time for questions later." I hoped. "But no more touching."

With my dark sweatpants and sweatshirt, I probably looked a lot like a prowler as I stealthily crossed the street, ducked under the crime-scene tape, and pressed my back against the pub's exterior. I inched my way toward the light.

Whump-whump-whump-whump.

I knew the feeling. My heart pounded, my palms dampened, and I wondered how I had gotten myself into this crazy situation. Out here before dawn, letting a ghost boss me around . . .

Almost to the light I stopped. Maybe I should turn back. Get Ve. Notify the Elder. Nick. Someone.

Another hot nudge on my arm startled me.

I drew in a sharp breath. "You're pushing your luck."

Michael flashed three times.

"I'm taking that as 'I'm sorry.'"

He flashed once.

"You're forgiven."

His urging propelled me to investigate. I inched along the wall, tentatively nearing the glow. The brilliant white light cast far and wide, creating eerie shapes and shadows across the lot and the building. At the edge of the light, I held my breath and plunged forward. As soon as I stepped into the brilliance, I felt all my anxiety ebb. It was replaced with a feeling of calm. Of contentment.

And then I saw why.

She was sitting, cross-legged on the dirt path near the spot where her brother's body had been found. Even in her grief, this Illumicrafter emitted peace and serenity—even if she wasn't *feeling* it. It was simply her nature.

"Amy?" I said softly. She really did look a lot like a young Sally Field, even with her messy hair and mascara-streaked face.

She didn't seem to notice me.

"Amy?" I said again, approaching her slowly.

Her head came up, and she studied me. Tears swam in her eyes.

"Hi, Darcy."

"Hi," I said. "Can I sit down?"

She motioned to a spot next to her.

I'd expected the ground to be icy cold, but it was warm—almost hot. Now that I was here, I wasn't sure what to say.

"Michael's dead," she said, choking on the words.

"I know. I'm sorry."

"Someone put him in there." She nodded to the copse of trees and dense underbrush. "He would have hated that. He didn't like the woods. It was too dark. Too dark."

I swallowed hard.

She looked at me. "Why would someone do that?"

"I don't know."

A tear slid down her cheek, and I put my arm around her. "Have you slept?"

She shook her head.

"Eaten?"

"Not hungry."

I understood. When my mother died, I didn't have a proper meal for almost three months.

I heard a car in the distance and almost immediately felt an insistent nudging. I leaned away from it. "Amy, you need to turn off your glow."

"My glow?"

I gestured to the bright light. "You're visible for miles." Maybe even from space — but I left that part out. "A mortal might come along." And there was no explaining how this brilliance was coming from a nineteen-year-old girl.

She blinked, then seemed to focus. "I can't."

"Can't what?"

"Turn it off."

Whump-whump-whump-whump.

Panic fluttered in my stomach. "Why not?"

"Strong emotions make it uncontrollable." She swiped at her eyes.

Strong emotions like grief. Great. I had to hide her. *How* was another matter altogether. I looked around, wondering if the tree canopy would give her any shelter, but as most of the leaves had fallen already, it provided no screen.

If I could get her back to Ve's, to an interior room, she could stay there until the glow started to fade. As I tried to figure this out, her light suddenly flickered and died.

I blinked — momentarily blinded by the lack of light. The ground grew cold as I rubbed my eyes and then slowly opened them. I was thankful the parking lot lights cast a soft glow around us.

Amy cried softly.

I took hold of her hand. "Come on, we have to go before you light up again."

"Where?" She hiccupped. "I don't think I can stand to go back to the apartment. . . ."

"My house," I said, helping her to her feet. "We can figure the rest out later."

I realized as I held on to her that I no longer felt Michael, his presence. He was gone. For now. I could only wonder for how long. He seemed a persistent sort of ghost.

Shaky, Amy stood. As soon as she straightened, however, she lit up again.

I winced, blinded again.

As my eyes slowly adjusted, I heard a familiar noise getting closer.

"What's that?" Amy whispered.

"Reinforcements," I said, looking upward. Archie's flapping made a distinct noise.

As he flew into the light, he yelled, "Incoming!" as he dropped something, then flew off again.

I spotted a shadow falling out of the sky and smiled when I recognized my mouse friend, Pepe. He floated downward, using a tiny umbrella as a parachute. I cupped my hands and caught him.

The mouse bowed. He was dressed in his usual outfit—a tiny three-button red vest. His whiskers were twirled into a fancy mustache, and a pair of round glasses perched on the bridge of his nose. *"Ma chère."*

"It's good to see you. I need all the help I can get right now." I kissed the top of his head as he closed his umbrella. "Where did Archie go?"

With cheeks red, Pepe said, "Reporting this latest development to the Elder." Then, addressing Amy, he said, *"Mademoiselle*, my deepest condolences on your loss." He bowed again.

His French accent was enchanting.

"Thanks, Pepe." She sniffled and patted his head. Her light flickered but remained shining brightly.

"We have to hide her," I said to Pepe. "Soon. Before a mortal comes along."

"There is only one thing that can hide a light this brilliant," he said.

"What?"

"A Crafter cloak. Godfrey is on his way with one. He's a slight bit slower than I with that girth of his."

"Never mind that you had a ride from Archie," I pointed out.

His whiskers twitched. "Mere details."

Pepe, a familiar, had lived with Godfrey Baleaux's family for generations. The Cloakcrafters had become like family to Pepe, and he and Godfrey acted more than a little like squabbling siblings. Both of them worked magic with fabric as premier clothiers and tailors at the Bewitching Boutique, though Pepe often boasted that he was the more masterful Crafter of the two. Which might explain why Godfrey was forever threatening to adopt a cat for the shop.

The thought of a cat had me thinking about Tilda again, but I had to push worries about her aside for now and focus on Amy. My anxiety grew the longer we waited. "How soon before Godfrey gets here?"

"He had to finish casting the spell on the cloak," Pepe said. "It is not a normal cloak used in a case such as this."

"Why?" The usual Crafter cloak, which reminded me of Darth Vader's cape in *Star Wars*, was a long, hooded satin cape. When worn by a Crafter, it provided invisibility so mortals couldn't see us when we visited the Elder.

"It needs to be . . . How do you say?" He paused, twirling his mustache. "Extra-strength. To contain all the light."

Amy burst into tears. "I'm causing so much trouble!"

The light around us dimmed intermittently, reminding me of a lighthouse beacon.

A voice came out of the darkness. "What on earth is going on over here?" Harper stepped into the circle of light.

She saw me and said, "Why am I not surprised?"

"It's my fault," Amy cried.

Harper brushed passed me and pulled Amy into a hug. "Nonsense. I'm sure it's Darcy's fault somehow."

I rolled my eyes. "What are you doing here?"

"The light shining through my apartment window woke me up. I'm pretty sure this glow can be seen from space."

I bit back a smile, since I'd thought the same thing.

"Oui," Pepe agreed.

"We have to hide her," Harper said. "If a mortal comes along . . ."

"Sœurs," Pepe mumbled.

Sisters. "Yeah, yeah," I murmured to him, though I didn't mind being compared to Harper. I was proud of my sister, proud of the way I'd raised her. Well, except for those brushes with the law, but there was no need to go into that. To Harper, I said, "Already on it."

Pepe cupped his big ear. "I hear Godfrey now."

I strained to listen and heard nothing. "You do?"

"Can you not? The huffing and puffing is deafening."

I stared at the mouse. "You're making that up."

"You shall see, *ma chère.*"

"Here I am," a voice cried from the shadows, "to save the day."

I felt Pepe tense in my hand at the Mighty Mouse reference Godfrey used. "That is my line," Pepe murmured. He had a penchant for chomping on Godfrey's ankle when displeased with the man, and I had a feeling there would be some nipping going on later.

Godfrey hustled into the light, breathing heavily. Sweat beaded along on his forehead, around the deep wrinkles around his eyes, and on his jowls. His white hair had lost a little of its usual pomp. He wasn't dressed in his customary three-piece suit, either, but rather in fancy silk pajamas with robe tied around his large waist. "Here, here," he huffed and puffed, thrusting the cloak forward. He dabbed his face with a handkerchief.

"Told you," Pepe whispered with a smile.

"I shall never doubt you again," I said.

"Wise woman."

Harper took the cape and wrapped it around Amy. It wasn't until the hood had been pulled over Amy's dark hair that her light vanished.

That *she* vanished.

She was gone.

"Whoa," I said. "Where'd she go?"

"I'm right here," Amy said, her voice ringing out in the darkness.

Usually with the cloaks, even though Crafters were invisible to mortals, we were still visible to one another. "Extra-strength" indeed.

Harper reached out like a mime. "She's there." She must have found Amy's hand, because she seemed to be holding it.

"The only way," Godfrey explained, "to hide the light is to hide the whole Illumicrafter."

"I want one of those cloaks," Harper said, her eyes wide.

"*Non,*" Pepe said. "It will only work for the Illumicrafters."

Harper eyed him. "You wouldn't be lying to me, would you?"

"*Moi?*" he asked innocently.

"We should go," I said, hearing another car in the distance. "Someone is bound to get suspicious. Let's take Amy back to Ve's and figure out what to do from there."

Godfrey rubbed his hands in anticipation. "Yes, let's."

He'd once been married to Aunt Ve, and though she sometimes referred to him as a rat-toad bottom-dweller, they'd remained friends. It was an unusual relationship.

We'd just started up the dirt path to the Enchanted Trail, when a sharp voice rang out. "Stop right there!"

Chapter Eight

Caught in the act.

I froze, then slowly turned around. A beam of light (one not coming from Amy or Michael) blinded me, and I brought my hand up to block my eyes. Pepe dove for cover under my hair at the back of my neck, and I was doing my best not to laugh—he tickled.

"What's going on here?" the voice—female—demanded.

Godfrey puffed up. He had cupped his eyes, too, against the light. "Who's asking?"

The beam of light lowered, revealing Glinda Hansel. Her khaki uniform pants had been starched to within an inch of their life, but even at five thirty in the morning she looked glamorous, like an old-fashioned movie star.

Great.

"Glinda, is that you?" Godfrey said. "You nearly scared me to death. I'm an old man, you know."

She wasn't falling for his "old man" routine. "What are you doing here? You've violated a crime scene." Glinda was a Broomcrafter who knew Pepe well, so he came out of hiding. She gave him the evil eye. "What is going on? Explain yourselves."

"Well," Godfrey said, "Amy—"

Glinda snapped to attention. "Amy Healey? You've seen her? I've been looking for her all night. Me and every other officer on the force."

I made a snap decision. "We *thought* we saw her. We saw a light over here, but by the time we arrived, it was gone."

Glinda aimed her flashlight at each of our faces. I felt Harper tense behind me, and I hoped she'd hold her tongue.

She did, though I could tell it was taking effort on her part. I could practically feel her agitation.

Glinda flashed her light around the area. "You shouldn't be here."

"We were just leaving," Pepe said.

Glinda's perfectly plucked eyebrows dipped. "What are all of you doing out and about this early, anyway? Together?" She eyed Godfrey. "With you in your pajamas?"

"I asked for his help," I said quickly.

"With what?" she demanded.

"Tilda, my aunt Ve's cat, is missing. You know her, right? Tilda, not Ve. I know you know Ve." I didn't add— though I wanted to—that she knew Ve because her bimbo mother ran off and eloped with Ve's ex-fiancé. "Tilda's white and gray with blue eyes. Himalayan."

"Bad attitude," Harper added.

"Sharp claws," Pepe said sincerely. I felt him tense on my shoulder as if he could practically feel those claws.

"We were looking for her," I said. "She's missing, and she's not really an outdoor cat, so we're very worried."

Glinda's eyes narrowed on me. "Just so you know, I don't believe you're telling me everything."

I shrugged. "It's the truth. Tilda's lost. If you see her, can you let me know? Ve's worried sick."

"Personally," Pepe said, "I am glad she's gone, but I am not one to ignore a friend in need. If Darcy needs my help, all she need do is ask."

I said, "I forgive you for wanting Tilda to stay missing."

He bowed. "I speak only the truth. Tilda has tried more than once to eat me, to gobble me right up. I would rather that did not happen."

"Perfectly understandable," Harper said.

"Merci," Pepe returned, giving her a nod.

"Enough," Glinda snapped. "Get out of here, all of you, before I bring you in."

Since the Enchanted Village police cars were pastel-colored MINI Coopers, I kind of wanted to see her try. She might be able to fit Godfrey in her pink cruiser. Might. She'd need lots of backup for the rest of us.

She continued, saying, "I will keep an eye out for Tilda, if you keep an eye out for Amy. If you see her, please tell her to come see me at the police station. It's imperative she come sooner rather than later."

"Yes, ma'am," Godfrey said, bowing.

Glinda bristled at "ma'am," and I wanted to kiss Godfrey.

"Go!" she ordered.

We spun around and hurried away. Ahead of me, Harper whispered harshly, "What are you doing?" Then she stopped short and looked back at me. Under her breath, she said, "Amy let go of my hand."

"Uh-oh," I said. "We have a runaway."

Suddenly, I heard a little scream and looked back at Glinda. She was flat on her rear on the ground.

Godfrey started toward her, but she held up a hand to stop him and jumped up. "I'm fine," she said. "Just tripped on something." She looked at the ground as if perplexed, then rushed off.

Next to me, Amy's voice suddenly rang out, loud and clear. "Okay, I'm ready now."

Godfrey chuckled. "Were you, perchance, the object over which Glinda tripped?"

Amy said, "My foot may have gotten in her way."

"Why?" I asked. I mean, *I* kind of wanted to trip her, but I had my own issues with Glinda.

"Because she stupidly thinks Fisk killed Michael and that I know where he ran off to."

"Fisk ran off?" I asked.

"Last night, after he found out about Michael's death," she said, her voice hitching.

Harper met my gaze, and I could tell she was thinking the same thing as I was—guilty behavior. I wondered if that was the phone call Dash Khoury had received while talking to me last night—that Fisk had flown the coop.

"*Do* you know where he is?" I asked.

"No, I don't," she said after a long pause. "And even if I did, I'd never rat him out."

"Why, *ma chère*, do the police think Fisk is involved?" Pepe asked. "Were not he and Michael the closest of friends?"

"Because he and Michael got into a huge fight last night," Amy said. "A fistfight."

"Over what, my dear?" Godfrey asked.

"I don't know," she said softly.

"But you're sure Fisk wasn't involved in . . ." Harper gestured to the path.

"I'm sure," Amy said, her voice strong. "He's innocent."

As we headed for As You Wish, I hoped for Amy's sake that she was right.

*   *   *

Ve didn't seem the least bit surprised to see us. In fact, she had a fresh pot of coffee brewed and pancakes cooking.

"Archie," she explained when I gave her a questioning look. "He dropped by a few minutes ago and mentioned I might be having company."

"Is Mimi up yet?" I asked, looking toward the stairs.

"Sound asleep last I checked. It was quite the picture, seeing Higgins and Missy in bed with her, one on each side with Mimi nestled in the middle."

Alarmed, I asked, "Higgins was in my bed?" When I left, he'd been dozing on the floor.

"With his head on your pillow. He drools in his sleep. Did you know?" Ve asked, an amused lilt in her voice.

This was payback, I was quite sure, for letting Higgins slobber all over her last night. She'd probably coaxed him into my bed and put my pillow under his head.

"Speaking of, am I drooling?" Godfrey asked, parking himself on a stool. He sniffed the air, rubbed his bulging tummy, and made goo-goo eyes at Ve.

She winked and coyly patted her hair. "Not in front of the kids, Godfrey!"

He pinked right up. "Oh, you!"

"You two are making me queasy," Harper said. "Knock off all that phony flirting."

I set Pepe on the counter. He sat, letting his feet and tail dangle. "Yes, it is *quel* disturbing," he said.

"No one makes better pancakes than you, Ve," Godfrey said, ignoring us.

She laughed. "It's probably the only thing you miss about me."

"Not true," he insisted. "I also miss your vanilla raspberry trifle. I simply cannot replicate your recipe. Care to share it?"

She shook a spatula at him. "It's a family recipe, and you, my dear friend, are no longer family."

He pouted.

Missy must have heard the excitement, because she came clattering down the steps at full speed. She reached the bottom step and fairly launched herself at the invisible force in the room—a force that caught her.

Ve stared at Missy—who appeared to be hanging in midair—and grabbed her chest. "What's going on? Has Mrs. Pennywhistle returned? Is that you, Eugenia?"

Eugenia Pennywhistle, Mrs. P, was a Vaporcrafter who had the ability to make herself disappear at will. I envied her that particular gift. "No, she's still in Florida visiting friends," I said. "This is Amy. Didn't Archie mention she'd be with us?"

"He neglected to mention that she'd be invisible," Ve said darkly, as if envisioning plucking one or two of Archie's feathers in retribution. "I thought she'd simply changed her mind about coming here." Ve looked among all of us. "Why is Amy . . . invisible?"

Harper smiled wide and said, "Let me." She walked over to where Missy hung in midair, reached up, fumbled around, and lowered the hood of the cloak.

Amy's face appeared amid startling bright light. "Peekaboo," she said, giving a little wave with her free hand.

Ve covered her eyes. "Good God! I'm blind!"

"Temporarily," I said, squinting.

Harper put the hood back up, and Amy vanished again. Missy, however, didn't seem to have any trouble seeing her as she set about licking Amy's face. Amy giggled.

Ve stared in wonder. "Are you hungry, Amy dear?"

"Not really," Amy said. "I'm just a little tired. Would it be possible to lie down for a while?"

"Of course! Darcy," Ve said, "show her upstairs to Harper's old room. Stay as long as you like, Amy."

"Thank you," she said. "I'll try not to be too much trouble."

Missy was lowered to the ground, where she immediately went over to Godfrey and started sniffing.

I held out my hand to Amy. It was strange to feel her palm on mine but not be able to see it. Slowly, I guided her up the steps and into the guest room. I made sure all the shades (I was thankful they were the room-darkening kind) had been drawn, and for extra precaution, I draped dark sheets over the windows as well. "I think it's okay to take the cloak off in here now. No one will be able to see the light. Just be careful when you're in the hallway or the guest bath."

She slipped off her hood, and I winced at the light. Sitting on the edge of the bed, she seemed to fold into herself, and she looked about ten years old.

Glancing at me, she said, "Thanks for letting me stay here. And for lying to Glinda about me."

"You can stay as long as you want." I bit my lip. It had been easy to lie to Glinda, but it wouldn't be so easy to keep a secret from Nick, especially with his daughter staying here. "It's probably in your best interest to talk to the police at some point."

"I know." She stared at her dark purple fingernails. "Just not Glinda. Fisk and I overheard her last night telling someone that she thought Fisk was guilty and they should just arrest him. All because of one little fight." She shook her head. "That was when Fisk took off. He's not guilty," she added.

I nodded, because I didn't know what to say. I had no idea whether he was guilty or not. The circumstantial evidence against him was starting to pile up, however. "And you really don't know why he and Michael were fighting?"

She swiped a tear away. "They told me to keep out of it."

"You didn't overhear any of it?"

"Bits and pieces. Nothing that made sense. Something about the moon." She yawned.

"The moon? As in the one in the sky?"

Yawning again, she said, "I told you it didn't make sense."

"Why don't you get some rest?" I said.

She nodded, and as I left the room, I had to wonder if she was telling me all she knew about the fight.

The moon.

I shook my head. Why would they be fighting about the moon?

Amy was right—it made no sense. And it certainly didn't explain why Michael was now dead.

Chapter Nine

By ten, the house had pretty much cleared out. Nick had called to say he'd be late in stopping by; Harper and Mimi were currently walking Missy and Higgins; Lost flyers had been made; Amy was still asleep; and I had been stood up.

By Lydia Wentworth.

She was supposed to have stopped by this morning to sign contracts so I could get to work in tracking down the mysterious Louis. I had called and left a message on her home phone, but so far, she hadn't called me back.

I almost hoped she didn't. The whole Louis thing had a sordid feel to it, and I didn't know if I wanted to be involved.

Plus, I had other matters to deal with. Namely, a ghost. Michael was back—I could feel him around me, much like a hovering cloud.

Whump, whump.

Ve and I were in the office, which made me twitch with anxiety. The office was a source of contention between us—I wanted desperately to organize it, and Ve wanted desperately for it to remain the same cluttered mess it had always been.

As I was the type-A sort, it was enough to send my blood pressure through the roof. Hence, the twitching. I focused on blocking out my surroundings and sat in the chair opposite her desk. "Can I ask you something?"

She glanced up from her computer keyboard. "No, I have no interest in getting back together with Godfrey. We were just having fun."

"Good to know," I said, smiling. "But that wasn't what I was going to ask."

"Oh?"

"No."

"Well, then." She leaned back in her chair. "What were you going to ask?"

"Can a Crafter become a ghost? A spirit stuck between two worlds?"

Her blue eyes widened, their golden flecks sparkling. "Why do you ask?"

"Well," I said, drawing the word out into four syllables. "I have a new friend hanging around. Michael Healey."

Reddish eyebrows snapped downward as she leaned forward. "Darcy, dear, what are you talking about?"

"Michael Healey. His spirit, his ghost, has been following me around since I found his body last night. He's why Amy's here, as a matter of fact. He guided me to her this morning."

She blinked slowly, probably questioning my sanity.

I sighed. "Michael, say hi to Ve, will you?"

Next to me, a light flickered.

"Have mercy!" Ve cried, clutching her heart. "Do it again."

The light sputtered a few more times.

Ve looked at me. "Why's he following you?"

"Your guess is as good as mine. I was hoping you would know."

"I—I don't know." Her hand rested at her throat. "I've seen many things in my years as a Crafter, but I've never seen anything like this. You need to bring this to the attention of the Elder, Darcy. She can help you."

I itched to arrange a stack of papers on the desk. "I was afraid you were going to say that."

"You need to set aside your feelings for the Elder and think of Michael. He obviously needs your help in some way."

"Why me?"

"No clue."

"Big help."

"The Elder," she singsonged.

I groaned.

There was a knock on the back door; then someone yelled, "Darcy! You'll never believe what happened!"

"Starla," I said to Ve as I stood up. As I headed for the kitchen, I ran straight into something hot, thick, and squishy that blocked my way. I jumped back. "Ew!"

"Ew what?" Ve asked.

"I think I ran into Michael."

Ve shuddered. "What did he feel like?"

"I don't know. Like hot thick gel."

"Ew," Ve said, hurrying for the door.

"Darcy!" Starla called from the kitchen.

"Coming!" I yelled back.

I reached a hand out to make sure the path was clear and followed her voice. In the kitchen, Starla practically glowed like Amy had this morning. She had her hands set atop a jack-o'-lantern.

"Look!" she said, pointing at the pumpkin.

"It's cute," I said. It had two big star-shaped eyes, an

upside-down heart-shaped nose, and a gaping mouth with mismatched teeth. "Did you make it?"

"No," she said, rolling her eyes. "It was on my front step this morning."

"Who put it there?" Ve asked, pouring another cup of coffee.

"I don't know. But look." She lifted its top and reached inside.

I shuddered a little. I hated touching pumpkin guts, and even the thought of it gave me the willies.

She pulled out a note, cut into the shape of a star.

I eyed it. "What's that?"

"Read! Read!" Her blue eyes were alight with happiness as she thrust the paper at me.

> *Like the moon, you glow*
> *Like the stars, you shine*

I flipped the card over. "That's it?"

"Sounds like you have yourself an admirer, Starla," Ve said, wiggling her eyebrows.

Starla snatched the note back. "I don't know whether to be excited that someone likes me enough to go to this trouble, or scared that I have a stalker. Who do you think it could be?"

Ve started throwing out names, including Godfrey's and Pepe's. Starla giggled, and I loved seeing her so happy, especially in light of what had happened with Michael.

The phone rang in the office, and Ve went to answer it.

"Who do you think it is, Darcy?" Starla asked.

"On the phone?"

She elbowed me. "Who dropped off the jack-o'-lantern?"

I didn't have any idea who it could be and only hoped

this wasn't some sort of a joke. "Someone with good taste."

A light behind Starla flicked once. Michael agreed with me. So help me, I was getting used to his hanging around.

"Awww!" Her eyes glimmered. "Now, who do you think that would be?"

I was saved from having to come up with possible suitors by Ve. "Darcy, dear, the phone is for you. Lydia Wentworth."

"I'll be right back," I said to Starla.

In the office, I couldn't help but put some wayward pens back into their cup as I picked up the phone. "Darcy Merriweather."

"Darcy, it's Lydia. I'm so sorry I missed our appointment this morning." She sounded breathless.

"Is everything okay?"

"No." Her breath hitched. "Everything is terribly wrong. There's been a bit of a crisis here at the Elysian Fields."

"What kind of crisis?"

"It's h-horrible. Is it possible . . . Can you . . ."

"What?" I asked.

"Can you possibly meet me here, at the greenhouse?"

I didn't even need to think about it. "I'll be right over."

Chapter Ten

Whump-whump-whump-whump.

Michael was agitated as I drove to the Elysian Fields. It was a short drive, maybe ten minutes tops, but it felt like it was taking longer because I had to keep stopping to let tourists cross the road.

I finally made it around the green and into the wooded village neighborhoods behind the square. The Elysian Fields were located at the end of Starry Hollow Road, which ran along the village's boundary with Salem. It was a beautiful street with expensive houses—the priciest in town.

Tall oak trees lined the cobbled lane, their branches all but bare. A few shriveled reddish leaves remained, hanging precariously until a stiff breeze came along to whisk them away. It reminded me of O. Henry's bittersweet "The Last Leaf." Which reminded me of death.

"Can you talk?" I asked the ghost next to me.

He flickered twice.

No.

So it definitely hadn't been Michael who whispered to

me this morning. I wondered who had, but there were more important things to focus on right now.

I drove slowly down the street, past beautifully crafted houses. Nothing ostentatious, just pretty, like grown-up dollhouses in fanciful colors and gingerbread trim. "Do you know who killed you?"

He flickered twice.

No.

"Do you think it was a random act?"

No.

I slowed to turn into Harriette Harkette's driveway, the mouth of which was framed by a stacked-stone archway nearly covered in snaking star jasmine vines. Twin metal gates had been pushed open.

Whump-whump-whump-whump.

I said, "You're nervous to come here."

Yes.

"Do you think your murder has something to do with this place?"

Yes.

Well, now I was nervous, too.

The tumbled-brick drive forked, one branch headed toward Harriette's house (and Lydia and Willard's carriage house), the other toward the fields. As Lydia asked me to meet her at the greenhouse, I turned left.

"But you don't know who?"

No.

I glanced in his direction, even though I couldn't see him. "You didn't see the person?"

No.

Great. I drove beneath another stone arch. The road was bordered on each side by a low stone wall and led to a small gravel parking lot that had three silver sedans parked in it, side by side. Straight in front of me lay acres of fields, recently plowed under. To my left were two identical greenhouses; to my right, two more.

"Ready?" I turned off the car and stashed the keys in my coat pocket.

No answer.

"Michael?"

Yes.

I opened the car door and stepped out, shivering against the chill in the air. Winter would be here soon. "Which one is Harriette's greenhouse?"

I felt a hot nudge, guiding me to my right. "Thanks."

A bluestone walkway that started at the edge of the lot was bordered by low evergreen hedges and flower beds filled with colorful hearty annuals. Dwarf trees that had already lost their leaves lent a magical gnarly charm to the landscape.

Tucked away in the hollow of a copse of woods were two gorgeous greenhouses. Framed in white, they appeared to be traditionally built, but I knew they were high-tech with state-of-the-art operating systems and even alarms.

Illusion was part of the village's charm.

The pathway branched, and a small wooden guidepost pointed left to the inscripted name, IMOGENE and right to HARRIETTE.

The other two greenhouses across the lot had to be Bertie's and Ophelia's.

The Floracrafters were clearly separated from the Terracrafters.

For the love, as Harper would say. Segregation among Crafters—it reeked of injustice.

I was headed for the door of Harriette's greenhouse when it burst open.

"Darcy!" Lydia cried, rushing toward me. "Thank you

for coming. There was no way I could get away." She was dressed all in black from her turtleneck to her black gardening clogs.

As she neared, I could see that she'd been crying. Dark circles rimmed puffy red eyes.

"What happened?" I asked. She'd said it was "horrible." "Is everything okay? Your mother?"

Whump-whump-whump.

"Mother's as okay as she can be after what happened. Come, let me show you."

I followed her down the path and into the greenhouse. When she closed the door behind me, I immediately felt the warmth and humidity of the space. The heady scent of roses nearly knocked me over. The smell was so strong it was almost overpowering.

"Just look," she said, her voice hitching.

I gasped.

Whump-whump-whump-whump.

Silently, I walked the length of the greenhouse. Two aisles divided three long multitiered benches of plants—two benches ran along the sides of the greenhouse and one straight down the center.

I tried to take in what I was seeing.

On the right bench, dozens and dozens of colorful roses sat in various stages of bloom. From pink buds to full red roses, it was a rainbow of color.

On the left side, however . . .

There were dozens and dozens of black roses. Every last one of them had shriveled and died.

"How did this happen?" I asked in a whisper. The moment seemed to call for a reverent tone.

"I'm not sure." Her voice shook. "The flowers hadn't been faring well lately, but as of last night they were all still alive. For them all to die like this so suddenly, we're working on the assumption that someone sneaked in here and poisoned them."

"Who would do such a thing?" I asked.

"We have many enemies, Darcy. People who are jealous of our success. This," she said, gesturing, "is bad enough, but what's even worse is that several black rosebushes are missing."

Whump-whump-whump-whump.

"Smugglers," she said on a long, drawn-out sigh.

"Smugglers?" I repeated.

"It's a big business in the flower world, Darcy. Especially when rare breeds are involved. Last year in Europe, the police arrested an orchid smuggler at the airport. He'd been trying to get a dozen rare orchid seedlings across the border. Those seedlings were worth tens of thousands of dollars. Keep in mind that our Witching Hour roses are the only ones on earth that are naturally black."

"How much would they be worth on the black market?"

"Millions," she said without hesitation. "I guarantee that whoever stole those bushes is at this very minute having the plant's DNA tested, trying to figure out how the rose was cultivated."

"How was it cultivated?" I asked, wanting to know.

"A lot of hard work." She shifted on her feet. "And a little bit of magic. A spell my mother created."

Whump-whump-whump-whump-whump.

I fidgeted from Michael's angst. Something Lydia had said really upset him. The spell? "What kind of spell? To turn the flowers black?"

"It's complicated," she said. "And also top secret. Mother won't share the spell with anyone. Not with the other Wickeds"—she frowned—"and not even with me."

The door burst open. Harriette strode in with Willard, Lydia's husband, hot on her heels.

Ashen-faced, Harriette stopped short when she saw me. "Darcy. I didn't expect to see you. What are you doing here?" Her eyes cut between Lydia and me.

I couldn't very well admit that I'd come bearing papers for Lydia to sign so I could uncover details about Harriette's supposed fiancé. "I ah—" I had no idea.

"I asked her to come over," Lydia blurted.

Harriette skewered her daughter with a piercing glare. "Why?"

Willard hovered in the background, seemingly trying to blend in with the dead plants. He was a hair taller than I, with dark hair streaked through with patches of gray. Ordinarily, I'd describe him as having a pleasant face and a happy—yet a bit snobby—demeanor. But today he looked pained as he shifted and twitched as if suffering from a nervous disorder.

Maybe he was.

The disorder's name was Harriette.

Lydia threw her hands in the air. "I was so impressed with As You Wish's planning of your birthday party last night that I decided to hire them to plan a surprise engagement party for you and Louis. I was supposed to meet Darcy this morning to sign the paperwork, but with this crisis, I haven't been able to get away. Darcy graciously agreed to come here. But alas, I guess the surprise is ruined now."

Harriette wore a black cashmere sweater and black pants tucked into knee-high boots—black, of course. Her white hair had been combed back into a tight bun, revealing a sharp widow's peak. A perfectly arched white eyebrow shot up. "A party?"

I tried to look as innocent as possible by glancing around as if interested in the workings of the greenhouse. A rack near the door held many gardening tools (a trowel, a cultivator, a dibber) in an almost-perfect row except for one empty hook. Beautiful tools, too. Spotlessly shiny with worn leather grips.

Lydia nodded. "I'd still like to throw one. Perhaps you'd like to plan it with me? It's the perfect chance to introduce Louis to all your friends."

As Lydia talked, Willard had abandoned his spot by the door and had picked up a basket from a spot near the tool rack. He pulled open a drawer in a worktable and rummaged around until he came up with a pair of ordinary household scissors. I watched as he avoided the black roses and went about snipping fresh roses—probably gathering stock for the Black Thorn. As he cut stems, I blinked in wonder, as another bud magically bloomed in its place.

The village motto was Where Magic Lives. It truly did—and sometimes took me by surprise. Entranced, I watched him work, enraptured with the way stems regenerated with every snip.

Harriette noticed him, too. "Are you using scissors, Willard?" She said "scissors" as if they were the spawn of the devil. "Where are the snips?"

"I—I don't know."

Harriette swiveled to look at the tool rack, then spun back around and speared Lydia with a glare. "The snips?"

She shrugged. "They weren't here when I came in."

"I suggest you find them," Harriette said tightly. She turned her beady eyes toward me. "In light of what transpired here last night, a party doesn't seem appropriate. I'm afraid my daughter has wasted your time, Darcy."

Lydia, still sticking to the story, said, "It doesn't have to be soon, Moth—"

"No," Harriette hissed, cutting her off.

The viper had come out to play.

Lydia straightened. "You're being—"

"I said no." Harriette's snake eyes zeroed in on me.

I tried not to shake in my boots.

"Again, I am sorry my daughter wasted your time, Darcy," she said.

"It was no trouble on my part at all." I glanced around. "I am sorry to see what happened to these beautiful flowers. Have you called the police?"

"We will handle the matter on our own," Harriette seethed. "If not for someone leaving the greenhouse unsecured last night, this might not have happened."

Willard sputtered. "I—I'm sure I set the alarm."

"In light of the alarm not going off when someone came inside and destroyed our year of hard work, then I suspect you are mistaken in your recollection, Willard." The viper's fangs dripped with venom.

He gulped. "Perhaps so." He barely looked at Lydia as he said, "I need to open the shop. I'll be home for dinner." Clumsily, he made his way out the door.

"Mother, aren't you being a bit—"

"Enough, Lydia."

Lydia clamped her jaw closed and rocked on her heels.

Harriette pressed her fingertips to her temples. "I have a searing headache and must rest."

"That's a good idea. I'll take care of things here."

Harriette arched an eyebrow as though she had her doubts.

"All my flowers are fine, aren't they?" Lydia countered, gesturing to the colorful roses.

Harriette pursed her lips, spun around, and strode out, one long step after another.

As soon as the door closed, Lydia slumped, sitting on the edge of a bench. "I hate seeing her so agitated. She's not been well lately, and I'm afraid this crisis will cause a setback."

"Not well?"

"Her heart," Lydia said. "She has an appointment with Dennis Goodwin next week."

Dr. Dennis Goodwin was the most sought-after Cure-crafter around. If he couldn't heal Harriette, no one could. I could only imagine what this stress was doing to someone with a heart issue and hoped Harriette rested as she said she would.

"Mother . . ." She strove to find words, and I could see anger flashing in her eyes. "She's a difficult woman who has trouble letting go, even though until last night's incident, I've more than proven I can handle this green-house."

"You're solely in charge now?" Harriette seemed too much of a control freak to let anyone else handle her business.

"Yes, except for the cultivation of the black roses, which is Mother's pet project. She turned over the rest of the day-to-day operations to Willard and me a couple of months ago. And she shouldn't be so hard on him. He set that alarm last night. He always does."

"How many people have the code?"

"Not many. The Wickeds. Me, Willard."

Whump-whump-whump.

"What about people who work here? Maintenance people, that sort of thing?"

"They're not allowed in here," Lydia said.

A tiny light behind her flickered twice. *No.*

"Not even Michael Healey?" I asked. "Didn't you say he worked closely with the plants?"

She flushed. "You're right. He was an exception to the rule, one Mother made because she appreciated his talent with the roses."

Whump-whump-whump.

"Who hired him? Was it Harriette?"

"Actually, no. Bertie hired him against Mother's wishes."

Bertie Braun—the Terracrafter who raised lilies in one of these greenhouses.

Before I could ask another question, Lydia stood up. "I think it's time for you to leave, Darcy. I'm already in trouble for having you in here. Mother's probably lurking outside, waiting for you to go before giving me hell."

"Does she do that often?"

Lydia smiled weakly. "She used to, but lately she's been . . . nicer. To me, to the other Wickeds. She's been more generous, helpful, happy."

It sounded to me as if she had fallen in love, and suddenly, I wanted to change my bet at Spellbound.

"I thought she was finally changing her ways," Lydia said, "but apparently, old habits run deep. Do you have the papers for me to sign?"

I fished them out of my bag and handed them to her. "May I ask you something personal?"

She shrugged. "I guess."

"Why don't you and Willard move?"

Something darted across her eyes. It looked a lot like fear. "Mother would never let us."

"Why is it her decision?"

"Don't you understand, Darcy? She controls everything I do. Always has. Always will."

"Why not walk away? Between you and Willard, you can start your own flower farm. Open your own shop."

She shook her head. "I've worked too hard to walk away now. This place is mine." Her eyes flashed—and I realized how snakelike hers were as well. "I just have to be patient."

Patient. Until her mother dies.

As she bent down to sign the papers, I watched behind her as a tiny flicker of light grew into a glowing, pulsing orb. When the sphere touched one of the dead black roses, its shriveled leaves unfurled, its stem straightened, and its bloom reopened one petal at a time. It had come alive.

The light flickered, then vanished, leaving behind a beautiful lush, perfectly healthy black rose.

I swallowed hard.

Lydia, who was oblivious to what was happening behind her, handed the papers back. "I worked my whole life under the belief that this place would one day be my own. I don't want someone who's never even had dirt under his fingernails coming along and taking it away from me."

Nodding, I tucked the papers away. "I'll be in touch."

"I'll be here," she said mournfully, "trying to figure out how to replace a year of mother's hard work."

The air temperature outside seemed even colder after I had been in the warmth of the greenhouse. I hurried to the car, turned on the heater, and sat staring at the churned fields.

Whump-whump-whump-whump.

My heart beat just as wildly as I replayed what I'd seen with that black rose over and over in my mind. Finally, I said, "Those roses weren't poisoned, were they?"

No response.

"They died," I said, "because you died. Am I right?"

He flickered once.

Yes.

Chapter Eleven

I tried to figure out what that even meant. "Why?"

There was no response. Obviously, since it wasn't a yes or no question.

I bit my lip and tried to figure out how I could discover the reason. As I glanced around, I saw someone walking around inside a greenhouse to my left. I squinted at the guidepost.

The arrow directed me to Bertie's greenhouse.

Perfect.

I cut the engine. I wanted to find out what Bertie knew about the Witching Hour roses—and what Michael had to do with them. And why, too, she had hired Michael when Harriette was against the decision.

I glanced his way. "Can we trust Bertie?"

No response.

"You don't know who to trust, do you?"

No.

"Oh, Michael." My lip quivered and I bit it. "What did you get mixed up in?"

No response.

I sighed. "Come on, then. Let's go see what we can find out from Bertie."

Following an identical bluestone pathway to Bertie's greenhouse, I hoped Harriette wasn't lurking as Lydia suspected. I didn't want her to see me going inside. Mostly because I didn't want to face Harriette's wrath if she found out I was snooping around in her business.

I turned the latch on the door and stepped inside. Warmth flooded over me, and I was grateful for it. I'd been chilled to the bone. A sweet scent hung in the air as dozens of lilies bloomed along long worktables in a lay-out identical to that of the other greenhouse.

Bertie looked up from her work and smiled. "Darcy, hello."

Bertie was the second youngest of the Wickeds—in her mid-sixties. She wore much the same kind of outfit as Lydia, right down to the clogs. Her silver-streaked blond hair was cut into a severe bob that tended to hang in her face. She pushed a section of hair behind her ear and assessed me from behind a pair of rectangular glasses. "I'm surprised to see you here."

"I came to see Lydia."

"She's across the way," Bertie said, pointing to the rose greenhouse as if I'd lost my way.

"I know. I was just there. I saw what happened to the Witching Hour roses. . . ."

Bertie's face, soft and glowing with good health, suddenly lost color. She ran a finger over a pearlescent lily petal. "It's . . . shocking."

"Do you know what happened to the roses?"

"No, but maybe it wouldn't have happened if Harriette had shared the Witching Hour spell with the rest of us Wickeds. Among the four of us and our skills, we could probably find the solution to the problem. But no,

Harriette insists on being selfish. She won't even share the spell with her daughter, who's practically begged to be let in on the secret. No surprise there, really. Harriette's known for caring about only one person. Harriette."

Bitterness laced her tone, and I noted the anger in her eyes. "Have you tried to create your own black flowers?"

"Of course! It's an ingenious creation, but none of us has been able to replicate it."

I could see Bertie and Imogene wanting the spell for their lilies and orchids, but Ophelia? "Black saffron doesn't seem like a good idea. . . ."

Bertie adjusted a pot on the bench. "For Ophelia, it's sport. And trying to prove that as a Terracrafter she's just as good as Harriette."

"But that's not your goal as well?"

Her gaze snapped to me. "What is it you want, Darcy?"

I hedged for only a second. "Information about Michael," I said honestly.

"Why?" she asked.

"I was the one who found his body," I said. "I feel . . . obligated to figure out what happened to him."

"That's not your duty," Bertie said.

"It is now."

She suddenly startled. Her gaze darted around. "Oh my good God, he's here, isn't he?"

I tried to look innocent.

"I feel him," she said. "He's . . ." She stared at me. "He's imprinted on you, hasn't he?"

"He's what?" I asked.

"Come away from the front windows," she said, drawing me farther back into the greenhouse. "It's too easy for passersby to see you standing there."

"What does that mean, he's imprinted on me?"

"It means his spirit form has latched onto you because you were the first one to find him. He has unfinished business here—something he has to take care of before he can cross over. He's stuck." She smiled. "To you."

"How do you know all this?" Ve hadn't had a clue about why Michael was following me around.

"I had an imprinter once." She shook her head. "Craziest three days of my life. You won't be rid of him until his mission is complete. Finding his killer really is your duty. He won't be able to leave you until he can rest in peace."

Great. Wonderful. Fantastic. Nothing like a little pressure.

"Good lord," Bertie said, wiping her brow. "I never should have hired him." She marched along the aisle, mumbling to herself.

"Why did you hire him?"

"As a favor to Trista Harkette. I'm the one who introduced Dash to her—yet another source of contention between Harriette and me. I couldn't turn her down when she called me one day and asked a favor. One of her son's Crafter friends needed a good-paying job. He'd just lost his mother and was trying to take care of his little sister. Harriette threw a fit, but Imogene backed me up. She has a soft spot for Trista. In hindsight, I wish I hadn't brought him here. Maybe then he'd be alive right now."

Whump-whump-whump.

"All right, calm down, Michael. I'm just telling it how it is."

"You can feel him?" I asked.

"Of course. Once you've been imprinted, you recognize the sensation easily. Others might not feel him at all, unless they're finely attuned to the other side—even mortals have the ability if they're sensitive enough."

I thought of Harper and how she'd felt him. She'd once worked in a nursing home and had eerily been able to predict when residents were close to death. It didn't surprise me that she sensed Michael's presence.

"Has he touched you yet?" She shuddered.

"A few times."

"Better you than me, kid. Imprinters, fortunately, can only touch the person they're connected to."

Wonderful.

"Anyway, Harriette eventually got over her snit when she met Michael, and he won her over. He was quite charming."

"He would be as an Il—"

An urgent hot nudge cut me off.

"A what?" Bertie asked.

"Lost my train of thought," I fibbed, wondering why Michael hadn't wanted me to mention his Craft. His caution also made me double-think asking about his connection to the black roses and why they may have died. After all, Michael had already expressed that we didn't know if we could trust Bertie. "So much going on today that my mind is whirring. Do you know why Michael quit?"

She glanced around and lowered her voice. "I don't know for sure, but I'm beginning to suspect that he had some—" She stopped talking and stared over my shoulder.

Turning, I followed her gaze. Ophelia and Imogene were coming up the walkway.

Bertie said, "Michael, you'd better skedaddle. You don't want them realizing you're hanging around. Go on, hurry."

"You don't want them to know he's here?"

"It's better that way."

"Why?"

Before she could answer, the door swung open.

The two women who walked in stopped midconversation when they saw me.

"Ophelia, Imogene!" Bertie said brightly. "Look who stopped by for a visit."

Each regarded me with thinly veiled suspicion.

Ophelia, Bertie's daughter-in-law, was the youngest of the Wickeds—in her early forties. Stylish in a dark pencil skirt, form-flattering blue sweater, and heels, she was petite and thin, with long tawny hair and intelligent blue eyes. I could feel the tension between Bertie and her, and it made me uncomfortable.

Of average height and weight, Imogene was in her mid-seventies and by far the most laid-back looking of the group, with wild pale white-blond frizzy hair, no makeup, and comfy in jeans and a long-sleeve T-shirt. I wanted to like her despite the look she was giving me.

"Why are you here, Darcy?" Ophelia asked pointedly.

I could practically hear her "You don't belong here" tacked onto the sentence.

I borrowed Lydia's made-up excuse, which also suited my snooping needs. "Lydia wants to throw a surprise engagement party for Harriette and Louis. I was hoping you could help me out a bit, to get a better feel for them as a couple. What's Louis like?"

Bertie leaned back on her heels, and I could sense her Cheshire cat smile. She was pleased with the excuse I'd come up with.

"Harriette won't like a party," Ophelia said. She stood off to the side, segregating herself from both Bertie and Imogene.

Why anyone wanted to work in these greenhouses— magical land or not—I couldn't imagine. The atmosphere had to be stifling between Harriette's controlling nature and the multiple conflicts.

"No," Imogene agreed, "she wouldn't."

"Be that as it may," I said, "I was hired to throw one. Does anyone know Louis's interests? I always like to incorporate personality into a party."

They looked between each other and shook their heads.

"I don't even know his last name," Imogene said.

Bertie and Ophelia admitted they also didn't know.

"You've never met him?" I asked them.

All three shook their heads again.

"I did see his car once," Imogene said. "I'd stopped by to have drinks with Harriette, and he was just leaving."

"You saw his car?" Bertie asked.

"What kind was it?" Ophelia added.

Imogene shrugged. "It was small and black."

Ophelia sighed and leaned against a workbench. "Of course it was black. Harriette wouldn't have had it any other way."

Bertie stepped up next to her and pulled a potted lily from behind Ophelia, relocating it to the center bench.

Ophelia rolled her eyes.

"The car had some sort of fish sticker in the window," Imogene added, oblivious to what was going on between Ophelia and Bertie.

We all stared at her.

"A fish sticker?" Ophelia said, her voice light with humor. "Who puts a fish sticker on his car?"

"Lots of people," Bertie said with a haughty tone. "The ichthus symbol? I've even seen those as bumper stickers," she said, directing her words to Ophelia.

It was ridiculous, this back-and-forth between them.

"No, nothing religious about it." Imogene shook her head. "Just a fish. White background, dark fish. Very unusual."

Ophelia shot Bertie a smug smile.

The mother hen in me wanted to take them both to task.

I could see that I was going to get nowhere with them about the mysterious Louis, so I said, "Well, if you think of anything, let me know. I should be going."

"I'll walk you out," Bertie said.

Two sets of curious eyes followed us.

I stepped out into the cold, and Bertie followed, tugging the door partly closed. "Listen, Darcy," she said in a whisper, "be very careful whom you tell about the imprinting, okay? Because if the killer finds out that Michael is still around, it puts you in very real danger."

Chapter Twelve

Well, that visit had been illuminating, as Starla would say.

After I left the Elysian Fields, I drove toward As You Wish. I had to pick up the Lost flyers and distribute them around town. Then I planned to stop in and see Vince Paxton at Lotions and Potions. Archie said that Vince had broken up the fight between Fisk and Michael last night. Maybe the Seeker had heard a little more about what the argument had been about.

As I drove, my mind kept slipping back to my visit to the greenhouses. One thing in particular was bothering me about my trip to Lydia's. For whatever reason, the black roses had died because Michael had died, but that didn't explain why a few of the plants were missing. Who had stolen them?

"Do you know what happened to those missing Witching Hour roses?" I asked Michael. It was a beautiful autumn afternoon, and the village was packed with tourists. The Harvest Festival was crowded with long lines and happy faces.

Only the police crime-scene tape fluttering in the

light breeze hinted that anything bad had happened here recently.

Michael fluttered twice. *No*.

"Had something like that ever happened before? Plants that have gone missing?"

Yes.

I felt I was on to something. "Recently?"

Yes.

"While you were still working for Harriette?"

Yes.

Multiple times. It made me question exactly how tight Harriette's security had been.

"Someone is trying to replicate the black roses?" I asked.

Yes.

"Do you think the black roses are why you were killed?"

There was a long hesitation before he flashed once. *Yes*.

"Any chance you could be wrong?" I asked.

No.

I was missing something big. "Why would you be killed over the black flowers?"

He, of course, had no answer.

I bit the inside of my cheek as I pulled into Ve's driveway, parking outside the detached garage. The two-story structure hadn't been used to house a car in decades. It was too full of clutter—which included most of my things. I stored them there when Harper and I had arrived in town. Five months later, it might be time to start pulling them out.

"Okay," I said to him. "Let me ask you this. Do you think whoever killed you is someone you know personally? Another Crafter?"

Yes.

I'd been afraid of that. I'd been holding out hope that a plant smuggler had come along and Michael had gotten in the way, but his murder seemed too much related to magic.

But if it wasn't a stranger, that left me with a pit in my stomach.

Because that meant I probably knew Michael's killer.

Pushing open the back door at As You Wish, I pulled off my boots and smiled at Ve and an invisible Amy as they played a quiet game of gin rummy at the kitchen counter. Michael, I realized, hadn't come in with me. Where he was off to was anyone's guess, but I knew he'd be back. I'd been imprinted.

Ve held a finger to her lips and pointed toward the living room.

I followed the direction of Ve's finger and found Higgins snoring on the area rug and Nick sound asleep on the sofa.

I crept over to Nick and just took in the sight of him for a moment.

His arms were folded across his chest, his five-o'clock shadow had crossed the line to a beard, and he looked utterly peaceful, his face slack, his mind, while asleep, worry free.

I couldn't help but reach out and touch his messy hair, twisting a soft strand around my finger. He shifted, and I quickly backed up, leaving him be.

Back in the kitchen, I whispered, "How long has he been like that?"

"About half an hour," Ve said. "He came to pick up Mimi, sat down, and was out like a light. I didn't have the heart to wake him."

I looked around. "Where is Mimi? And Missy?"

"With Harper at the bookshop. I thought it best to

keep Mimi out of the house as much as possible with our current houseguest, and she asked if she could bring Missy along."

Our current houseguest. Amy.

I watched a playing card be picked up from the pile and float through thin air.

"How's the glow?" I asked her.

Suddenly, light filled the kitchen. Amy smiled at me, keeping one hand on the hood of her cloak. "The same."

She put the hood back up and vanished. Before she had, I'd seen the dark circles under her eyes. The grief etched in her face. "Did you sleep?"

"A little."

"How was your visit with Lydia?" Ve asked me.

I filled her in on what had happened to the black roses.

Ve's eyes took on a troubled expression. "The flowers all died? How strange. What happened?"

"Lydia thinks they were poisoned. . . ."

"But?" Ve asked.

"I think it had something to do with Michael." I wished I could see Amy's facial expressions. It was disconcerting to be unable to gauge her emotions. I didn't know if she could sense Michael's ghost, so I didn't mention *why* I thought it had to do with him—that he'd pretty much told me so.

"How?" Ve asked.

I poured myself a glass of ice water. "That, I'm not sure."

Amy's voice cracked as she said, "If the roses died at the exact same time Michael did, there is only one explanation."

"What's that, dear?" Ve asked, her eyes full of curiosity.

"It was his spell cast over the flowers," Amy said

simply. "When an Illumicrafter's light is taken from the earthly world, any light used in a spell is taken, too. . . ."

I'd been missing something big—and this revelation certainly qualified.

"If that's the case with the roses," I speculated, "Michael had to have used his light to grow them, but that doesn't make sense, either. Illumicrafters *create* light. Blackness is the *absence* of light."

Ve tipped her head, apparently thinking it through. "No, it doesn't make sense."

We both looked in Amy's direction.

"Don't look at me," she said. "I have no idea *how* he did it, but I guarantee it was his spell."

It wasn't likely that Michael could tell me how in yes and no answers, either.

What I really didn't understand was why Harriette would claim the spell was hers, taking credit for its success, especially when in doing so, she was eliminating any potential ability for Michael to use his Craft for a profitable career. Had she tricked him somehow? It was clear that no one at the Elysian Fields knew he had been an Illumicrafter—or that he'd created that spell. Even Lydia didn't know the truth—she had told me this morning that the spell was her mother's.

I ran a finger down the side of my glass. "Amy, did you have any idea that Michael had something to do with those roses?"

"He never said anything to me. He never said much about any of his jobs. I don't think he liked me to worry about how hard he worked to support me." She sniffled as if trying to hold back tears.

"What other jobs did he have?" I went in search of some lunch, something quick, because I had plans to head back out. "The Elysian Fields. The bakery. Anything else?"

"I know he had at least one other job he was working since quitting the greenhouses. He also had some sort of master plan in place for his future. He'd been spending a lot of time with Fisk's dad, Dash."

I frowned as I set a tub of peanut butter on the counter. I remembered what Dash had said about trying to warn Michael.... "Were they working on something together?"

"I don't know. He wouldn't say for sure. He said he didn't want to jinx it."

I bit my lip. That was interesting. "What about this other job? What was he doing?"

"I don't know that, either. Something at night, which he hated because he—"

"Doesn't like the dark," I finished for her.

She tapped her cards on the counter. "Right."

Lydia had mentioned that when she offered Michael his job back, he'd claimed he didn't need the money. Why was that, exactly? Because of this new night job? Or because of what he was working on with Dash?

I let that roll around in my head. If Michael had been working with Dash, it most likely involved flowers. I'd bet my last Peppermint Pattie that it had to do with black flowers....

"I'm out," Amy said, laying a playing card facedown on the pile. She revealed her hand.

With Amy being invisible and all, it was as if I had two ghosts around. The fact that I wasn't bothered about that surprised me. I really wasn't a go-with-the-flow kind of girl. But, I supposed maybe I was a go-with-the-flow kind of witch. I'd slipped into this magical life pretty easily.

Ve groaned. "Card shark. Another hand, Amy?"

"Actually, I think I'm going to go lie down again."

"After that," Ve said, "you must eat something. You'll

just feel weaker and weaker until you get some suste-
nance in you."

Fondly, Amy said, "Yes, ma'am."

Ve quirked an eyebrow.

I'd yet to meet any woman who liked the term.

Footsteps sounded on the stairs as Amy climbed
them, and we heard the soft click of the bedroom door
latching.

I slathered peanut butter. "Does Nick know she's
here?"

"Not yet, but I think you should tell him."

I nodded. I didn't like keeping secrets from him. "Any
word about Tilda?"

"Not a peep," she said, sweeping the playing cards
into one massive pile.

I eyed her. "Why don't you seem worried about that?"

She adopted a surprised expression. "I don't know
what you mean. Mimi and Harper littered the town with
the flyers this morning while you were with Lydia. I'm
sure we'll get a call soon. Believe it or not, I think Tilda
is highly capable of taking care of herself for a day."

I crossed handing out flyers off my afternoon to-do
list, but I still had to meet with Vince. I was about to ask
Ve again if Tilda was a familiar, when I remembered how
Archie had behaved this morning. It wasn't likely Ve
would be able to tell me, either, if the Elder wanted me
to figure out familiars on my own.

I swallowed the last of my sandwich. "Archie wants
me to go see Vince Paxton. Apparently, he broke up the
fight last night between Fisk and Michael. The Elder
wants to know what he might have overheard."

Ve nodded. "Is Michael still hanging around?"

"Not at the moment. But yes." I told her what Bertie
had said about imprinting.

"Of course!" Ve said. "That makes perfect sense."

I rolled my eyes and rinsed my plate before setting it in the dishwasher. "I'm going to head out now."

"I have a few errands to run as well," she said, then glanced at the stairs and frowned. "Do you think our guest will be fine here on her own?"

"I think so." Amy was, after all, nineteen.

Ve headed up the stairs to tidy up before she went out, and I turned toward the family room for one more glance at Nick before I left.

He was still sleeping peacefully—as was Higgins, who had rolled onto his back and stretched out. Posed that way, he was almost longer than the couch.

I couldn't resist the temptation to run my fingers through Nick's hair again. While I was at it, I leaned over the back of the couch to kiss him good-bye as well.

Before I even realized what was happening, I was being dragged downward. I squealed as Nick settled me on top of him, nose to nose, toe to toe.

Well, *hello*.

I leaned up on my elbows so I could see his face.

Smiling at me, he said, "You're getting better at your screaming."

He was being kind. I still hadn't mastered projecting, and my shrieks sounded more like mewls. "I get lots of practice. You know, when bony hands grab me in parking lots, and you yank me over the back of the couch."

His dark eyes narrowed. "Who's grabbing you in parking lots?"

"Lydia."

"Wentworth?"

"She hired me to look into Harriette's supposed fiancé."

He ran his fingers through my hair. "Don't look too hard. My bet is that he's made up."

"Yours, mine, and just about everyone else's in the

village." The payout would be pennies at this rate. "How long have you been awake?"

"Not long. Who were you and Ve talking to?"

"When?" I asked, trying to play dumb.

"In the kitchen. A few minutes ago."

Ve saved me from answering as she came down the back stairs and into the living room. She took one look at us, sprawled on the couch and started singing "Love Is in the Air." I should have been embarrassed, but I wasn't. Being here with him . . . like this . . . It felt too right.

"I'm headed out, Darcy," Ve said, still humming. "Are you still planning to see Vince?"

I levered myself up and climbed off the couch. I'd have much rather stayed, but I really didn't want to answer Nick's question about the voices in the kitchen. Not yet. "Just leaving now."

"I'll check in with you later then." She gave me an overexaggerated wink. "Ta-ta!"

As she danced her way to the back door, she began singing again. I rolled my eyes. Subtle she wasn't.

"Vince?" Nick sat up and ran a hand over his head, smoothing wayward hairs.

Higgins's feet twitched in his sleep.

"Archie, via orders from the Elder, wants me to ask Vince a few questions. Apparently, Vince broke up the fight between Michael and Fisk in the alley behind the bakery last night."

"What are you hoping to find out?" He stood, then stretched.

His shirt rose up with the motion, and I tried not to stare at the muscled abs that peeked out. As Ve would say, have mercy!

"It would be nice to know what Michael and Fisk had been fighting about."

He gave a curt nod. "Yes, it would. I didn't know that Vince had been there last night. How'd you find out?"

"Archie."

"How'd he find out?"

"No clue. You'll have to ask him."

He smiled. "I will. Just as soon as we get back from Vince's."

"We?"

He tucked in his shirt (darn!) and said, "I'm coming with you."

Chapter Thirteen

"I still owe you a caramel apple," Nick said, squeezing my hand.

We'd dropped off Mimi's overnight bag and Higgins at his house and were on our way to Lotions and Potions.

My shoulder brushed against his as we threaded through the crowded sidewalk. Colorful leaves skittered across the cobblestone road, and the scent of cinnamon hung heavily in the air—the fried dough booth had a line that stretched down the block.

"That you do," I said. My gaze skipped to the Scarish Wheel (the festival's Ferris wheel), and I enjoyed the hokey fantasy I had of Nick kissing me while stopped at the top. Which might, in fact, be completely cheesy, but it brought a warm, fuzzy feeling to my stomach.

He stole a sideways glance at me. There was heat in his eyes that made me believe he had similar Ferris wheel thoughts. Then his jaw tightened and he said, "I just don't know when. This case . . ."

Tamping down disappointment, I said, "There's time enough." Another whole week before the festival wrapped up. But whether or not I got my kiss atop that Ferris wheel—or a caramel apple—seemed silly in comparison to what had happened to Michael.

Whump, whump.

He followed a few paces behind us, and I was grateful that he was no longer nipping at my heels. I could still feel him, but it wasn't the uncomfortable weight of last night.

Or maybe I was simply getting used to having him around.

What a crazy life I led.

"Are you cold?" Nick asked, releasing his hand and wrapping an arm around me.

"That's better." I hadn't been cold, but I wasn't going to say so. I liked having his arm around me. "Any new leads in your investigation? Did you talk to Dash Khoury about his warning to Michael?"

"I sent Glinda to interview him, but he wasn't available. Hopefully by tonight we'll have his statement. We're still looking for Fisk Khoury, and now Amy Healey is missing as well. We think they might be together."

I swallowed. Now might be the best time to tell him about my houseguest. Before I could get a word out, however, he said, "This case is more complicated than it appears."

"How so?"

"The medical examiner called this morning." Stopping, he tugged me out of the way of oncoming foot traffic.

I leaned against a gaslight, instinctively knowing I was going to have to brace myself for the news he was about to give me.

"Michael wasn't just killed once last night." Nick dragged a hand over his face and looked to the heavens as if they'd impart some answers he clearly needed.

"What does that mean?"

Nick's brown eyes clouded as he looked at me. "He wasn't killed once. He was killed four times."

Whump-whump-whump.

I scrunched my face, not understanding.

Nick said, "Preliminary autopsy shows Michael Healey was stabbed, bludgeoned, strangled, and poisoned."

Wrapping my arms around the light post, I held on tight so I wouldn't sink to the ground. "What?"

"The poison is the official cause of death—it appears as though the other methods weren't thorough enough to be fatal."

I shuddered. *Now* I was cold. Completely chilled.

"We haven't recovered any of the weapons except for the poison. It was in the sports drink in the delivery van. Antifreeze is easily masked in sweet drinks."

"Antifreeze?" I echoed, my teeth chattering. Shock was setting in.

"Just a couple of tablespoons can be deadly," Nick said. "It appears as though Michael drank it between leaving the bakery and arriving at the pub. There's evidence that he had been ill in the bushes. I think that's when someone came up behind him, stabbed him in the back, and hit him over the head."

His face had lost color, and I could easily see the dark circles under his eyes. The half hour of sleep he'd had on Ve's couch was probably all he'd had in the past twenty-four hours.

"Why?" was all I could ask.

"We'll find out, Darcy. We'll find out." He pried my fingers from the pole and put his arm around me again—this time to pretty much hold me up. "Let's find out what Vince overheard, okay? And we'll go from there."

I nodded. I had to tell him about Amy. And the black roses. But for now, I was too numb to walk along with him and think about poor Michael.

And about how someone had really, *really* wanted him dead.

The bell jangled on the door of Lotions and Potions as we went inside, and I could hardly believe my eyes at the sight before me.

Vince Paxton sat at the head of a rectangular wooden worktable surrounded by Brownie Scouts. Six sweet faces watched him in awe and wonder as he dramatically pushed a button on a food processor.

As the machine whirred, his gaze flicked up to meet mine. Surprise widened his eyes, and he nodded, letting us know he'd be with us in a moment.

"And voilà!" he declared, removing the lid from the processor. "Pumpkin puree."

The girls clapped. Each had a small mixing bowl and wooden spoon set in front of her, along with smaller ramekins filled with spices. I could pick out the cinnamon and cloves easily, but the others were a mystery.

Whump, whump.

Michael lurked, but if others in the shop could sense his presence, they didn't let on.

The store was busy with shoppers loading wooden baskets with beauty supplies. I waved to Colleen Curtis, a local college freshman who was working the cash register. She, her mother, Angela (who worked for Harper), Vince, Harper, Marcus, and I had taken that ill-fated cooking class together. We'd bonded over the trauma of it all. Colleen worked part-time at the library, and I hadn't realized she had taken a job here as well.

Chest-high display shelves lined one half of the store—the demonstration area took up the other side. Along two walls there were clear containers as at a candy shop, except these weren't filled with gumballs and gummy worms but with herbs and spices Vince (with

Mrs. Pennywhistle's help) used to make his lotions and potions that ranged from moisturizers to lip balm to bath fizz.

Vince scooped the puree into a large orange ceramic dish. "One scoop of this into each of your bowls. After that, we'll add the scrubby and spicy part of the recipe. You girls get started, and I'll be right back."

Spoons dove for the pumpkin puree as Vince wiped his hands on a black smock and came toward us. He and Nick shook hands, and he smiled at me. "In the market for a pumpkin spice body scrub? Freshly made."

I leaned on my tiptoes to get a better view of the table. "Is it edible? Because it smells delicious."

"Sadly, no, though it probably explains why I've had a craving for pumpkin pie lately." He smiled as he adjusted his glasses and said, "Why do I feel like you two aren't here to shop?"

I was thankful that with Nick along I didn't have to resort to sneaky tactics to question Vince about the fight he'd witnessed last night. I let Nick take the lead.

He said, "Can we go somewhere a little more private?"

Vince glanced at his Brownie Scouts, then at Colleen. "Can you take over for a second, Colleen?"

"Sure." She bustled out from behind the counter and started *ooh*ing and *aah*ing over the Scouts' progress.

Vince led us to the back of the shop, to a tiny office space. I wondered if Nick was having the same flashbacks I was. It wasn't all that long ago that we'd broken into this place looking for evidence of a killer. Well. *I* had broken in, and Nick had reluctantly followed.

Vince's puppy dog eyes had grown wide with concern. "You're here about the fight last night between Fisk Khoury and Michael Healey?"

Nick said, "Unofficially. Just trying to piece together a timeline."

Vince sat on the edge of the desk. He was boy-next-door cute, but I knew he had a dark side. It was bad enough he was a Seeker, but he was a Seeker on a mission to learn everything he could about any possible witchcraft in the village. Four months ago, that exploration had put him front and center of a murder case, and revealed that he'd go to just about any lengths to get what he wanted. Including cheating on his girlfriend at the time to woo someone he thought was a Crafter.

At one point, Harper had a crush on him, but she had quickly snapped out of her infatuation. Thank goodness. I had the queasy feeling that whoever got too close to Vince would come away the worse for wear.

"If only I'd known what was going to happen." Vince shook his head, sending his brown shaggy curls flopping this way and that. "Maybe I could have stopped it. Somehow."

His voice held such sincerity that I was inclined to believe him. Pain sketched across his face in the tightness of his lips, the wariness of his eyes.

"I think," I said, "that someone was determined. There was nothing you could have done."

Vince sat on the edge of his desk. "Even still."

Even still. I knew how he was feeling, wondering if I could have somehow prevented what had happened. If I'd called to check on the cake earlier ... or met Michael when he arrived in the parking lot. Something. Anything that could have stopped what happened.

Then I thought about what Nick had said. Stabbed, strangled, bludgeoned, poisoned.

Someone had wanted Michael dead. And I had no doubt it would have happened whether in the parking lot last night or somewhere else.

I had to listen to my own advice. There was nothing I could have done.

"What time did you come across the two fighting?" Nick asked.

There was a no-nonsense air about him. And even though his uniform might look better suited to a camp counselor, and he drove a black and yellow MINI Cooper (that I had nicknamed the Bumblebeemobile), he meant business. He'd once been a Rhode Island state trooper before being shot in the line of duty. His wife at the time, Melina (a Wishcrafter), had insisted he quit the force out of fear of losing him.

He did, but their marriage fell apart anyway. She cheated on him, he left, they divorced. Then the unthinkable happened. Melina was stricken with terminal pancreatic cancer. Nick had moved back to the family home to take care of her, not because he had to but because he wanted to. It was the kind of man he was—loyal, loving. By the time Melina passed away, they had pieced together a friendship, and I think that had brought him comfort during the dark days when he probably wondered if there was anything he could have done to save her.

Growing up a mortal, he'd been oblivious to the Craft until Melina revealed her powers to him. In doing so, she lost her ability to Wishcraft (another Wishcraft Law), but it was alive and strong within Mimi. Nick had wanted what was best for his daughter, so after Melina died, he'd packed up Mimi and moved her here so she could learn more about her Craft.

Vince clasped his hands together. "There's not much to tell. I had been at the festival, and I was taking a shortcut through the back alley to the shop when I came across them going at it. Amy was there, crying, begging them to stop. I pulled them apart, gave them a lecture about friendship, and Fisk stomped away with Amy trailing after him. Last I saw, Michael had climbed into the delivery van and driven off."

Nick said, "Did you hear what they were fighting about?"

"Bits," Vince admitted, "but none of it really made sense."

Whump-whump-whump.

I noticed Nick glance around, his eyes taking in every detail.

Had he felt Michael?

I bit my lip, then said, "Anything about the moon?"

Whump-whump-whump-whump.

Nick shifted, on alert.

Oh yeah, he definitely felt Michael.

I felt him, too, his agitation. What was it about the moon that was so important?

Vince snapped his fingers. "Actually, yes."

Nick threw me a questioning look.

I tried for an innocent expression despite knowing I probably looked guilty as sin.

"Now that you mention it," Vince continued, "as Fisk marched off last night, I heard him mumbling about the moon under his breath"—he glanced up at me and held my gaze—"and how he was running out of time."

Chapter Fourteen

Back outside, I'd taken just two steps before Nick grabbed my forearm, pulling me to a stop.

So much for a clean getaway.

"Darcy?" he said, his brown eyes probing.

I sidestepped out of the way of a stroller. "Yes?"

Nick tugged me into the passageway separating Spellbound's storefront from Lotions and Potions. "Something you want to tell me?"

A group of kids from the back alley ran past us, darting across the street to the festival, barely looking for oncoming traffic. My heart clutched until they made it safely across.

I glanced at Nick, who was waiting patiently for me to answer. "Actually," I said, "I have a couple of things to tell you."

"Spill."

"You look very handsome today." I batted my eyelashes.

His tight lips loosened into a half smile. "On any other day, flattery might get you everywhere, but today? I want some answers."

"You're no fun," I teased.

"Darcy."

I sighed. "Okay, well there's this thing with the black roses."

"Wait." He held up a hand. "Black roses? What black roses?"

"Harriette Harkette's black roses. They're officially called the Witching Hour roses."

"The ones she won awards for?"

I nodded.

"What do they have to do with Michael?"

"Everything. They're why he's dead."

Whump-whump-whump-whump.

Nick jumped a little, and his head swiveled back and forth, apparently looking for the source of what he could feel but not see. Finally, he stared at me. Questions churned in his eyes.

"I don't know where to begin," he said on a drawn-out sigh. "I've been looking into Michael's death for more than twelve hours now, and I haven't come across anything to do with *roses.*"

"They're magic roses," I said.

"Magic?"

I heard his skepticism and couldn't fault him for it. After all, he'd grown up a mortal and hadn't quite adjusted to the fact that magic was happening around him at all times.

"Did Glinda mention Michael was an Illumicrafter?"

"No, she didn't. What kind of Crafter is that?"

He sounded annoyed, and for some reason I felt the need to say, "She may not have known he was one. He kept it kind of hush-hush." I thought back to the run-in with Glinda that morning and realized that none of us had actually revealed that Amy was an Illumicrafter. I'd made a vague reference to light, but that could have been taken many ways.

I quickly explained to Nick the abilities of Illumicrafters and how Michael had been working at the Elysian Fields until two months ago.

"Harriette's flower farm, right?" he asked.

"Right. Apparently it was his spell that turned the roses black."

"How do you know all this?"

"Which part?" I asked.

"Any of it. All of it. What was with that moon question? How did you know about the spell?"

I winced. He wasn't going to like this part. "Well." I cleared my throat. "The moon thing? I heard that from Amy Healey."

His eyes widened. "You've seen Amy?"

I wanted to joke that all of outer space could have seen her this morning, but I didn't think he was in the mood for my humor. "I kind of ran into her this morning while I was jogging. She was, ah, glowing."

He glanced around as if wanting to find a chair to sit down. But only leaves rustled behind him, and somewhere nearby, was Michael.

Whump, whump.

"Literally?" he asked.

Ah, the Halfcrafter in him was finally catching on. I nodded. "Illumicrafters have the ability to glow. And apparently, when there is strong emotion involved, they can't shut the glow off. She practically lit up three blocks this morning." I quickly told him how Godfrey had come to the rescue.

"Where is she now?" he asked.

"At Ve's. Sleeping. She says she's more than willing to talk to you. Just not to Glinda."

"Why?"

"Something about how Glinda was ready to arrest Fisk last night . . ."

"You do realize Fisk is our top suspect at this point, right?"

Whump-whump-whump.

With a puzzled expression, Nick looked around.

"An understandable suspect," I said, "before you learned about the roses. But Fisk has nothing to do with those."

Whump-whump-whump.

I frowned at Michael's reaction. *Did* Fisk have something to do with the roses?

Nick tucked his hands into his fleece's pockets. "I'm almost afraid to ask, but why do you think the roses are the reason Michael is dead?"

I scrunched my nose. "Because Michael told me. Well, not told *literally*. He can't talk. But he flashed me. With light. I mean, because he's not visible, either. He's a" — I dropped my voice — "ghost."

"I need a drink," Nick said. His gaze zoomed into the distance, across the square to the Cauldron. Then he focused on me. "You're serious?"

"He imprinted on me last night when I found his body. He's been with us the whole time. You've felt him here."

"I have?"

"*Feel,*" I said to Nick, then said to Michael, "Black roses, spell, moon."

Whump-whump-whump.

Nick rubbed his arms as though a million goose bumps had just risen. Wide eyes blinked slowly. "You are serious."

"Michael, say hi to Nick, will you?"

A few feet away, a tiny light flickered on and off, on and off.

Nick slowly turned his head to me, then back to the light, then back to me.

"I know," I said. "I could hardly believe it, either. He can't talk, but he can answer yes and no questions. He flashes once for yes, twice for no, and oh, three times for I'm sorry."

" 'I'm sorry'?" Nick echoed.

"There was a shoving incident. . . ."

He shook his head. I told him all about my trip to see Lydia this morning, what had happened with the roses, what Bertie had said, and how Amy had linked the death of the roses to Michael's death and how that meant Harriette was a big fraud.

"This is . . . incredible."

It really was. There was something I wanted to ask Michael because of his earlier reaction to something I said. "Michael, earlier you were agitated when I mentioned that Fisk had nothing to do with the roses." I took a deep breath. "Was I wrong? Is he involved with what's going on with the black roses?"

He flashed once. *Yes.*

Nick rubbed his eyes. The cop in him was taking over. "Do you know where Fisk is now?"

No.

"Do you," Nick said, "think that Fisk had something to do with your death?"

No response.

Nick looked at me. "What does that mean when he doesn't answer?"

"It means he's unsure," I said softly.

Which meant that Fisk could very well be Michael's killer.

Nick had only another few minutes before he had to head back to work. With this new twist in Michael's case, he had other avenues to investigate—namely, Harriette Harkette and the Elysian Fields.

Nick pulled open the door to Spellbound and held it open for me—and me alone. Michael hadn't followed me in. Nick was present physically, but I could tell his mind was elsewhere. Probably awash in magical possibilities.

I saw the Lost notice featuring Tilda hanging on the glass, and I felt a little pang. Where could she possibly be?

The bell on the door was still jingling as Missy came charging toward us—bypassing me and going straight to Nick. He barely even noticed her, so it didn't surprise me in the least when she nipped his ankle to get his attention.

She wasn't one to be overlooked—unless it was on her own terms.

Nick jumped back and glanced down at her. She blinked innocently, turned tail, and strutted away.

Nick shot me a shocked look. I shrugged and said, "You shouldn't ignore her. She doesn't like it."

Angela Curtis, Colleen's mom and Harper's part-time employee, was helping a customer in the cookbook section, Harper was finishing ringing up a sale, and I spotted Mimi in the kids' nook. I nudged Nick to take a look. Mimi had Pie sitting on her lap as she read a storybook to a group of enraptured preschoolers.

A breathtaking smile bloomed on Nick's face, and I fell just a little bit harder for him. The unabashed love he felt for his daughter made my heart turn to mush.

Angela led her customer to the cash register and then came over to us, putting an arm around my shoulders. "Mimi's a natural with the kids."

She looked it. I couldn't see the story she was reading, but she was quite the dramatic storyteller, letting her voice rise and fall. Grand arm gestures punctuated sentences. The group of kids seemed to inch closer and closer to her toadstool, as if they, too, wanted to climb atop her lap like the spoiled tabby kitten.

She looked up and gave a smile that matched Nick's. It made my heart mushy, too.

Mimi had been "helping" Harper at the bookshop for the last two months—ever since school started. Technically, she couldn't work for Harper yet—Mimi wasn't old enough—but Harper paid her a decent hourly wage under the table. Mimi had been hoarding the money, saving up to buy a new iPod.

"How long has she been reading to them?" Nick asked.

Angela glanced at her watch. "Going on an hour now. I don't think she even realizes how much time has passed. I'll tell you what, it's good for business. The kids' parents are shopping like crazy."

I glanced around. Sure enough, the store was packed. I felt a little kick in my stomach when I spotted Ophelia Braun-Wickham across the shop. She was staring at me. I offered a smile just as she turned to whisper in Hammond Wickham's ear.

I elbowed Nick. "That's Ophelia, one of the Wicked Widows."

He straightened. Each of the Wickeds was now on his list to be interviewed.

Angela said, "She and Hammond have been browsing for an hour now, waiting for Ophelia's little boy, Jacob." She pointed to a small dark-haired boy who stared, besotted, at Mimi.

"Oh, and there's Imogene, too," I whispered to Nick, though he already knew Imogene, having met her before at town meetings.

Imogene stood off to the side of the children's nook, watching Mimi read to the little ones. She appeared as besotted as little Jacob. After a moment, she glanced up, noticed us, and came right over.

"Your daughter is lovely, Chief Sawyer," Imogene said.

"I couldn't agree more," Nick said with a smile.

"Do you have grandchildren, Imogene?" Angela asked.

"Never blessed with children at all," she said with a wistful sigh. "It's my biggest regret."

"Understandable," Angela said with a knowing nod.

"My orchids have kept me busy," Imogene said. Then she laughed as she added, "They practically need as much coddling as babies."

"They need more!" Angela smiled. "I tried my hand at growing some at the cottage this past summer and had some success."

Imogene pushed her glasses atop her head, where they acted as a headband for her out-of-control hair. Her eyes had lit with enthusiasm. "What kind?"

The two slipped into a conversation about orchids that had me zoning out. My black thumb would never cut it at the Elysian Fields.

Imogene laughed at something Angela said, snapping me out of my fugue.

Angela smiled and said, "Listen to me chatter on. You'd think I was petitioning to become a Wicked Widow."

"Should Harmony be worried?" I joked.

Angela gave me a playful shove. She and her partner, Harmony Atchison, owner of the Pixie Cottage, had been together for a while now and as far as I could tell were as happy as could be.

"Not hardly," Angela said. "Well, I should probably get back to work."

"Call me if you have any questions about your gardening," Imogene said.

I was surprised by the offer, considering Angela was a home-gardener and Imogene was a Floracrafter known for her high-and-mightiness.

Angela thanked her and ducked away.

Not long after that, Ophelia strode over—and I real-ized that she moved a lot like Harriette. They slinked very much alike.

For a Terracrafter, Ophelia had quite the pretentious air about her—no wonder I had assumed she was a Flora. "Do you know Nick Sawyer?" I made introduc-tions.

Ophelia shook his hand. "You're the new police chief. A pleasure to meet you."

The glow from watching Mimi had faded, and Nick was back in cop mode. "I hope you retain that impress-sion, Ms. Braun-Wickham."

She tipped her head. "Why wouldn't I? And please call me Ophelia."

"I'd like to set up a time to ask you a few questions. Both of you," he said, including Imogene in his response.

"Us?" Ophelia's hand flew to her chest. "Why ever?"

Nick dropped his voice so as not to be overheard. "It's about Michael Healey's death."

A little of Ophelia's confidence vanished. Lowering her voice, she said, "I still don't understand. I barely knew Michael."

"Because he worked at the Elysian Fields?" Imogene asked.

Nick nodded. "I'm trying to fill in some blanks about his last few months. I'm investigating all loose ends, and his work at the Elysian Fields is a loose end."

Imogene said, "We don't know much other than his tasks at the farm, but we'll certainly help any way we can. It's tragic what happened to that boy."

Ophelia said, "Terribly tragic. He was a nice young man. Do you have any leads on the case?"

I saw Harper lurking behind Nick, fussing with some books on a shelf. She was clearly eavesdropping.

"A few. Nothing concrete yet," Nick said.

"Well." Ophelia drew her shoulders back. "I'll certainly be glad to tell you all I know. Which unfortunately for your investigation isn't much. You may want to speak with Harriette. She was much closer to Michael than any of us other Wickeds."

Nick smiled thinly and pulled a vibrating cell phone from his hip. He glanced at the readout and said, "Please excuse me for a second." He trotted off to a quiet corner of the shop.

Ophelia tapped a diamond watch. "We should be off now, Imogene." To me, she said, "We're meeting Bertie at the festival to judge the pie contest today. It's a Wicked Widow tradition."

"Just the three of you?" I asked.

"Harriette's under the weather but promised to join us if she feels better." Ophelia turned away, walked over to whisper something to her husband, and then slinked toward the door where she waited for Imogene to join her.

Imogene lingered at my side, and I had the feeling she liked to keep Ophelia waiting. Finally, she said, "Darcy, please give Mimi my accolades for her performance. She's a charming girl."

"I will," I said.

Imogene leaned in to me and whispered, "Is Ophelia tapping her foot yet?"

I glanced over my shoulder. "Tapping her foot and drumming her fingertips on the door."

With an amused gleam in her eye, Imogene nodded. "Take care, Darcy." She shuffled off, clearly dragging her feet. I'd never seen her move so slowly.

Nick was back a second later. "I have to go. There's been a break in the case."

"What kind?" I asked.

"One of the murder weapons has been uncovered." He gave me a quick kiss and rushed out the door.

Harper immediately stepped up next to me. "What did he mean 'one of'?"

As I leaned against a bookshelf, I watched Nick run at a dead sprint across the square.

I quietly explained about Michael's death.

"Ooh," Harper said. "Shades of *Murder on the Orient Express*."

Running my hand over the rough bark of the bookshelf, I said, "What do you mean by that?"

"Don't you remember? The man died from something like thirteen stab wounds—each inflicted by a different person?"

The story slowly came back to me, and I suddenly realized what Harper was saying. Four methods of murder.

Four perpetrators.

Out the window, I saw Ophelia and Imogene meet up with Bertie. All three turned and looked at the bookshop.

Bumps rose on my arms.

Was it just a coincidence that there were *four* Wicked Widows?

Chapter Fifteen

A few minutes later, I was still in the bookshop, and I had just wrangled a promise from Harper that she would ask Marcus about Harriette's will. She was more than willing to be my coconspirator.

I realized how far I'd come in my relationship with her, at least in terms of my moral code. Since we'd moved to the Enchanted Village, it seemed like my moral compass had aligned itself with hers, rather than the other way around.

It was a little disconcerting how willing I was to be unethical just because I had a good reason. . . .

Which was how Harper had been explaining her exasperating behavior for years.

Maybe all that time she'd been right—and I'd been wrong.

It was a painful admission, even making it to myself.

Was it possible the Wickeds were guilty of Michael's death? Plausible?

I tried to sort it out. Michael had left the bakery around seven. I had found his body at eight thirty. That was an hour and a half of unaccounted time. When had he actually arrived at the lot? And when had he been killed?

Thinking back to last night, I remembered that Ophelia, Imogene, and Bertie had all arrived at Harriette's party together at eight sharp. Harriette had come in later. With respect to time, it could have worked. But plausibility?

Why would all four of them want him dead?

He said he'd died because of something to do with the Witching Hour roses. . . . But *why* exactly? What about them led to his murder?

I needed to find out how many people knew that it was his spell that created those black roses. Harriette had to know, of course. But who else? I wished that Michael were here so I could pepper him with questions, but he had yet to return.

I needed to find someone who knew more about what Michael was doing at the Elysian Fields—someone who knew Michael inside and out.

I needed to find Fisk.

I'd just clipped on Missy's leash to take her home before I went to the festival when Angela, standing behind the cash register, let out a small cry.

I spun around and saw panic filling her eyes. Her hand shook as she held a cell phone. "I have to go," she said to Harper as she ran to the door, stopped, ran to the back storeroom and came out with her coat.

Harper said, "What's happened?"

"It's Harmony."

"Is she okay?" I asked, anxiety twisting through me.

"She sent me a text message." Looking around, she lowered her voice. "Apparently she found the weapon used to stab Michael Healey. I have to go."

I took a peek at Harper, who looked disappointed that she couldn't leave Mimi to run the shop so she could accompany Angela. She shooed me with her hands. "Go with her, Darcy! She's a friend in need."

I bit back an exasperated sigh. This had nothing to do with friendship and everything to do with Harper wanting the scoop on what Harmony had found.

Angela grabbed my hand. "Come on!" She yanked open the door, sending the bells into a jingly fit, and took off down the sidewalk.

I jogged to keep up with her. Missy trotted at my side. "Where are we going?"

"Harmony has been working in the Dumpster behind the Sorcerer's Stove. The new owner is renovating the restaurant before reopening," she said, "so Harmony thought it would be great pickings."

In addition to owning the Pixie Cottage, Harmony was also what she liked to call an "article relocator." In plain terms, she was a Dumpster diver, who had the talent to transform junk into masterpieces. I once saw a table she'd made from a broken window frame; it was gorgeous.

Angela gulped for breath by the time we reached the restaurant. The architecture of the building was one of my favorite styles in the village. A stone cottage with a central chimney, leaded glass windows, and a board and batten door, the place looked as though it had fallen out of *Hansel and Gretel*. The police had already cordoned off the street, and I didn't see Harmony in the crowd. "Do you know where she is?"

Angela shook her head and sent a quick text message.

We waited impatiently. A moment later, Angela's phone buzzed, and she said to me, "Around back, on the Enchanted Trail."

We skirted the crowd and accessed the path near Third Eye Optometry. We found Harmony sitting alone on a bench in the garden behind the Sorcerer's Stove. Police officers swarmed the area.

Angela hugged Harmony and said, "Are you okay?"
She held her at arm's length, checking for herself.

I was alarmed to see a bandage on Harmony's hand.
"Were you cut?"

"Just nicked," Harmony said.

I shuddered.

"Nicked?" Angela gasped. "Let me see." She examined the wound. "I think you should have a doctor look
at this. It might need a stitch or two."

Harmony laid a hand atop Angela's. "I'm fine. The
paramedic already cleaned it up. Someone's trying to
track down Michael's medical records to make sure I
don't have to worry about any blood-borne diseases."

I shuddered again. I couldn't help myself.

Harmony smiled at me. "And the paramedic gave me
a Valium, which is why I'm so damn calm."

I kind of wished the paramedic would give me one,
too. I was freaking out.

Missy set her paws on Harmony's legs and wagged
her tail. Harmony rubbed her ears. "You're such a good
dog," she sang.

I smiled. Missy had a calming effect on people.

Angela asked what had happened, and Harmony said,
"I was digging—oh my gosh, I found the most beautiful
window; you should see it—and as I was pulling it out, I
felt something poke me. I thought maybe there was
broken glass in the Dumpster, but when I dug farther, I
found a pair of gardening snips. Razor-sharp ones at
that. At first, I was thrilled. They're beautifully made—
expensive, I can tell, with a leather grip. I probably could
have sold them online for more than a hundred dollars.
Then I saw the dried blood on them, and my brain put it
together that this was probably the weapon used on Michael. I practically fell out of the Dumpster to get away

from them. I called the police ... and now here we are."
She was the one shivering now.

Angela looked around at the officers combing the
area. "Are you allowed to leave?"

Harmony nodded. "Nick just didn't want me walking
home alone."

Angela tugged her to her feet. "Come on then. Let's
go. Darcy, can you let Harper know that I won't be back
to the bookshop?"

I said I would. Harmony patted Missy's head and gave
me a wan smile; then they headed along the trail and
disappeared from view.

When I looked back at the Dumpster, I saw Nick
coming toward me. This time when Missy pranced
toward him, he didn't ignore her. In fact, he knelt down
and scratched her chin.

I crouched next to him. "How sure are you that those
snips are one of the murder weapons?"

"Fairly sure. I've sent them to the crime lab. I wish
they hadn't been found in a Dumpster, though. Too many
contaminants."

As Nick was part Wishcrafter by marriage, I couldn't
grant his wishes, so I didn't even attempt to cast the spell.

"With the renovation going on, the dirt alone ... ," I
said.

"The strange thing was that the snips had feathers
stuck to them." He smiled wryly. "I wonder what's been
cooking in the restaurant."

I tipped my head. "Feathers?"

"White ones."

"Thin? Fluffy?"

"Where are you going with this, Darcy?"

"It's just that last night Harriette was wearing a black
dress that was trimmed in white feathers to her party."

Nick stood. "I think it's time I paid Harriette a visit."

I agreed. "Those snips . . ."

"What?" he asked. "Do you know something about them?"

"I'm not sure. It's just that this morning, when I was at Harriette's greenhouse, there was a rack with gardening tools with leather handles. There was an empty spot that indicated one was missing—according to Harriette, it was the pair of snips."

Nick cursed under his breath.

"So," I said, catching his eye, "when you go to question Harriette, you might want to bring along a warrant."

As I didn't think the festival was the best place for Missy, I dropped her off at home to keep Amy company, and I headed for the pie-tasting contest to spy on the Wickeds.

On my way there, I stopped at the fried dough booth. I really wanted a caramel apple, but I would wait for Nick to fulfill his promise.

I was starting to get a little worried about Michael. He still hadn't returned. What could he possibly be doing?

I'd just stuffed a piece of dough into my mouth when I practically ran into Starla, who was working the festival as a freelance photographer for the local newspaper, the *Toil and Trouble*.

Starla had been appropriately named. With her bright eyes, her white-blond hair, and radiant personality, she simply shone like a glimmering star in a dark night sky. "Darcy! You're not going to believe it." She was suddenly distracted by my fried dough. "That looks amazing."

"Believe what?"

She grabbed a hunk of my dough and took a bite.

"Hey!" I said.

"Friends share." She grinned as she wiped powdered sugar from her mouth with the back of her hand. "I didn't realize how hungry I was until I saw that." She blinked prettily.

Reluctantly, I handed the whole plate over to her. She beamed as I went and bought myself another one. When I came back, she was already done with hers.

Although she was my first best friend ever, she was not getting this dough, too. I held it close and said, "Now, what am I not going to believe?"

"Oh! That. I got another one."

"Another what?"

"Jack-o'-lantern." Starla took a quick picture of a baby being handed a spider-shaped balloon. "It was sitting outside Hocus-Pocus late this morning when I opened up the shop."

"Did it have another note inside?"

She nodded, her eyes alight.

Again, I hoped this wasn't some creep playing tricks on her. It was, after all, the season of trickery.

"It said, 'Beautiful are you; Beast am I.'"

I nearly choked on a nibble of fried dough. "Beast?"

"I know," Starla said, adjusting her camera strap. "That sounds ominous, doesn't it? Yet, it's kind of romantic. I mean, *Beauty and the Beast* is a love story. It's about looking deeper into someone's soul and not being deterred by what's on the surface."

She'd obviously been putting a lot of thought into this.

"I could use a happily-ever-after for a change," she added on a sigh.

Her last few relationships had been big duds, so I couldn't blame her for wanting something long lasting.

Just as long as it wasn't with some pumpkin-freak stalker.

"I wonder who it is," she said dreamily.

I had absolutely no idea. "I'm sure you'll find out soon."

"You think so?"

I nodded.

Looking like a kid at Christmas, she smiled ear to ear, then straightened and tried to erase the grin from her face. "Okay, I'm going to just pretend like none of this happened. I have work to do. Besides, I don't want to get my hopes up."

I didn't know who she thought she was fooling. Her hopes had risen higher than a kite caught in a windstorm.

"I'll catch you later." She skipped away.

Actually skipped.

Whoever her secret admirer was, he couldn't have planned this better. I half believed that Starla had already fallen for this mystery man from the sheer romance of it all.

I just hoped she didn't fall as hard as that kite when the wind died down.

I stood on tiptoe and glanced around, trying to get a feel for the layout of the festival.

It looked like the pie judging was being held under a tent near the haunted house. I could see it was standing room only, and I hoped I could edge my way inside.

As I scooted past a little girl whose face was painted like a panda bear, I yelped when a hand grabbed my arm and yanked me to a stop.

Chapter Sixteen

"Sorry," Trista Harkette said. "You didn't hear me calling you."

Sœurs.

Pepe's term for sisters jumped into my head. Even though they didn't have much contact with each other, Trista and Lydia certainly had the same method of getting a witch's attention.

"I need to talk to you," Trista said. "Something important."

"Is this about Louis? Because I already have that covered."

"Who?" she asked.

"Your mother's fiancé?"

"Don't make me laugh," she said. "I couldn't care less about Harriette's love life, though I did hear about the betting pool."

"And did you place a bet?"

"Of course."

The Ghoulousel piped a jaunty tune, and I smiled at the grins on children's faces as they rode an assortment of ceramic ghosts. "Which side are you on?"

"He's real. Harriette would never lie about a man."

Harriette. Interesting that she called her mother by her first name. I supposed twenty years of not speaking to each other led to dropping familial terms.

Short and plump, Trista seemed to be the complete opposite of her mother and sister. Big light blue eyes, blond hair, fair skin. Unlike Lydia, she looked younger than her age, and unlike her mother, she didn't appear to have a dark side. There was nothing viperous about her.

She glanced around the festival. "Can you spare a minute?"

I threw a look toward the pie-judging tent and figured there was time enough to spy on the Wickeds. "Sure."

"Come with me. We can talk at the shop, where it's quieter."

We crossed the street, and I waved to Godfrey inside the Bewitching Boutique. Gone were his silk pajamas, replaced now with a zippy three-piece suit. Trista's shop was a little farther down the road. The building reminded me a lot of the Gingerbread Shack, but on a smaller scale. Painted a pale lavender, it was only one story, with a pitched roof and delicate trim. A window box was full of dark purple flowers and cascading ivy that reminded me of the Elysian Fields. I waited on a narrow porch for her to unlock the front door of Something Wicked. A CLOSED sign dangled from a multipaned glass door, beneath which a small placard read DEATH IN THE FAMILY.

Sympathy flowed through me. If Trista and Dash had been like family to Michael, then losing him must feel like losing a son. And if Fisk was somehow involved in Michael's death, it would be a double whammy. I truly hoped that wasn't the case.

Skylights spilled sunshine into the already bright shop, highlighting sexy nighties, silk pajamas, delicate underwear, and the biggest assortment of bras I'd ever seen. I'd never seen an AbracadaBra up close and personal, and I smiled when I realized that you couldn't take the flora out of a Floracrafter. The bra's cups weren't traditionally round, but more of a wide triangle—they were shaped like leaves. And the colors in the store? All floral colors—pinks, reds, purples, yellows, whites. Not a black garment to be seen. Trista had incorporated her floral background into an incredibly successful business.

"Coffee?" Trista asked, heading for a kitchenette. "I already have a pot made."

"Sounds good," I said, taking a seat in a small lounge area.

A few minutes later, she set a tray on a leather ottoman and handed me a mug of coffee. Steam rose enticingly from the rim of the cup. I gratefully wrapped my hands around it.

Sitting back, she drew her legs beneath her on a tufted purple couch and smoothed a wrinkle in her jeans.

I stirred sugar into my mug and said softly, "Is this about Michael?"

Tears filled her eyes. "Darcy, our lives are falling apart. Michael is dead, Fisk is missing, and Dash went into his greenhouse last night and refuses to come out."

"I'm so sorry for all you're going through." I blew on my coffee and tried to think of a way to pry that didn't sound too nosy. Finally, I gave up on pretenses and said, "I hadn't realized Dash had his own greenhouse. I thought he was strictly a landscaper. . . . Is it near here?"

Sipping her coffee, she said casually, "It's in a secret location."

"Why is it secret?" I asked, both amused and intrigued.

She appeared to be waging an internal debate before she finally said, "He's breeding special flowers. It's kind of a secret project."

"*Black* flowers?" I asked.

Her eyebrows dipped. "How'd you know that?"

"Black roses were what Michael had been working on at the Elysian Fields, so when I heard that Michael and Dash were working on a project together . . . it makes sense that it would be on black flowers."

"Well," she said, her cheeks growing red, "this is starting to make some sense now. I had no idea Michael had been working on the black roses. I thought he was doing simple maintenance over there." Her eyes took on a distant look, as if she were trying to piece together a puzzle. With shaky hands, she set her mug on the tray, and coffee sloshed over the rim.

I really wanted to blot up the spilled liquid, but I held myself in check. "He wasn't just *working* on the roses. I'm fairly certain that Michael was the one who created the spell for the flowers."

Her face paled. "Not Harriette?"

I shook my head.

"Do you have proof?"

"No," I said. "Just speculation. But you can ask Dash about the spell. He probably knows more about it than I do, especially if he has pure black flowers in his greenhouse. Michael probably created those, too."

"I should have figured this out, especially after I heard the news about Harriette retiring."

"She's what?"

"Retiring. She called an emergency meeting of the Wickeds this week and announced it. A little birdie, or should I say Bertie, told me. If the Witching Hour roses were Michael's creation, then Harriette's probably retiring to save face since she wouldn't be able to produce any more of them." Her nose scrunched, and tears sprang to her eyes. "Does his death have something to do with those black roses?"

"Yes." Harriette's retiring *was* the perfect cover for not producing any roses. Of course, she was also eighty years old, long past the usual age to stop working. Then I recalled that Lydia had mentioned Imogene was retiring soon, too. Lydia was halfway to her wish of having the Elysian Fields revert back to family.

Letting out a little moan, Trista leaned forward, putting her elbows on her knees and her face into her hands. "Dash was so excited about working with Michael and Fisk to create a line of black flowers. Orchids, lilies, carnations—anything. Everything. I didn't realize how involved Michael was—I believed he was just helping out, helping them. It seems the opposite was true if it was his spell. . . ." She tipped her head. "Wait. How did he create black flowers? He was an *Illumicrafter*."

"Right now it's a mystery. Maybe Dash or Fisk knows?"

"Maybe."

She didn't seem too eager to find out. I finally gave in and wiped the spilled coffee with a napkin. "Why wouldn't Dash tell you about Michael working on the black roses at the Elysian Fields? He had to have known the truth. . . ."

"He knows I don't like hearing anything about Harriette or the Elysian Fields. He was probably trying to shelter me as much as possible. See, when Harriette cut me out of her life, I cut her out of mine as well."

I fiddled with the end of my braid. "What about Fisk? Does Harriette have any kind of relationship with him?"

"Once or twice a year, Fisk gets a written invitation to visit with her. Written, for God's sake. Heaven forbid the woman pick up the phone."

I could feel her anger and resentment. "Does he go?"

"Absolutely not." Trista shook her head. "If she doesn't accept my husband, she doesn't accept my child. Period."

A hard line to toe, but I supposed it was her right to choose to do so. "What's Fisk's predominate Craft?" As a Crosser, he could go either way, Terra or Flora.

"Fisk is a rare Crafter who has equal abilities. Maybe because the two Crafts are complementary—we're not sure. He's an incredibly gifted gardener." Her eyebrow quirked. "And he has a passion for it, too. He's going to make quite a name for himself. Put Harriette out of business."

She seemed pleased about that. "But," I said, "isn't it your business, too? Technically?" I was fishing, trying to find out if Trista was named in Harriette's will.

"Not in the least. When my mother disowned me, she cut me off from *everything*. The Elysian Fields will undoubtedly go to Little Goody Two-Shoes."

"Lydia?"

Trista rolled her eyes. "She complains about being unhappy working for Harriette, but she doesn't *do* anything about it."

"Do you two see much of each other?" I asked.

"We try to meet for lunch a couple of times a year, just to keep in touch. There's not much of a relationship."

I heard the note of sadness in her tone and wanted to shout, "But you don't *do* anything about it!"

I kept quiet, though. I had enough on my plate without trying to heal a decades-old rift between sisters. I was heartened to hear that Trista hadn't cut her sister completely out of her life. It was something. A small something, but still.

"I've never met Fisk, but I've heard him play guitar," I said. "At the Witch's Brew. He's good, though his song selections . . ." The funeral tunes were enough to give me the willies.

Trista laughed. "I think he likes to shock people. Kids. Sheesh. Do you have any?"

My heart double-clutched. While I was married, I'd wanted a baby so badly, but my ex, Troy, had wanted to wait. So I waited. I was still waiting when I found out he'd been cheating on me. He ended up marrying that woman, and within a year they'd had a baby together. It had been like a knife to my heart. "No." Then, on impulse, I added, "Not yet."

I wasn't ready to give up that dream quite yet, and my mind automatically wandered to Nick and the kind of father he was to Mimi, and the kind of family we could have together. . . .

Giving myself a good hard mental shake, I pushed the thoughts aside. For now. Maybe later when I was curled up in bed, the covers tucked tight to my chin, I'd close my eyes and let that picture fully form. And let myself keep dreaming. Hoping. Wishing.

I added a little more coffee to my cup. "I did help raise my sister, Harper, though, and can understand. She certainly has a mind of her own and knows how to use it." I left out the part where Harper, believing her honors teachers unjust for assigning homework over spring break (when the other students had none), hacked into the mainframe of her high school and deleted all academic records.

It had taken a computer whiz to resurrect the files, some fast-talking on my father's part, a hefty donation to the athletic fund (which further infuriated Harper), and a suspension on her record to get her out of that mess. We were lucky the police hadn't been involved.

"Harper's wonderful," Trista said. "I know Amy adores her." She looked off into the distance, but she said no more about Amy—and how she'd disappeared. I wondered if Trista believed, like everyone else in the village, that she was with Fisk.

"She really is," I said. Flaws and all.

Thinking about Amy led me to another question that had been bothering me. "Do you know why Michael and Fisk may have been fighting last night?"

Her eyes darkened. "I heard about that. I can't imagine why. I know they'd both been under a lot of pressure over creating the new business, but I can't imagine what would cause them to be physical with each other."

"I heard . . ." It sounded so silly. "I heard they'd been fighting over something to do with the moon."

She'd been bringing her cup to her lips and stopped midway. "The moon?"

I nodded.

"That's strange."

I agreed with her. It was strange. There had to be more to it, but to know how much more, I needed to find Fisk. But first, I needed to learn as much about Michael's life over the past couple of months as I could.

In my head, I was trying to piece together all the information I knew. For verification, I said, "This morning, Bertie told me that it was you who asked her to hire Michael. True?"

She nodded. "I knew Harriette would pay Michael a decent wage. The boy wouldn't take a cent from us, no matter how much we offered. He was proud. And he wasn't afraid to work hard—a quality he needed if he was going to work for Harriette."

I could see that about him.

"So I asked a favor from Bertie." She pulled her bottom lip into her mouth and blinked back tears. "I suddenly feel like that one phone call put this whole situation in motion." Trista wiped her eyes. "I guess I need your help more now than ever."

"Why's that?"

I heard sirens in the distance as she said, "I want to hire you. I want you to find Fisk. Originally, I just wanted to find him before the police found him and arrested him for something he didn't do . . . but now, I need you to find him, because if Michael had been killed for having something to do with those flowers, then Fisk might be in danger, too."

Chapter Seventeen

Since locating Fisk had already been on my mind, I left Trista with a promise to do my best to find him. I couldn't help but feel he held the key to solving this whole case.

I'd also spent my last few minutes silently wishing that Trista would just wish to know where he was. It would have made my job so much easier.

But as it was against Wishcraft Laws to solicit wishes, I couldn't say so aloud. Unfortunately, because Trista hadn't picked up on my silent pleading, I was going to have to find Fisk the hard way.

My first inclination was to ask Amy if she had any thoughts about where he might be hiding out. It was, in fact, my only inclination, so I hoped she had some suggestions for me.

Even though I'd recently acquired a PI license, I had come about it in a magical way, and hadn't (yet) put in the necessary requirements.

Which boiled down to the fact that I had no idea what I was doing.

On the front porch of Something Wicked, I buttoned

my coat and tucked my hands in my pockets. I glanced at the sky. Dark clouds had moved in, and I could smell rain in the air.

I smiled. I loved rain.

But if the temperature dropped any more, the rain would surely turn to snow. Beautiful, yes, but not good for the festival.

As I headed down the sidewalk, I listened to the wind whistling down the street and suddenly realized how quiet it was.

Deathly quiet.

I kicked up my pace and headed for the village green. As I neared, I could see the flashing lights of emergency vehicles, a crowd, and Evan standing in front of the Gingerbread Shack, taking it all in.

Jogging over to him, I said, "What's happened now? Not another murder?"

I didn't see the medical examiner's van, but it might not have arrived yet.

Evan said, "Someone didn't like the judgment of the pie contest."

The pie contest? The one the Wickeds were judging? "What happened?"

"Imogene Millikan became horribly ill shortly after awarding the winner of the pie." He rolled his eyes. "A plain old apple pie." *Tsk*ing, he added, "How boring. I would have made chocolate raspberry mousse pie, but alas, professional bakers are disqualified. Apple. So boring."

I hated that my stomach rumbled at a time like this. "Not all of us are as refined as you are."

His blue eyes gleamed. "More's the pity."

"Imogene," I said, trying to refocus his attention. "What happened to her?"

"No one's sure. Starla keeps running back and forth

to give me updates. The latest rumor is that someone poisoned a pumpkin smoothie Imogene drank after the contest as retaliation for not winning."

"Seems a little severe."

"Oh, Darcy. No one is more cutthroat than bakers."

I wasn't so sure. Because I wasn't thinking a frustrated (psychotic) baker had anything to do with Imogene's being poisoned.

More likely, it was someone who had something to do with what happened to Michael. Which reinforced my growing suspicion that the Wickeds knew more than they were letting on about Michael's death.

Four murder methods. Four Wickeds.

But now someone had poisoned Imogene. . . . I didn't know how that factored into everything going on, and not knowing scared me. I hoped Nick had made some headway in the case.

Evan put an arm around me and pulled me close. He kissed my temple.

"What was that for?" I asked.

"You looked like you needed it."

I smiled at him and gave his cheek a quick peck. "I did. It's been a long, crazy day."

"This business with Michael?" he asked.

A glimpse of red in the sky caught my eye as Archie flew toward the village green. He'd been a busy bird today.

"Trista Harkette just hired me to find Fisk."

"Really?"

"She thinks he might be in danger. That whoever killed Michael might come after Fisk, too."

Evan motioned me into the bakery. Slipping behind the glass display case, he took out a cake pop and handed it to me. "Has she been sampling magic mushrooms?"

"You don't think he's in danger?"

He filled a mug with coffee and sat with me at a table. We had a good view of the excitement outside, including the ambulance that was pulling away from the festival.

"I think he *is* the danger," Evan said.

The cake pop had chocolate coating that glistened under the lights. I took a bite. Moist vanilla-bean cake melted in my mouth. It was nice to have friends who owned bakeries. "Why do you think so? Just because of the way he looks?"

Tipping his head side to side as if thinking about it, he said, "Maybe."

I nudged his arm. "Evan Sullivan, a fashion snob. I'm shocked. Just shocked."

"Don't make me take your cake pop away, Darcy Merriweather. Have you seen the way he dresses? A crime in itself."

He had a point. But still. "Trista seems nice enough. Dash is a great guy. I can't imagine their offspring would be anything other than a good kid, even if it's disguised under doom and gloom attire."

Evan picked a piece of lint off his sweater. "The jury's out."

I had a feeling it would stay out until Fisk underwent a fashion intervention.

"I don't suppose you know where Fisk hangs out. Or with whom?" Maybe a friend would know where he was.

Speaking of friends, Michael still hadn't returned. I didn't feel his pulsing energy in the shop. He had been gone for a while now, and I was starting to worry.

Then I checked myself. What could possibly happen to him? He was already dead. This took my mother-hen worrying to a whole new level.

Evan ran his finger along the edge of the table. "I only know of Michael and Amy. . . . Did you hear that she's now missing, too? Probably ran off with that delinquent."

Large photos Starla had taken decorated the walls.
Beautiful close-ups of all kinds of treats. My favorite was
the shot of the double chocolate mocha cake. It made
me crave it every time I saw that picture. "Actually, she
didn't."

Eagerly, he leaned in. "You know where she is?"

I winced. "At Ve's."

His blue eyes grew wide. "Do the police know? Of
course they don't know," he said, "or else Glinda wouldn't
have stopped by here three times today already, asking
if I'd seen or heard Amy come home."

That's right. She lived upstairs. "Maybe Glinda just
likes your cake pops."

"That is possible," he acceded. "Now tell me everything. Why is Amy at Ve's?"

I told him all I knew, and as I finished the tale, I stared
in wonder at a spot on the wooden floor. One of the slats
was moving, an eensy bit at a time, sliding to reveal a
dark cavity.

"Uh, Evan?" I said, motioning.

He looked down. "It's all clear, Pepe," he yelled.

Pepe, his little mouse whiskers twitching, pulled himself up and out of the hole. He dusted himself off, adjusted his vest, and pushed his glasses farther up his
nose. "It took you long enough."

"I didn't hear you knocking," Evan said, bending over
and placing his cupped hands on the ground. Pepe
climbed into them, and Evan lifted him onto the table.

It seemed to be a familiar routine to them.

With a smile, Evan added, "Darcy was yammering on
and on."

"Hey!" I said. "I do not yammer."

Pepe bowed. "*Ma chère*, how is the glowing one?"

"Still glowing. And resting," I said. "Missy's keeping
her company. Do you come here often?"

His tail swished. "*Oui*. I cannot keep away from the chocolate cheesecake. It is a weakness." He rubbed his belly and looked longingly at Evan.

"Subtle." Evan stood and cut off a nibble of cheesecake. He placed it on a teacup saucer and brought it back to the table.

"*Non*. Effective," Pepe said with a toothy grin as he picked up his treat.

Out the front window, I saw the crowd slowly start to dissipate. I was curious to know what exactly had happened to Imogene. I spotted Nick walking along with Glinda at his elbow, and I ignored a sharp stab of jealousy. On the bright side, she looked exhausted. Yes, still gorgeous, but droopy. That cheered me up a little.

Behind them, I was a little surprised to see solemn-faced Lydia and Willard Wentworth standing off to the side watching what was going on. I presumed that Willard had called her when he saw the hubbub at the festival because I had thought Lydia said she'd be working in her greenhouse all day. Willard wore a BLACK THORN apron, as if he'd left his shop in a hurry.

Starla was bustling around snapping pictures of anything and everything. Despite the seriousness of the situation, she still had an air of happiness about her.

"What do you two think of Starla's secret admirer?" I assumed Pepe knew about the jack-o'-lanterns. In a village this small, word tended to get around.

Evan blew out a breath. "She's over the moon. I just don't want her to get hurt. Do you have any idea who it is?"

"Not a clue," I said. "Did you hear about his latest note? 'Beautiful are you; Beast am I'? What kind of man goes into a potential relationship comparing himself to a beast? It's as if he's warning her off before he even meets her."

Evan tapped his chin. "Who's the furriest in the village?"

"Hands down, Roger Merrick." He was a local Geocrafter, and I was pretty sure he had hair coming out of every pore on his body.

Evan scrunched his nose. "He's happily married, plus he's old enough to be her father. Gross."

"You asked," I said.

Pepe coughed. "Perhaps the Beast reference was not literal."

"What do you mean?" Evan asked.

"Perhaps," Pepe said, dusting his paws free of cheesecake crumbs, "Starla's admirer is concerned that there's an element to his being that she will not find attractive."

"But not literal," I said, musing. "More like a personality trait."

"*Oui.*"

I leaned down and looked him in the eye. "You know something, don't you?"

A bead of sweat popped out on his forehead. He glanced down, pulled a tiny pocket watch from his vest pocket, and made a show of looking at it. "Look at the time! I must be going."

He darted for the edge of the table. Evan grabbed Pepe's tail, stopping his progress.

"Unhand me!" Pepe demanded.

"You know who it is, don't you?" Evan prodded.

Pepe looked nervously at me. "I may have seen a man dropping a pumpkin off at Hocus-Pocus this morning. . . ."

"Who?" I asked. "Who is he?"

"*Non!* I cannot say! Now let me go."

"Not until you give up the information," Evan said.

"Ruffian!" Pepe said, gnashing his teeth.

I had the feeling he was about to take a bite out of Evan's hand, and I was about to warn him when Evan suddenly let go.

In a flash, Pepe leapt off the table, scurried to the hole in the floor, and dove in headfirst, leaving Evan and me staring after him in wonder.

"For such a chubby familiar, he sure is fast," Evan remarked with wonder in his voice.

I stood up. "I won't tell him you called him chubby. His teeth are really sharp."

Evan smirked. "Thanks. Where are you off to?"

Truth was, I wasn't sure. "I have to uncover whether the elusive Louis is real or make-believe, find Fisk, look for Tilda, see what I can find out about Imogene's poisoning, check on Amy, ask Marcus Debrowski about wills, and figure out why Fisk and Michael were fighting over the moon. So . . . a nap sounds good."

Evan's laughter rang in my ears as I gave him a quick kiss on the cheek, thanked him for the cake pop, and left the shop. As I stepped outside, the chilly wind felt like it was boring into my soul. It was time to dig out my winter coat from Aunt Ve's garage. Another thing to add to my to-do list. I glanced up at the bakery building, taking note of the windows on the second floor. As I watched, I could have sworn that a curtain shifted.

I turned around and went back inside the bakery.

Evan gave me a puzzled look. "All right," he joked. "You can have another cake pop."

I smiled. "Actually, I was wondering . . ."

"What's that look in your eye?"

"As landlord, you have keys to Michael and Amy's upstairs apartment, right?"

"Yes . . ."

I batted my eyelashes. "Can we take a quick look?" I

wanted to make sure no one was up there, snooping around. If I had any measure of luck, I'd find Fisk hiding out.

"You know," Evan said as he rummaged around drawers, "there are rules that protect tenants' privacy."

"Your point?"

"Aha!" He pulled out a key ring and jangled the keys hanging from it. "No point at all. Let's go."

Chapter Eighteen

Evan unlocked the apartment door and pushed it open.
Whump, whump.

Ah, so this was where Michael had been.

His energy was calm, so I hoped that meant he'd found some peace being in the space. Rightfully so—it was an adorable apartment, and amazingly clean for housing two young adults.

The walls had been painted a light grayish blue, and were adorned with bold-colored artwork. The furniture was sparse, just a couch and a couple of chairs in the living space. In the adjoining dining area, a wooden table had been painted a bright cheery yellow. A vase of flowers sat on the tabletop. Black roses. Dead black roses.

I swallowed over the sudden lump in my throat.

There was a lumpy sofa that looked like it was a pull-out. Which made sense since there was only one bedroom.

"The police have already been through here," Evan said. "Last night. They took a laptop and a couple of files. Nothing much else."

I glanced around. No landline phone, so checking for

messages was out. I remembered seeing Michael's phone on the seat of the van. I wondered if the police had found anything on it—a text message identifying his killer would be nice. But probably too much to hope for.

I walked over to the window and pushed the curtain aside. Had it been Michael doing the same earlier? Or had someone else been in the apartment? Someone like Fisk.

"Was there something in particular you were looking for, Darcy?" Evan asked.

A floorboard creaked, and a voice said, "Yes. Was there?"

Evan and I spun around. Glinda Hansel stood in the doorway to the only bedroom. She wore a pair of gloves and a seriously ticked-off expression.

Evan dramatically grabbed his heart and said, "Scare a man to death, why don't you?"

Glinda ignored him and focused on me. If her bright blue eyes could kill, I'd be out cold on the floor. "You shouldn't be in here."

"We—ah, heard a noise," I lied.

Evan caught on. "As a landlord, I had a duty to check it out since I know the apartment is supposed to be empty." He lifted an eyebrow, challenging her.

She didn't take the bait. As a police officer investigating a crime, she had every right to be here.

I silently groused at Michael, however. He could have warned me we weren't alone. An extra *whump* or something. It wasn't too much to ask.

Glinda leaned against the bedroom doorjamb. "A word of warning, Darcy. I know you fancy yourself some kind of sleuth, but sticking your nose into a police investigation is going to get you in trouble. And not only that," she added with a touch of malice in her voice, "if it's discovered that any officer of the law has been sharing confidential information with you, then that person would be in trouble, too. Maybe even lose his job. Get my drift?"

Next to me, I heard Evan meow under his breath.

I could feel my anger simmering. "Is that a threat, Glinda?"

"Not at all, Darcy," she said, saccharine-sweet. "Like I said, it's a warning. What you do with it is entirely your choice."

Do No Harm, Do No Harm.

I kept repeating the phrase over and over as I took the Enchanted Trail home from the Gingerbread Shack. It was longer, yes, but it would give me time to get my temper under control before I made it home and took it out on innocent family members.

As I walked, I kept an eye out for Tilda and called her name intermittently. I even made kissy noises, though to my knowledge she had never once responded to the sound before (she was above such things). It just seemed the thing to do.

Oooh, that Glinda. All shreds of civility were gone. *Meow* was right. The claws had come out. War had been declared.

But as I walked along, one thing kept nagging at me.

She was right.

I picked up a stone and hurled it into the woods, throwing it as hard as I could. Whisking away the angry tears in my eyes, I tried to calm down.

I felt a gentle nudge on my upper arm.

Whump, whump.

"I'm okay," I said.

Another nudge.

I sent a watery smile in Michael's direction. "I will be okay. Soon." I picked up a small twig and hurled that into the woods. Throwing things was making me feel a smidge better.

Glinda was right. I wasn't a police officer. I was a civilian. Nick could lose his job for sharing information with me. And though he often held back a lot of what he knew about cases, he probably told me a little too much.

"You could have warned me that she was in the apartment," I said.

He flashed three times. *I'm sorry*.

"No," I said, shaking my head. "*I'm* sorry. For what happened to you." It was crucial to keep in mind what was truly important. "I promise you I'll figure it out."

He blinked four times.

"Thank you?" I guessed.

Yes.

"You're welcome." What few leaves were left on the trees rustled in the breeze. "I do have some questions for you. Okay?"

Yes.

"Did you create the Witching Hour spell?"

Yes.

"Did Harriette help in any way?"

No.

"Did you give her permission to call the spell her own?"

Yes.

"Why would you do that?"

He, of course, didn't answer. I was going to have to pay a visit to Harriette. I drew in a deep breath. "Other than you, how many people know the spell?"

He blinked two times.

Two others. "Harriette?"

No.

"Fisk?"

No.

"Dash?"

No.

"Any of the Wickeds?"

No.

"Lydia?"

No.

"Amy?"

No.

"I'm stumped." And worn out. It had been a long day already. "I'll keep thinking on it." I'd list every person in the village if I had to.

A small footbridge led from the trail to a small path behind As You Wish. I passed Ve's massive garage and debated about going inside to get a winter coat. I bypassed it for now, feeling the need for food that didn't have a high sugar content. Not that I didn't love fried dough or cake pops, but my body was craving something warm and comforting. Soup, maybe.

Opening the back gate, I saw Archie in his cage, regaling a small group of tourists with the narrative prologue from Disney's *Beauty and the Beast* movie. Dramatically, he quoted, "'As the years passed, he fell into despair, and lost all hope'"—he threw a look my way and winked— "'for who could ever learn to love a beast?'"

Amazed, the tourists clapped and clapped as if Archie's version were the greatest thing they'd ever heard. He basked in the glow, lapping up the accolades. I was surprised he didn't take a bow, but then that might have tipped off his audience that something magical had just happened, rather than a macaw with good memory repeating something it heard on TV.

Was it a coincidence he was quoting from *Beauty and the Beast*? I doubted it. My guess was that he also knew the identity of Starla's secret admirer. Maybe I could get the information out of him later. He was easily bribed with games of Trivial Pursuit, *The Lord of the Rings* version.

I waved to him and unlocked the mudroom door. As I stepped into the kitchen, I hoped with all my might to see Tilda peering dismissively at me from her favorite spot at the top of the staircase, but she wasn't there.

As I started up the steps, I didn't see Tilda, but I did hear voices. Ve's and another woman's. Not Amy's. No, this was the woman I'd heard several times over the past few months. The one Ve denied existed. The one I suspected was a familiar. I always believed it to be Tilda or Missy — but with Tilda out of the house, that only left Missy.

Was she really a familiar? Or . . . was there another critter in the house I wasn't aware of — a mouse, a fly, a bird?

I stealthily crept up the steps, hoping to catch a glimpse of whom Ve was speaking to — and as I did so, I blatantly eavesdropped on the conversation.

"I wish you wouldn't be so hard on yourself," Ve was saying. "You couldn't have known."

"I should have known. He came to me with concerns, and I didn't take him seriously enough."

Ve said, "Again, you couldn't have known."

"I have to figure out what happened."

"I believe Nick and Darcy are working on that. The investigation is in good hands."

The woman said, "I will continue my investigation as well. And Amy . . . We must protect her as well. If Michael's killer realizes . . ."

"She's safe here staying with Darcy and me," Ve said.

"You misunderstand, Ve. It is not about location. We must protect her from *herself*. She is young, naive, and entirely too trusting. She has no idea of the power she holds within and the lengths to which someone will go to get that power if it is uncovered that she holds it. Michael didn't fully understand, either, but he trusted me enough to indulge my wishes about keeping the true ownership spell a secret. I failed him by not realizing the extent of the danger he was in. I will not fail the girl as well. She is safe here as long as she stays invisible. It is her only true protection right now."

Whump-whump-whump-whump.

My curiosity was killing me. As I lifted my leg to take another step up, the office phone rang. I was momentarily torn. Answer it or spy on Ve? But then I realized that if Ve came out of her bedroom and found me lurking on the stairs . . . Not good.

I quickly backtracked to the kitchen as the phone rang a second time. I yelled, "I got it!" up the steps to let Ve know I was home more than anything. I dashed into the office and grabbed the phone. "As You Wish, this is Darcy. What is the wish you wish today?"

"Hi, Darcy," a man's voice said. "This is Rod Stiffington."

I sat down and automatically started straightening piles of papers. "Rod, hi. Is there something I can help you with?"

"Yes. It appears as though, well . . . It appears as though I've been stiffed, Darcy."

Oh, the images that flashed through my head. I wasn't proud.

"I'm not sure I understand," I said carefully.

"I went to cash the check Ve wrote me last night. There had been a stop payment made on it."

I was speechless. I fumbled for something to say. "Can you hold for a moment?"

"Certainly."

I pressed the HOLD button on the phone and hurried to the stairs. Ve was coming down them.

"Ve," I said.

"Yes, dear?"

"Did you put a stop payment order on Hot Rod's check?"

Her cheeks immediately flamed. "I may have."

"Oh, Ve. Why?"

"Did I mention that he was cute?"

I groaned. "He's on the phone, looking for an explanation."

"Let me handle this, Darcy, dear."

Ve brushed past me, practically sashaying.

I followed her. She picked up the phone and said, "Rodney, this is Ve Devaney. I understand there's a problem?" She listened for a moment. "I am not sure how such a mix-up was made. I'm so very sorry," she purred. "We must rectify this error at once. Would it be possible for you to stop by the office later today? I'll gladly cut you another check — or pay you in cash, if you prefer."

Oh, she was good. Very good.

"Wonderful! I'll see you then. Good-bye."

Her smile was wide and triumphant as she turned to face me.

I clapped.

She bowed.

"Any word about Tilda?" I asked.

"Not a thing. I'm sure she'll turn up soon." She hurriedly brushed past me.

"Do you know something about Tilda, Ve?"

"What? No. Of course not. I just have faith. You should, too, Darcy."

Hmm. Ve was up to something.

I heard footsteps on the stairs and turned. Amy, without her cloak and without a glow, was coming down the steps with Missy in her arms, and for a moment, I was stunned silent.

"I know," Amy said. "It shocked me, too."

"Wh-what happened?" The bright light was gone, but

her hair had turned a shocking blond color—the palest platinum. Her eyebrows, too. She looked like a moon goddess out of a mythology book.

Ve said, "An external manifestation of her grief."

As if the glow hadn't been enough.

But it was a sight better than the black-dyed hair she'd had before. "I kind of like it."

"Me, too," Amy said.

"I was about to make soup," I said. "You want some?"

She nodded and Ve gave her an encouraging smile, then disappeared back upstairs.

To continue her conversation with the mystery woman?

As I set about making lunch, I couldn't help but think back to the conversation I'd overheard. About how Amy had a power someone would kill for.

It had to be about the spell, the black flowers—and being an Illumicrafter.

I just couldn't piece it together. Not enough information.

Amy sat on the stool, and her bare foot swung back and forth. I caught a peek of color on her foot. A tattoo. "What is that?" I squinted.

She smiled. "A trout."

"A what?" I leaned down to get a better look.

"A trout."

Sure enough, it was a trout. I laughed. "Why?"

"Silly joke with Fisk. His name means 'fish.' I think it's cute."

Ah, young love.

"I thought the fish was a better choice than getting his named tattooed, just in case things don't work out. I mean, I'm only nineteen. It's not likely to work out."

I shrugged. "You never know." The soup came to a simmer. "Can I ask you something?"

"Sure."

"Why did you dye your hair black in the first place?"

"Ah," she said. "You think Fisk made me do it."

"I heard a rumor," I admitted. "About that, and failing grades . . ."

"It wasn't Fisk. It was me. I'm just trying to find myself, you know?"

"It took me thirty years," I said as I set out three bowls and a sleeve of crackers. "And how does Fisk fit into finding yourself?"

"He . . ."

Her face softened, and her eyes turned dewy. Definitely young love.

"He lets me be me. No judgments. No criticisms. He's sweet and kind and tries in all kinds of little ways to make my life better. He drives me to school so I don't have to spend hours on public transportation. He gets me my favorite drink from the Witch's Brew every morning. He's tolerant when I want to browse bookstores and museums for hours on end, even though those aren't things he's into."

Heck, after hearing that, I wanted to set him up with Harper. "He sounds like a keeper."

"Do the police really think he had something to do with Michael's death?" she asked.

I ladled the soup. "Right now they just want to ask some questions. Because he might have information about who did do it. Do you recall anything more about Fisk and Michael's fight?"

She shook her head. "Not really. I arrived at the tail end of it. They were both so angry with each other. Shouting about what was right and wrong and the moon and Harriette. It was all so confusing. I just wanted them to stop yelling."

"Harriette?" This was new information.

She nodded. "Fisk had just come from seeing his grandmother at the Elysian Fields, and Michael wasn't happy about it."

Wait a sec. Trista had said Fisk didn't have a relationship with Harriette. "Why did Fisk go see her?"

Something flickered in her eyes, and I had the feeling she revealed something she hadn't wanted to.

"I'm not sure. He's been spending time with her lately. I don't think Michael liked it."

Whump-whump-whump-whump.

No, apparently Michael didn't. Fisk's mother wasn't going to like it, either, if she found out.

As I dished out the soup, I suddenly found myself thinking about that conversation I overheard between Ve and the mystery woman. About how the woman had failed Michael. And how Amy needed protecting from a power she held within.

I studied Amy as she delicately sipped soup from her spoon.

What power?

As I watched, she flickered. I blinked at the blinding light, and the answer hit me.

Her power was her glow.

The Witching Hour spell could *only* be cast by an Illumicrafter.

I failed him by not realizing the extent of the danger he was in. I will not fail the girl as well.

The woman's voice haunted my thoughts and sent my mind churning.

Suddenly, without a doubt, I realized a big truth.

Ve had been speaking to the Elder.

Chapter Nineteen

During lunch I figured out what I needed to do.
I had to talk to the Elder.

If I was going to determine who killed Michael, then I needed to have all the information I could. I just hoped she'd give it to me.

I let Ve know I was going to fish some belongings out of the garage, and I left Missy cuddling with Amy. Michael, too, had stayed inside.

I was happy to see that Archie wasn't entertaining a group of tourists. One of his bright tail feathers had floated to the ground. I picked it up and twirled it as I moseyed over to his cage. " 'This feather may seem worthless. But it carries with it all my good intentions.' "

He crossed his wings over his chest, tapped his head, then his chin. "You've stumped me. I've been defeated. I shall never work in this business again."

"*The Joy Luck Club*," I said, enjoying the way he carried on.

He grabbed his heart and fell backward onto the floor of his cage as if mortally wounded. Closing his eyes, he coughed and sputtered a few times. "I shall never recover."

"Well, that's too bad, because I need to send a message to the Elder. I suppose I can have Pepe do it. . . ."

He leapt up and brushed himself off. "Don't you dare!" He hopped closer to me. "Why do you want to see the Elder?"

"I have some questions for her about Michael Healey's death, and I think she has some answers I need."

He nodded. "I shall go at once."

"Whoa, hold on there, my little feathered friend. There's something I want to ask you."

His beady black eyes narrowed. "Like what?"

"Like, do you know who Starla's secret admirer is?"

"Of course!" He primped and preened.

I leaned in. "Who is it?"

"I cannot say."

Groaning, I said, "Why?"

"It ruins the joy of the surprise, no?"

"But what about the Beast part of his latest clue? Is he a beast? What's wrong with him? Is he destined to break her heart?"

"'Hearts will never be practical until they can be made unbreakable.'"

"That doesn't help me." I leaned on the fence. "*The Wizard of Oz*, by the way."

"Curse you!" he cried. "I'm going to see the Elder now. My shame and I." He nudged open his cage door and flew out.

"Tell her I said hi!"

He made a sound like a big wet raspberry and flew out of sight.

I watched him head off over the woods behind the house.

Thinking about Michael and Amy made my stomach
hurt as I struggled to put the pieces together. For a
change, I couldn't wait to speak to the Elder.

Shivering, I turned my sights to the garage and my
quest to find a winter coat. I went in the side door and
was glad to see that the organization I'd done over the
summer still remained. Ve hadn't had a chance to blow
through and mess everything up again — yet.

The stuff I'd brought with me from Ohio was stacked
neatly on one side of the spacious garage. There were
dozens of boxes containing everything from clothes to
Troy's favorite Little League uniform shirt (that I'd denied I had). Pots, pans. Books and knickknacks.

I went immediately to the container I'd labeled WIN-
TER OUTERWEAR, opened it, and pulled out my favorite
dark red wool coat. It would need to be dry-cleaned, so
I made a mental note to drop it off Monday morning.

I was about to head back into the house when I spotted a plastic tub labeled PERSONAL.

I debated opening it. Most often trips down my memory lane were draining, and I was already feeling emo-
tionally raw, but I couldn't resist the allure of that
box — the allure of peeking at my past. It was a nice di-
version from all that was going on around me.

I dragged the box out of its corner and dusted the top.
Across the garage, I found a folding chair, cleaned off the
seat, and sat down. I opened the tub's lid and just sat and
stared at the contents for a good long minute. My heartbeat had kicked up a notch, and I had to wipe my hands
on my pants to rid my palms of moisture.

It was amazing that this one box held so many of my
little treasures. My first spelling bee ribbon, a lock of my
baby hair. My baby book that only had entries till I was
seven, because my father hadn't thought to keep it up after my mother died. My first fake driver's license, needed

because the state of Ohio refused to give me one because my picture never turned out. Ah, if only I'd known then the reason behind *why*. Most people had fake licenses with other people's information on it. Mine had all the proper information, but someone else's picture. She could be a doppelganger she looked so much like me. Enough to fool anyone at first glance, anyway. I moved aside some of my treasured childhood books, digging past worn copies of *Watership Down* and *Little Women*.

I kept digging. There was one thing in particular I was looking for. The one thing that could always comfort me, no matter my emotional state. And right now, I needed a little comforting. I shifted papers and set aside trinkets. Finally, at the bottom of the box was the treasure I sought.

A sketch pad. I lifted the cover and inhaled softly at the images on the paper. I bit the inside of my cheek as I flipped through pages, holding in tears as I looked at the images on the page.

Images of my mother.

I ran my finger along the colored pencil drawings as if I could actually touch my mother's soft skin.

It was her death that had prompted me to learn how to draw. We'd had no pictures of her in the house at all (of course). My pictures had been pretty terrible when I was only seven. But as I got older, my hand became steadier, and my talent became a way to keep my mother alive.

By the end of high school, I'd filled this sketchbook with images of her. A tear slid down my cheek, and I wiped it away.

I heard a creak and looked up to find Mimi poking her head in the door. "Aunt Ve said to let you know that my dad is on his way over. What're you doing? Are you crying? Why're you crying?"

I smiled. Mimi reminded me a lot of Harper.

"I'm just looking at my mom." I sniffled. "I miss her."

She left the door open as she came inside. "Your mom? How?"

I held up the sketch pad.

Mimi came running over. "Can I see?" she asked, scooting close to me.

I handed her the book and watched as she flipped pages. Her eyes grew bigger and bigger with each image. She glanced up at me, confusion etched on her face.

"Why is her face different in every picture? In some of these she has your eyes and Harper's smile. But in others she has Harper's eyes and your smile."

I blinked away tears, and my heart ached at the sad truth of the matter. "I couldn't quite remember her face. It was fuzzy, going in and out of focus, so I drew different versions of her. And even though none of them is an exact replica, they're close enough that looking at them brings me peace."

Mimi's brown eyes immediately filled with tears. "You drew these? Wow," she breathed, making me feel as if I were Monet. "I wish I could draw."

She continued to flip through the pages, and as she did so, her bottom lip started to tremble.

I put my arm around her. "Mimi, what's wrong?"

A tear spilled from her eye and snaked down to her chin. "Am I going to forget what my mom looked like, too? I know my heart will never forget her, but . . ."

"You were older than I was when my mom died. Your memories are stronger."

She sniffled and nodded, but I could tell she was still worried.

Melina Sawyer had died two years ago, and as a Wish-crafter she couldn't be photographed, either. Though she had renounced her Craft to marry a mortal, she had still retained all the Wishcraft quirks. Such as no pictures.

On a whim, I said, "Grab a chair." Rummaging around in my bin, I came out with an additional sketchbook that still had some blank pages and a pack of charcoal pencils.

Mimi set her chair next to mine, so close our knees touched. Her eyes were bright with tears. "How can you draw her when you never met her?"

Dust mites floated on the weak light coming through the window. "I don't need to meet her. I've met you. You're all I need."

"Really?"

"It may take some trial and error, but I'm willing to put the effort in if you're willing."

"I'm willing!"

"Okay, close your eyes. Picture your mom. A happy memory. Maybe one where she's laughing."

Mimi's chin quivered and it was all I could do not to put my arms around her and hold her tight. I knew what she was experiencing.

"Do you see her?" I asked.

Mimi nodded.

"What shape face does she have? Is it the same as yours? Or more like mine? Or Harper's?"

"Mine," she said, "but her chin is a little bit bigger."

I sketched an oval face with a generous chin. "Her eyes? Like yours?"

"The same shape but hers were smaller. Closer together."

"Light or dark eyes?"

"Dark," Mimi said. "Like mine and Dad's."

I shaded in irises and asked, "Her nose?"

"Like mine. Long and straight, though hers fit her face and mine's too big."

"It is not too big," I said, nudging her with my elbow. "It's perfect."

Time was lost as we sat together, piecing together an

image of a woman I would never know, but to whom I'd always feel grateful. If not for her, her life, her Craft, Nick and Mimi would not be in my life.

We'd covered just about everything but her hair, and already the image on the paper before me revealed a beautiful woman. "Was your mom's hair curly like yours? Or straight like mine?"

"It was like yours," Mimi said. "But shorter. Just below her shoulders. I get my curls from my dad's side of the family."

I smiled as I drew in hair. "Did she part her hair in the middle? On the side? Did she have bangs?" I realized as I asked that Melina had probably been bald when she died. She had passed so quickly that I doubted her hair had time to regrow after the failed chemotherapy treatments. But as Mimi didn't mention anything about baldness or a head scarf, I had a feeling the image of her mother she had conjured had come before Melina's diagnosis.

"On the side, the left side," Mimi said.

I held the sketch pad at arm's length. "I think it's ready. You can open your eyes."

Mimi's eyelashes fluttered, and she blinked to focus on the pad. Her chin quivered again, and tears sprang to her eyes. "Her eyelashes were a little longer," she said thickly.

I sketched in longer lashes.

"And her lips ... They curved more at the ends, like she was always smiling. And she had a dimple. I forgot her dimple."

"Which side?" I asked.

"Right," Mimi said, pointing to her own cheek.

"Here?" I asked, poising the pencil.

"A little lower. There! There!"

I sketched in a dimple, gave it some shading. The tears in Mimi's eyes spilled over, and she suddenly bounded out of her chair and threw her arms around me. I set the pad down, settled her on my lap, and held her close.

"Thank you," she said into my ear.

"You're welcome," I whispered.

"You . . . gave me back my mom."

I could feel her tears seeping into the back of my shirt.

"No," I said, rubbing her back. "I didn't. Your mom's always been with you, Mimi. You just shared her with me, that's all."

I heard a sound and looked up to find Nick standing in the doorway and Missy sitting at his feet. I hadn't heard them come in and wondered how long they'd been standing there.

Nick's gaze met mine, and he held it for a long, long time.

Finally, I said, "We have company, Mimi."

Her head came up, and she quickly wiped away her tears. "Dad! Look!" She grabbed the sketch pad and ran over to him.

As I stood up, I heard his sharp intake of breath.

"It's Mom!" Mimi said.

"I can see that," he said hoarsely. "Beautiful."

Mimi nodded, and Missy pranced around their feet.

My heart squeezed—not in jealousy, but because it felt so full.

"Come on, Missy, let's go show Aunt Ve!" Mimi ran out the door, then turned around and ran back inside, nearly knocking Nick over in the process. She once again threw her arms around me. I kissed the top of her head, and she let go and dashed back outside. I felt her love for me in the pounding of her heart against mine, in the way she held me tight, and the glow in her eyes.

And my heart felt just a little bit fuller. Any more and it might burst.

I folded the two chairs and put them aside.

Nick wandered over to me. There was moisture in his eyes. "You just gave her the best present of her life," he said softly.

I shook my head. "You have that the wrong way round."

Pulling me into his arms, he looked me in the eye.

Kaboom! The fullness was too much to bear, and the mush and gush and love spilled over, filling me with warmth from head to toe.

Nick lowered his head and kissed me. I wrapped my arms around his neck and settled in. Here, in his arms, felt like home. His kiss made my knees weak, my soul sigh. I didn't want to let him go. Ever.

"Ever" came approximately ten seconds later when I heard Archie's imitation rooster cry—his calling card announcing his arrival.

"That's for me," I said to Nick, dragging myself away from him.

"Lousy timing."

"Agreed."

I grabbed my winter coat and my sketch pads, and Nick carried my box of trinkets for me. Archie in all his brilliant glory sat on the back porch. He blinked slowly at us, then started singing "Love Is in the Air."

I groaned. "You've been talking to Ve."

He laughed, then turned serious as he bowed and said, "The Elder has agreed to your request. She will see you at seven thirty tonight. Go alone and do not be late."

He flew off, continuing to sing as he settled into his cage. Tourists walking by stopped and stared at him. He was such a show-off.

"The Elder?" Nick asked as we walked into the mudroom.

"I think she may know something about Michael's

death." I shared with him my recent conversations with Trista and Michael, and what I'd overheard upstairs.

With an angry set to his jaw, he said, "Let me know what the Elder says. We're hitting nothing but dead ends." He winced. "Bad choice of words."

Ve was in the kitchen, pouring a cup of tea. Mimi sat at the counter, staring at the picture of her mother. Nick walked over and put his arm around her, and Ve gave me a loving smile.

"Did you talk to Harriette?" I asked him.

"Stonewalled," he said. "She's a tough cookie and lawyered up after the first couple of questions. If I want more answers from her, I'm going to have to arrest her."

Ve gasped. "Surely she had nothing to do with Michael's death. She's eighty years old!"

Nick said, "At this point I'm not ruling anyone out. We did uncover that she's been making large withdrawals every month for the last year. It's unclear where the money was going."

Were Lydia's fears founded—about Harriette's fiancé using her for money? Had she been doling cash out to him regularly? Or had the missing money been a payout for Michael's spell? "Have you checked Michael's bank accounts yet?"

"Still working on that," he said. "Is Michael here? We can ask him."

"Not right now. He disappears a lot. Did you search Harriette's house?" I asked.

He nodded. "I found the dress she wore last night and sent the feathers to the lab, but the snips you saw missing from the greenhouse had been returned by the time we arrived."

So either they hadn't been the pair used to stab Michael, or someone had replaced the lost pair pretty damn quick.

"I need to talk to Amy," Nick said, breaking the ensuing silence. "Is she still here?"

Ve sipped her tea. "Upstairs."

Mimi's head popped up. "Amy's here?"

"Long story," Ve said. "Long, long story."

I rubbed Missy's head and said, "I'll get her."

At the top of the steps, I poked my head into Ve's room. Nothing was amiss, and no one was there. The mystery woman—the Elder—had moved along. Across the hall, I tapped twice on the guest room's door before pushing it open. "Amy?"

Whump, whump. Michael was here—somewhere— but I didn't see his sister. "Amy?" I repeated, walking over to the bed and giving it a pat down. There was no sign of Amy or the cloak.

I checked the bathroom, and all the other rooms on the second floor. Finally, I walked back into Amy's room. I noticed her cell phone sitting by the bedside table. Without feeling a shred of guilt for violating her privacy, I flipped it open and scrolled through old messages. One had come in twenty minutes ago—just before five thirty.

It's Fisk. Meet me at R's.

"R? Who is R?" I said aloud.

Whump, whump.

"Do I know R?" I asked Michael.

Yes.

Well. That was interesting, because I couldn't think of a single R related to this case.

"So, Amy's definitely gone?" I asked.

He flickered once.

Yes.

I stared at the phone. The number Fisk used had come up *unknown*. Maybe tracing that number would lead to R. And Fisk. And now Amy. And maybe, I hoped, a killer.

Chapter Twenty

Mimi had just left to take Missy for a walk when I came down the steps. I set Amy's cell phone on the counter next to Nick's elbow and said, "She's gone. The cloak, too."

"Have mercy," Ve said. "She can move freely around the village in that cloak."

I thought about what the Elder had said about Amy's invisibility and hoped she was using the cloak at all times.

Nick picked up her phone and did the same thing I had done—scrolled through old messages.

"Who's R?" he asked.

"I don't know," I said, "but Michael says I do." I glanced at Ve. "Do you know an R related to this case?"

Ve started ticking off fingers, "Fisk, Amy, Dash, Trista, Lydia, Willard, Harriette, the elusive Louis, Imogene, Ophelia, Bertie ..." Ve snapped her fingers. "Bertie's real name is Roberta!"

"I'll send an officer over to her place," Nick said. "I need to make a call. I'll be right back." He went out the mudroom door just as the office phone rang.

"I'll get it," I said.

I rushed down the hallway and grabbed the phone as it trilled a second time. "As You Wish, this is Darcy. What is the wish you wish today?"

"Darcy, it's Hot Rod again."

"Oh, hi, Hot Rod," I said loudly.

I heard commotion in the kitchen, and Ve came scurrying into the room, rubbing her hands in delight.

"Listen," he said, "I was tied up at a job and can't make it there tonight. Just hang on to the money for me, okay? I'll pick it up Monday."

"Monday?" I echoed. "Not tomorrow?"

Ve's face fell.

"I already have plans," he said.

"Do you want me to just put it in the mail?" I asked.

Ve shook her head so vehemently that her hair twist came loose. Coppery strands framed her face.

"No. Monday's fine. I'll see you then."

I gently put the phone back in its cradle and went and put my arm around Ve.

"He's not coming?" she asked.

"Nope. Got held up at a job."

Ve drew in a deep breath and started worrying her hands, twisting her fingers. "Oh dear."

"Maybe this is a sign that you should focus on your relationship with Terry," I said.

She stuck her tongue out at me and went back into the kitchen.

With a smile on my face, I followed her. Nick came back inside, and a moment later, Mimi burst through the doors, saying, "Look who I found!"

For a second my hopes rose that she'd found Tilda while out on her walk—until I saw Glinda Hansel stroll in behind her.

Talk about deflation.

"Hansel?" Nick said. "What are you doing here?"

She still looked exhausted, which still cheered me up, but even with the puffy eyes, dark circles, and village police uniform she was stunning. I sat on a stool next to Nick.

Her gaze flicked to the drawing on the countertop, and her face lit up. "Oh my! Melina!"

Mimi bounced over, Missy cradled in her arms. "You knew my mom?"

Glinda's personality took a one hundred and eighty degree turn. She picked up the picture and smiled, ear to ear. She'd gone from beautiful to dazzling in a split second.

That didn't cheer me up at all.

"We grew up together," Glinda said, her eyes glittery.

"You did?" Nick asked. "I didn't know that."

"Melina never mentioned me to you?" Glinda asked.

"No," Nick murmured.

It wasn't odd to me that this was news to Nick because he once told me that Melina spoke little about her life in the village after she renounced her Craft. It was as if she had wanted to leave it all behind.

It *was* odd to me that Glinda hadn't mentioned it to him before now.

"We were best friends," Glinda said. "We lived right next door to each other until Mel's mom moved them to Rhode Island after graduation. Oh, the stories I could tell!"

Ve shot me a look. I didn't even try to decipher it.

Missy wiggled in Mimi's arms, and she set the dog on the floor. Missy walked over to her dog bed, turned three times, and settled in. She didn't close her eyes to sleep, however. She just lay there listening.

"Really?" Mimi's eyes were the size of saucers.

"Definitely." Glinda soaked in the artwork. "Where'd

you get this picture? I didn't think any existed. It's so good to see her again."

"Darcy drew it," Mimi said.

"Oh," Glinda said flatly.

Nick said, "What are you doing here, Hansel?"

Glinda set the drawing back on the counter, and her personality zipped back to tough-girl cop. "The phone company finally got back to us with a trace on Amy Healey's cell phone. Guess where it is?" she said with a bit of a snarky tone.

Nick picked it up off the counter and wiggled it. "Right here."

Glinda's eyes narrowed. "What is it doing *here*?"

"Amy left it here earlier," he said. "But she's gone now."

"Is she?" Glinda asked, eyebrows raised.

"Yes." Nick set the phone back on the counter.

"Can I see you outside, Chief?" Glinda said tightly.

He nodded once and didn't look back at me as he followed her outside.

"What's going on?" Mimi asked as the back door clicked shut.

"A power struggle, I'd say." Ve tucked the loose strands of her hair back in place.

My stomach ached a bit. I wondered if Glinda was giving him the same warning she'd given me. I'd debated whether to tell him about it—because it had seemed like it had been born of jealousy. But now I wondered if what Ve had said might be closer to the truth. Maybe this wasn't about jealousy at all. Maybe it was about Glinda's trying to move up the ladder at the police department.

Nick came back inside alone.

"Where's Glinda?" Mimi asked, craning her neck toward the door.

"I sent her to check Bertie's house."

Since he'd already sent an officer to do that, I had the feeling he just wanted to get rid of her.

I was beyond grateful for that.

There was, however, a set to his jaw that I didn't like. She'd definitely given him the same warning she'd given me.

What did he think about it?

"We should go," he said to Mimi.

Uh-oh. I didn't like his reserved tone.

Ve clapped her hands. "I've ordered pizza for dinner. Surely you and Mimi can stay a little longer."

"Higgins . . . ," Nick said.

"Oh, I checked on him a little while ago," Mimi said, "before I came back here. Walked him and fed him. He's fine. So we can stay?"

Nick looked pained, but I knew he'd never refuse his daughter. Slowly, he nodded.

"Good, good." Ve smiled. "Mimi, grab some plates. We'll set up in the family room like a picnic. Nick, while we have you, maybe you can share what happened at the festival today with poor Imogene. I heard some sore loser accosted her?"

Nick shook his head. "There was no accosting, but someone did slip something into her drink."

"Like a roofie?" Mimi asked as she opened a cabinet.

We all stared at her.

"What?" she said. "We learned about them in school."

"Not a roofie," Nick said with a slight smile. "She fell ill and was taken to the hospital. She's doing much better and has already been released. Fortunately, she hadn't had too much of the tampered drink or the situation could have been far worse."

"Sheesh," Mimi said. "Those bakers take their pies seriously."

I smiled. She sounded a little like Evan.

"Yeah," Nick murmured.

"Do you know what the drink was spiked with?" Ve asked.

"Not yet," he said, fussing with Amy's phone.

By his demeanor, I could tell he was lying. He knew. And because of the way he was acting, I could guess what had been in the drink.

Antifreeze.

The link was disturbing. The public didn't know that antifreeze poisoning had killed Michael. The only ones who knew were the police, me, the killer—and me. And now Imogene had nearly suffered the same fate? It worried me that the killer had an eye for more victims. I had gone from thinking that the Wickeds had been involved in Michael's death to being concerned for their safety. Did they know something about the killer's identity? Were they all going to be targets now?

Nick slid a surreptitious look my way, and I frowned at him.

This silence of his was because of Glinda. What she'd warned.

And, damn it, I couldn't blame him for keeping information important to the case to himself.

I sighed.

He put his hand on my leg and gave it a squeeze.

It didn't make me feel better.

"I'll be right back," I said, and went upstairs to get my laptop from my room. I figured I'd get a little work done while we waited for the pizza to arrive. And I hoped it would take my mind off the tension with Nick.

I brought my laptop downstairs and into the family room. I clicked on the gas fireplace and turned on a few crystal table lamps. It wasn't a large room, but it was my favorite in the house. It was comfy. Cozy. Home. Book-shelves lined one wall and were stuffed with everything from Harlequin romances to Chaucer. The couch was big, deep, and the most comfortable piece of furniture in the house. Club chairs upholstered in bold-colored florals faced the sofa, but I bypassed those and sat on the deep pile area rug in front of the coffee table. Mimi crowded in next to me.

"What are we looking for?" she asked.

"I'm not sure," I said to her. "I'm trying to find Fisk, and other than Michael and Amy, there aren't many people who know him well. I talked to his mom today, and she has no idea where he is."

"Would she tell you?" Mimi asked.

I smiled. She was a smart girl. "She's the one who hired me to find him."

"She did?" Nick said. He sat on the couch, holding a mug of coffee. I was pretty sure that Ve had laced it with bourbon—I could smell the sweetness of the liquor in the air.

"Trista thinks he might be in danger."

His face darkened. "And what would you do once you found him, since you know how hard we've been searching for him?"

Yep. Glinda had definitely gotten to him.

Great.

"Well," I said, "I'd let his mother know where he is. That's what I was hired to do."

Mimi said, "Maybe you should hire Darcy, Dad."

Missy barked as if in agreement.

Nick said nothing, but he fairly gulped his coffee.

I typed Fisk's name into the computer. There wasn't a single hit. Not even a Facebook account. Dead end. "Not even a little. It's hard to find someone based on only a first name."

Carrying a tray, Ve came in from the kitchen. "Have you had any luck finding Louis, Darcy?"

"Are there any Crafters named Louis?" I typed "Louis" and "Enchanted Village" into the search engine.

Ve tucked her legs beneath her. "Not that I can recall off the top of my head."

The search engine spit out some results, but nothing that seemed relevant.

"If Louis exists," I said, "he has to be a Crafter, right? With Harriette's snobbery, she'd never marry a mortal, would she?"

Ve chuckled. "The heart wants what the heart wants, Darcy."

I refused to look at Nick. "I suppose."

Mimi said, "Try typing it in the other way."

I glanced at her. "What do you mean?"

"We just finished reading 'Jabberwocky' in school. . . ."

"Lewis Carroll!" I exclaimed. "You're brilliant, Mimi."

"What am I missing?" Vc asked.

"Maybe I've been spelling Louis wrong," I said. I typed in "Lewis," "Enchanted Village," plus the village's zip code into the search engine.

I squealed when a White Pages listing came up.

"Lewis R. Renault," Mimi read.

Ve leaned forward. "Renault, Renault. I know that name. How do I know that name?" She looked at Nick.

He shrugged.

"It'll come to me. What's the address?"

"Divinity Ridge?"

Ve scooted to the edge of the couch. "Of course! Lew Renault. Wow. No one's seen him in decades."

"Who is he?" I asked.

"Oh, Darcy, he's a rare witch. An Emoticrafter."

I'd never heard of it.

"What kind of Craft is that?" Mimi asked.

"He has the ability to absorb the emotions of those around him," Ve said as she refilled Nick's mug from an urn on the table. "As you may imagine, it's an extremely difficult Craft, always feeling what others are feeling."

"I think that's so cool," Mimi said.

"Ah, but, child, imagine if Lew were in this room. He'd feel your joy, my worry, your father's anxiety, and Darcy's unhappiness."

"Darcy's unhappy?" Mimi asked, whipping her head to examine me.

I shot a "gee, thanks" look at Ve and turned the tables. "What are you worried about, Ve?"

"Yeah," Mimi piped in.

Nick kept sipping.

Ve laughed, but the humor didn't reach her eyes. "Posh, I was just giving a hypothetical situation! Now, can you imagine what that kind of scenario would do to an Emoticrafter?"

Mimi winced. "Maybe it's not so cool."

"Can he block the emotions?" I asked. I couldn't imagine living that way.

"If he's truly skilled, he can for short periods of time," Ve said.

Nick said, "Is that why he hasn't been seen in decades?"

Ve nodded. "Very wise of you, my friend. Lew cut himself off from society years ago because he couldn't deal with it. He bought a big house on acres of land and became the village hermit, if you will. The Crone's Cupboard delivers groceries once a week but leaves the items on his front porch. He hires a landscape team to keep his massive yard up to date. He'd be"—she counted off fingers—"around seventy, mid-seventies by now."

Whump-whump-whump.

Nick's head snapped up as if he'd forgotten Michael, who had decided to join us. Nick added a bigger splash of bourbon to his coffee as I wondered why Michael had reacted so strongly. How would he know a hermit? Then I realized what Ve had said. Lew had hired a landscape company. . . . Had it been Dash's? Had Michael worked for him at some point?

I wanted to ask Michael and ask about any payments from Harriette, but I didn't want to freak out Mimi—she didn't know about Michael's ghost.

Nick said, "Doesn't Divinity Ridge border the Elysian Fields?"

"And didn't Harriette say at her birthday party that her fiancé was a little younger than she was?" I asked.

Mimi clapped. "Harriette's fiancé is real! I'm going to win the betting pool!"

I smiled. She was going to have to share that money with Trista Harkette. "Is it possible?" I asked Ve.

Ve drew in a breath. "I don't know. I cannot imagine it. Harriette has a strong, abrasive personality—bane to an Emoticrafter."

"Ugh," Mimi moaned. "There goes the betting pool."

I wasn't as ready as Mimi to give up the thought that this Lew might be the Louis I'd been looking for. Tomorrow I'd take a ride to Divinity Ridge—which was a good five miles across town—and see what I could see.

The doorbell rang.

"That'll be the pizza," Ve said. She pushed herself off the couch and bustled to the front door.

"Mimi, go help Aunt Ve, will you?" Nick said.

Mimi nodded and bounced up.

Nick set his mug on the table and leaned forward. "I heard that you had a conversation with Glinda earlier."

I tucked my legs beneath me. "It didn't feel so much like a conversation as her marking her territory."

He quirked an eyebrow and gave me a small smile. "That may be the case, but she has some valid points."

"I know she does."

He held my gaze. "I can't keep sharing information with you. Not if I want to keep my job."

I nodded. I understood—I did. But I wasn't happy about it. Not when I was so invested in this case. I mean, really. There was a ghost imprinted on me who wouldn't—couldn't—move on until his murder was solved. "Do you think Glinda would actually report you if she had hard evidence that you gave me information?"

"In a heartbeat."

"Because you're dating me?" I knew she had no qualms about bending police procedures when it benefited her. Such as when her mother went around stalking people and Glinda didn't report it right away.

"Maybe a little comes from that, but I also think she's looking to prove herself as a competent officer, especially after what happened with her mother. And like I said, the fact is she's right. I've bent, if not broken, rules where you're concerned."

As Mimi's and Ve's voices carried as they joked with the pizza delivery boy, I tried to ignore the feeling that a huge wedge had just been shoved between Nick and me.

A wedge named Glinda.

"I hate that you're unhappy," he said, "but I can't keep sharing information with you."

I met his gaze. "I hate that you're filled with anxiety, but even though you can't share information, I have to keep investigating on my own. Michael's ghost is imprinted on me. I can't ignore that."

He dragged a hand down his face. "I can't argue that you're good at investigating, but it's not your job. It's mine."

He was right, of course, so I had nothing to counter with. I simply said, "I know."

"But it's not going to stop you, is it?"

I shook my head.

"Then we're at a bit of an impasse."

"A bit," I replied, feeling that wedge nudging us farther apart.

He wrung his hands. "We have to figure out some sort of compromise."

We did. "Like what?"

"I have no idea. You?"

"No." I swallowed over the lump in my throat. "Honestly, I don't think there's anything we can do about it right now."

"No, there probably isn't."

As we sat there in tense silence, I told myself to have faith that we would eventually figure it out.

Before Nick got fired.

Before Glinda arrested me for interfering with police business.

And before that wedge separated us permanently.

Chapter Twenty-one

Thanks to Ve and her endless village gossip and tall tales, dinner hadn't been a complete disaster. But as soon as the dishes had been set in the dishwasher, Nick and Mimi had gone home. Fortunately, before he left, he received a call from Glinda and shared with us the news that Bertie hadn't been the one housing Fisk and Amy.

I was surprised (yet grateful) he had told us at all after the conversation we had, but I supposed the information wasn't as confidential as discussing things like murder weapons.

Now, thirty minutes later, I was on the hunt for more information. I had to hurry, though—I had only forty-five minutes until my meeting with the Elder. I definitely did not want to be late for that. The Elder scared me.

The festival pulsed with life and energy as I skirted around the green. I noticed the crime-scene tape had been removed from the parking lot, and every spot was full. A minivan was parked in the spot where the Ginger-bread Shack van had been, and I shuddered.

Whump, whump.

"Which way now?" I asked as I came to an intersection.

Michael nudged me from behind to keep going straight. He was taking me to Dash's top secret greenhouse.

I wanted to ask Dash some questions, and I hoped he'd talk to me. In the absence of Fisk, Dash was my next big chance to sort out what had happened to Michael—and perhaps what had happened to Imogene.

As I walked, I quizzed Michael as best I could. "Did Harriette pay you for the Witching Hour spell?"

Yes.

That explained the withdrawals from Harriette's account. "Did the money stop coming in after you quit?"

Yes.

"So there haven't been any new black roses created since you left the Elysian Fields?"

No.

I recalled what Lydia had said earlier, about how the roses hadn't been doing well before they abruptly died. Probably because they needed Michael's light to thrive. "Harriette must have been desperate for you to come back to work."

Yes.

It wouldn't make sense, then, that she would be behind his death. She needed him—him or another Illumicrafter who knew the spell. . . . I fervently hoped that Amy was staying hidden.

"Did you give any of the black roses from Harriette's greenhouse to Dash?" I asked.

No.

"Do you think Dash or Fisk had anything to do with the theft of black roses from the Elysian Fields?"

No.

"You know," I said, "this would be easier if you could talk."

Yes.

"Earlier you were unhappy when Amy mentioned

Fisk had been spending time with Harriette. Has he been spending a lot of time there recently?"

Yes.

"Was he helping you with the black roses there?" Michael had said Fisk was involved in the roses somehow. Maybe the connection was through the Elysian Fields.

Yes.

"Does Lydia know Fisk has been hanging around?" It struck me that she wouldn't be too happy about it.

No.

"Does she have any idea how involved you were with the roses?"

No.

He guided me along the sidewalks of a neighborhood behind the square and tugged on my arm in front of a quaint Victorian-style house with charm to spare. I recognized it as Trista and Dash's house.

"Dash's greenhouse is here?"

Yes.

A covered portico connected the house to a garage, and I noticed two black cars parked in the open bays— someone was home. Michael nudged me under the portico and into the backyard. A stone patio arced out from the back of the house, surrounding a pool covered for the impending winter. The garden was meticulously groomed, and beautiful flowers still bloomed. The yard was contained by a fence covered in leafy vines. There was no greenhouse to be seen.

"Um," I said, looking around. Lights were on in the house, and I wondered if I should just knock on the door and plead my case to Trista.

Michael nudged me to the right. I stood firm. There was nothing over there but a viny fence. And for some reason, in the darkness, those vines resembled snakes.

Uh-uh. No way. No how.

He shoved me.

"Hey! I thought we talked about the shoving thing."

He flashed three times his apology, then nudged me toward the fence.

Reluctantly, I walked toward it. The wind rustled the leaves on the vines, making them look like *moving* snakes. Goose bumps popped, and I was ready to get the heck out of there.

He nudged again.

"There's nothing there!"

For a frustrating second, I stood there, staring at the wall. Suddenly, I felt a touch on my hand, hot—almost too hot to handle. It lifted my hand, curved my fingers around a vine that stuck out a touch more than the others, and then pulled.

The heat left my hand as a hidden door swung open. It had been so seamlessly hidden that I could have stood there for hours searching for it and never even come close to finding a hinge.

I felt my eyes grow wide as I took a tentative step into the breathtaking secret garden. Japanese lanterns hung from a wooden pergola covered in night-blooming jasmine, which shouldn't have been blooming after the first frost. But as this was a village where magic lived, I wasn't the least bit surprised. I breathed in the lovely fragrance and said loudly, "Dash?"

Gorgeous colorful flowers filled the lush area, peeking out from behind tumbled boulders and around a waterfall that drained into a small man-made stream. It was simply stunning back here.

At the back of the garden stood a small greenhouse surrounded by low-growing shrubs. The house itself was much smaller than Harriette's, maybe ten by twelve with only a two-tiered shelving unit on the left side, and a nar-

row workbench on the right. I followed a slate walkway
to the door, and I could easily see Dash inside, sitting on
a stool, his head in his hands, his dark hair hanging over
his eyes.

I paused for a moment and studied him. His regality
was gone, replaced with what looked like defeat.

Archie would be crushed to see him this way, engulfed
in grief.

All around Dash were dozens of dead black flowers.
They sat limply in pots on shelves, on the workbench,
on the floor. All had shriveled up, leaves crinkled and
curled.

Seeing the plants and knowing why they were dead
broke my heart all over again.

I tapped on the glass door. "Dash?"

His head snapped up. He didn't bother wiping the
tears from his eyes. "Darcy?"

Confusion filled his watery gaze, and I couldn't blame
him. It wasn't every day a witch you barely knew came
traipsing through your magical garden.

I didn't have time to beat around the bush. "I need to
ask you some questions." I didn't wait to be invited in,
but rather I forged my way inside, past the sad little
plants.

Whump-whump-whump.

I could feel Michael's sadness, too.

"How did you get in here?" Dash asked, looking past
me at the open gate.

"Michael showed me."

His eyebrows snapped downward. "When?"

"Just now."

He stood, towering over me, his dark brown eyes
troubled. "I don't know what kind of joke you're trying
to play."

"No joke, Dash," I said softly. "When Michael died, he

imprinted on me, apparently because I'd been the one to find his body. He's here now. Can you feel him?"

Whump-whump-whump.

Dash shook his head and still gazed at me suspiciously. "I don't feel anything."

"Michael? Do you want to do the resurrection thing?"

In front of one of the pots on the ground, a small light grew into a pulsing orb. The sphere moved to the base of a dead orchid, and I watched in awe as the plant slowly came back to life. Standing tall, the stem green, the beautiful flower a pure black.

"I need to figure out who killed Michael. It's the only way to get him to move on. And to do that, I need your help, Dash."

He didn't appear to be listening. He'd walked over to the orb and reached out his hands. The orb lowered into Dash's palms. "It's really him," he whispered.

It was an amazing experience to watch, and I walked around the greenhouse, letting the two of them have a moment. I heard Dash talking softly to Michael, but I couldn't understand the words. Maybe an apology. Maybe a good-bye.

Finally, Dash said, "I'll do whatever I can to help, Darcy."

When I turned back around, the orb was gone, but I could still feel Michael.

Whump, whump.

"Last night, you told me you'd warned Michael about something. What?"

Dash sat back on his stool. I watched in wonder as the orb flared up again before another plant. It slowly came back to life.

"To explain, I must go back a little."

I leaned against the workbench. "Please do."

"Trista told me you know that Michael created the Witching Hour spell. . . ."

I nodded. "But I'm still fuzzy on how it works, and how Harriette and Fisk became involved."

Dash dragged a hand over his face. "That's where it gets complicated."

Whump-whump.

"I heard all this through Fisk only yesterday, so if something isn't right, perhaps Michael can let us know."

Michael flashed once.

"That means yes," I translated.

Dash blinked slowly. "I can hardly believe this is happening."

It was incredible, but I didn't have time to get distracted. "What did Fisk tell you?"

"When Michael started working at the Elysian Fields, he was simply doing maintenance. Weeding, watering, that kind of thing. Slowly, over time, Harriette began to notice how the plants responded to Michael, and she struck up a friendship with him."

"Harriette?"

"I know. It surprised me as well. Over time, Fisk began visiting Michael at the farm and started getting to know—and growing close—to his grandmother, a fact Trista still doesn't know, and I'd appreciate it if you'd keep the secret for a while. I'm still coping with that bit of news."

I wasn't going to make any promises. "I'll do my best."

"Last winter, there was a huge snowstorm that knocked out power around the village. Michael was working, and Fisk was visiting him when the lights went out. They panicked as it grew colder and colder in the greenhouse, believing the roses would die and that Harriette would go on a rampage."

"They thought the roses would die, despite their being magical?"

Dash smiled. "In the moment, they simply forgot. Some of the blooms had wilted in the cold—nothing that couldn't be brought back easily, but they were young, tired, and didn't think things all the way through. It was Fisk who realized that Michael could keep them warm by using his glow. After a little while of using Michael's light, they noticed something strange happening."

Whump-whump.

Dash's eyes lit as he said, "The edges of some of the petals were turning black. It was right about then that Harriette burst in and found them—she'd seen the glow and had come to investigate."

I whistled low.

"Yes. Fisk related that it was quite the scene. Until Harriette realized that the black on the roses wasn't heat damage—it was hue. That incident sparked the creation of the black roses."

"But Michael hadn't used a spell that night, had he? Just his glow?"

"No," Dash said. "And try as they might, they couldn't replicate the black color until almost a month later. They finally achieved the same results—the edges of the roses turned black. It wasn't the product they were trying for, but that night they realized one crucial element."

A month later . . . "The moon!"

He nodded. "Not just any moon. Once that piece fell into place, Michael created a spell for the rest. The spell has to be cast by an Illumicrafter at midnight on the first night of a new moon. Otherwise, the spell is useless. The flowers use the light from the Illumicrafter to absorb darkness—turning the blooms black as night."

A stem blooms devoid of light, at the darkest time of night.

When was the darkest time of night? Midnight—the Witching Hour—on the night of a new moon.

I closed my eyes. It made sense now. "How did Harriette fit in?"

"They were her roses, of course, and she had the contacts, the reputation, to get the roses the recognition they deserved. She offered to pay Michael monthly for use of the spell, and in turn she'd claim the roses as hers. He came to me at that point and told me about what was going on and wanted my advice."

"Is this when you warned him?"

"Not yet," he said patiently, "though I begged him to make sure he was certain it was a deal he wanted to make. He believed it was. And at first it was mutually beneficial. But the more the roses received national acclaim, the more resentful Michael became of Harriette taking credit for his creation. He wanted her to publicly acknowledge his role, he wanted the fame, and he wanted a future for himself other than as Harriette's employee."

Whump-whump.

Michael didn't seem to be affected by this retelling. "Is that why he quit?" The timing coincided—he left the Elysian Fields right after the announcement that Harriette had won the big awards.

"Yes. He couldn't fathom how she could take all the credit even after he asked her to acknowledge his help with the roses. He even offered to return her money. She declined. I have to admit I took advantage when Michael quit the Elysian Fields and asked Michael to work with me creating black flowers. As you can see, we had great success until . . ."

Until he died.

Drawing in a deep breath, I said, "What—and when—was your warning to him?"

"It was yesterday. He mentioned that he was being pressured to do another Witching Hour rose spell at the Elysian Fields. I warned him against it."

"Who was pressuring him? Harriette?"

"I believed so, but no. Turns out it was Fisk. He confessed last night after Michael's body was found. That was when he told me he'd been growing close to Harriette, and how her roses were failing. He didn't want to see her fail, and he wanted Michael to help her out. The new moon is coming up in a few days...."

"Did Michael agree to do the spell?"

"No."

"Was that what they were fighting about last night behind the bakery?"

"Yes. Fisk had just come from Harriette's house and was upset because she told him to let it go. She was ready to move on, to retire, and said that she hoped Michael realized that the risk of raising black flowers was not worth the reward. Fisk took it as her giving up, and it ... He blamed Michael. They fought. Both were angry, yes, but Fisk didn't kill him."

"What risk was Harriette referring to?"

"Probably the constant scrutiny from the horticultural community and the threat of smugglers."

"Why didn't Michael ever take credit for the roses when he quit the farm and call Harriette out as a fraud?"

Puzzlement washed over Dash's face. "I don't know the answer to that."

I knew who did. "Michael, did you want to take credit publicly?"

There was a sudden flickering—nothing I could decipher.

Then something I overheard this afternoon clicked into place. I breathed in. "You went to the Elder for help."

Yes.

"But she couldn't help you."

No response.

"You don't know," I interpreted Michael's lack of response.

Interesting, because I overheard her saying she failed him.

"Dash, did you steal cultivations from Harriette's greenhouse?" I asked. Michael had said no, but he might not have been aware.

His dark eyes narrowed. "I haven't set foot on that property in decades."

"Did Fisk steal any?"

He said, "I don't believe so."

"Do you know where Fisk is?"

"No," he said, "but I received a text message from him about an hour ago that said he was safe and fine. It came from an unknown number."

It fit with the text Amy had received. I told him about the text on her phone, and how she was now missing. "Do you know anyone with an R name that Fisk would be friends with? Other than Bertie Braun—she's already been checked out."

Dash shook his head. "None at all."

I sighed. "Another dead end. Have you heard any rumors about the stolen rosebushes being sold on the black market?"

"None at all," he said. "But whoever stole the plants from Harriette's greenhouse is out of luck if the intent was to sell—or to replicate—the roses. Undoubtedly they all died when Michael died. And the spell died with him. He's the only one who can bring them back." Long fingers touched the petals of the black orchid Michael had resurrected.

"Who else knew that Michael *created* the spell?" I asked.

"Harriette, Trista, Fisk, and I did. I don't think anyone else knew. Harriette made sure everyone thought the spell was hers."

"Michael said only three people knew the actual spell. He and two others. Do you know who they are?"

"He kept it closely guarded—he wouldn't share it with anyone. Not me, not Fisk, not Harriette."

I told him about how I had run through a list of people in his personal circle who might know it, only to meet with Michael's nays.

Dash thought for a long minute, then snapped his fingers. "The Elder."

Yes.

Of course the Elder. Why hadn't I thought of it sooner? After all, he'd gone to her for help. It made sense that he'd share the spell with her.

Speaking of the Elder, I was running out of time. I needed to meet with her soon. "Who could the other person possibly be?"

"I'm out of ideas," Dash said.

Whump-whump-whump-whump.

I suddenly felt a burst of fear and anxiety from Michael. If this was what an Emoticrafter dealt with, no wonder Lew Renault chose to become a hermit.

Whump-whump-whump-whump.

"Michael, did you accept money in turn for sharing the spell with someone other than Harriette?" Maybe he'd sold the spell to another Crafter. One of the Wickeds, perhaps?

He flickered twice. *No.*

There went that theory.

Whump-whump-whump-whump-whump.

"I feel like Michael's trying to tell me something, a clue about who the third person is," I said. "He's fearful, desperate. . . ."

I felt my knees go weak, and I grabbed onto the table. I'd had the worst thought. Over a lump in my throat, I said, "Did you tell your killer the spell, Michael?" I had assumed he'd been killed because of the spell . . . not *for* the spell.

Yes.

And just like that his fear and anxiety were gone.

Mine remained.

Dash covered his mouth with his hand, and the pain in his eyes nearly crushed me.

I said, "Did the killer promise to let you go if you told?"

Yes.

"But you were killed anyway," I said softly.

Yes.

Sometimes locking myself away from the world like a hermit sounded wonderful. Like right now when I realized how evil some people could be.

"Does your killer know you were an Illumicrafter?"

There was no response; he didn't know. Which meant that right now his killer was either really confused as to why the spell wasn't working—or looking for Amy.

"I'm so sorry," I said. And suddenly I recognized the futility of my asking him earlier who else knew the spell. I'd run through the laundry list of people he knew and worked with, and he denied any of them knew. But one of them *could* know. If that person had killed him.

He gave me a little nudge.

I looked at my watch. "I need to get going, Dash. Thanks for telling me what you knew about the spell."

"I'll walk you out," he said, leading the way.

We walked through the gate, and a small cat came running toward Dash. He scooped it up, and I could hear its happy purrs. "This is Taboo," he said.

"She's beautiful," I said, feeling a pang for Tilda.

"I've seen the flyers around the village about Tilda. Has she come home yet?"

We stood under the portico. "Not yet."

He smiled, his beautiful teeth gleaming against his dark skin. "I wish you knew where she was."

My skin tingled, and I grinned. "I wish I might, I wish I may, grant this wish without delay." I blinked my left eye twice, and in an instant saw Tilda in the arms of a man, looking as happy as could be. My jaw dropped.

"Did the Elder grant the wish immediately?" Dash asked.

He had obviously heard about the amendment to the Wishcraft Laws that all wishes made by fellow Crafters had to be first approved by the Elder. I nodded.

He cocked his head. "Then why do you look so . . ."

"Dumbfounded?"

"That works."

"I'm just a little shocked at who she's with. It's—"

I was cut off by the sound of a revving engine. Dash quickly pushed me aside as one of the black cars in the garage came zooming out. It burned rubber as it peeled out of the driveway and sped off down the street.

Dash looked at me, shock etched on his face. "Was that car driving itself?"

I looked at him, feeling as shocked as he looked. "Was that a fish sticker in the back window?"

He nodded. "Fisk's car—he has a thing for fish. But I didn't see a driver. Did you see a driver?"

I suddenly realized that the car Wicked Widow Imogene had seen in front of Harriette's house hadn't belonged to Harriette's fiancé. It had belonged to her grandson.

"You didn't see her because she's invisible." I sighed. "Amy just stole Fisk's car."

Chapter Twenty-two

After I explained to Dash why Amy was invisible, I ran for home.

Dash had said he wouldn't call the police about the stolen car, but no sooner had the car fishtailed out of the driveway than a pink MINI Cooper zoomed after it. Glinda Hansel had been staking out the Khourys' house.

I could only hope that Amy knew she had an officer trailing her. I would have called to warn her, but Nick had taken her cell phone with him when he left Ve's earlier.

I had only fifteen minutes before my meeting with the Elder, and I needed to talk to Ve first to discuss the Tilda situation.

After I met with the Elder, I really wanted to go see Harriette Harkette.

I had a sneaking suspicion. A bad feeling.

Someone wanted to make it look like Harriette was involved in Michael's death.

The flower snips that were used to stab Michael—the ones that were identical to the ones from Harriette's greenhouse. The feathers stuck to the weapon.

It was all too obvious. Harriette wouldn't have been so careless.

I tried to wrap my head around this. Because now, Michael wasn't the only victim. Not really.

Now there was Harriette, too. Who hated her so much to pin a murder on her?

And what about Imogene? How did she fit in? Why was she poisoned? Does she know too much? If so, was she still in danger?

Then I remembered Harper's comment about *Murder on the Orient Express*. Four methods of murder ... four Wicked Widows.

Was someone out to get all of them?

I had a growing sense of unease. One I knew I should talk through with Nick—even if he couldn't share his thoughts about the case with me.

The festival was in full swing as As You Wish came into sight. The village green was packed; the shops looked to be doing great business. And I could still feel the magic in the air—but now there was something else, too.

Danger.

I shivered as I darted up the back steps of the house. Throwing open the mudroom door, I yelled, "Aunt Ve!" I kicked off my shoes and hurried into the kitchen. "Ve!"

She came running down the back staircase, her hand on her heart. "Darcy, dear! What is it? Are you okay?"

"Velma Devaney," I said, wagging a finger. "I want to know why Tilda is with Hot Rod Stiffington."

In the family room, Ve hugged a pillow and wore a contrite expression—her eyes wide and her lips pouty. "It wasn't supposed to be like this."

My leg jiggled nervously. The clock was ticking. "How was it supposed to be? You stuffed Tilda in Hot Rod's duffel bag!"

A guilty flush rose up her neck. "He was supposed to discover Tilda last night, bring her back, stay for a night-cap, and you know . . ." She batted her eyelashes.

She was incorrigible. Absolutely incorrigible.

"You had us searching for hours last night," I accused. All that time wasted.

"I couldn't very well tell you what I'd done, so I set the search in motion so I wouldn't look guilty. It was a diversionary tactic."

The way her mind worked baffled me sometimes.

"But when Rodney didn't return Tilda last night, I grew a wee bit concerned. Even more so when Rodney didn't come by this morning with her."

"Ah, so that's why you stopped payment on his check."

"I had to lure him back here. But now . . . he says he's not coming till Monday. And I'm frightfully concerned about that."

"Why now?"

"Why hasn't he returned her? She has her tags. . . ." She gulped. "What if she's still in that duffel bag? In the trunk of his car?"

Fine time to be thinking about that. I set her mind at ease, only because she was starting to hyperventilate. "She's not in his car. She's in his lap." I explained about Dash's wish, and how I'd seen Tilda.

"Lucky kitty," Ve said on a sigh.

I groaned. "We have to go to Rod's and get her back."

Ve shoved the pillow aside. "That's just it, Darcy. I've tried my hardest to locate a phone number or address for the man, but I have nothing."

"What about the caller ID? We can get a reverse trace done."

"The number he called from was blocked."

I nibbled my fingernail. I'd contacted Rodney through

a Web site—by filling out a form. There hadn't been a phone number or an address for the company. I checked my watch. I had five minutes before my appointment to see the Elder. "I have to go. But when I get back we'll figure this out."

Ve nodded.

I fetched my cloak from the front closet and slipped it on. As I headed for the back door, Ve said, "Did Tilda look like she enjoyed being in Rodney's lap?"

"Loving every minute of it."

Ve looked crushed.

I dialed Evan Sullivan as I hurried along the path to the Elder's meadow deep in the Enchanted Woods. The Gingerbread Shack was open late to profit from the festival, and he answered on the second ring.

"I need your help," I said after explaining how Ve had stuffed Tilda into Hot Rod's bag.

"How can I help?" he asked after he stopped laughing. I heard the dinging of a cash register in the background.

The woods were dark, eerie. Dark clouds blocked any moonlight from the crescent moon, but I'd brought along a flashlight to avoid any tripping hazards.

Michael was not with me. Apparently I wasn't the only one afraid of the Elder.

"You're the one who recommended Hot Rod's Web site to me. How did you know about it? Is he local?"

"I—ah," he stammered.

"What?" I pressed. "It's important. It's *Tilda*."

He cursed under his breath. "I promised I wouldn't say."

"Promised who, and why?"

"Michael."

I heard him swallow hard.

"Michael?" I repeated. "What does he have to do with

Hot ... Oh my gosh! Was Michael a stripper? Is that the night job he had that he wouldn't tell Amy about?"

"You didn't hear it from me," Evan said as if Michael were going to track him down and take him to task.

Actually, I guessed he still could. He certainly pushed me around enough.

"Michael worked for Hot Rod off and on over the past six months. Mostly when he needed some extra cash. Fisk, too, I believe."

I nearly dropped the phone. "Fisk certainly doesn't need the money."

"No," Evan said. "I think he just enjoyed it."

I tried to banish the images from my mind. When I'd hired Hot Rod, I hadn't scrolled through the other entertainers on the site. Rodney's was the first profile I saw, and I made up my mind then and there to hire him for Harriette's party.

"It's actually very tame," Evan said. "They don't go full monty. Just do a little dancing, collect some money. Have some fun. It's a good time."

"You sound like you know quite a bit about it, Evan Sullivan."

He coughed. "I don't know what you're trying to say."

Oh my. "Do not tell me you were a stripper!"

"I wasn't," he said, "but I've been to a few parties. . . ."

"La-la-la-la," I sang. "Not listening."

Evan laughed.

"I need an address," I said.

"I wish I knew one," he said.

Since he was half Wishcrafter, I couldn't grant his wish.

"Michael had to have pay stubs," I said.

"Paid under the table, I believe."

Curses!

"Fisk might know," Evan added, "if you can find him."

"That might be out of my hands at this point." I explained about Glinda following Fisk's car. If Amy was going to see her boyfriend at the mysterious R's house, and didn't realize she had a tail, then she had probably led the police straight to Fisk's doorstep—wherever that might be.

I stopped short in the path. *R. Rodney*. Could it be? I shared with Evan my supposition.

"You might be right, Darcy. I've never personally met this Hot Rod, but Michael spoke highly of him."

That meant if I found Rodney (and hence Tilda), then I'd also find Fisk and Amy. Win-win-win-win.

"But I still don't have any idea how to find them," Evan added, bursting my bubble.

"Keep thinking on it. Until then, I have another idea."

"What's that?" he asked.

"I'm bringing in the big guns." I needed someone to hack into a Web site, and I knew just the person to call.

"I already told you I'm out of ideas," Evan joked.

Laughing, I hung up and dialed my sister.

She answered on the first ring. "Spellbound Books, this is Harper. How may I help you?"

"It's me," I said, hearing my moral compass break just a little bit more.

"I was just about to call you. You won't believe what I spy with my little eye."

I smiled. I spy had been a favorite game of hers when she was little. "What?"

"A Wickeds convention under the beech tree on the green."

"You lost me, Harper."

"They're all out there, Darcy. Ophelia, Bertie, Imogene. They're gathered with their heads bent together. The only one missing is Harriette, who I spy near the creepy haunted house at the festival. Lydia and Willard are out there, too. You should see the looks they're throwing Harriette's way. Oooh-whee. If looks could kill. I spy daggers in their eyes."

It was an expression, yes, but one I suddenly couldn't discount. Lydia had a lot to gain if something happened to her mother. . . .

I moved Lydia to the top of my suspect list. I thought about Ve and her "diversionary tactic" of having us search for Tilda even though she knew where the cat was.

What if Lydia had hired me to look for Harriette's fiancé as a diversionary tactic as well? One to divert suspicion away from Michael's murder?

"I've got the shivvies just looking at them," Harper said. "I sense some seriously bad juju in the air."

I trusted no one's instincts more than Harper's. If she sensed something bad was going to happen, then something bad was going to happen.

"So how fast can you get here?" Harper asked.

I'd called to see if she could meet me at Ve's for a little hacking, but I supposed that could wait just a bit longer. It wasn't likely I'd get the chance to have all the Wickeds and Lydia in the same place again.

"I'll be there as soon as I'm done with the Elder."

"I'll keep an eye on them."

"Don't get too close."

"Are you kidding? I'm not going near that haunted house." She hung up.

I wandered deeper into the woods. The path was well marked, but I could probably find my way without the markers. My various trips to see the Elder were imprinted on my mind forever. This visit, however, was a little different. I had requested to see her. . . .

I turned right at a fork in the path, and tried to keep my jitters at bay. I was feeling anxious about this case, and about the danger I sensed.

Ahead, light burst from a clearing filled with wildflowers of every height and color. Beautiful, magical blooms. In the center of the clearing was a solitary tree. Wide trunked, its leafy canopy wept, making it look more like a mushroom. There was a notch in the tree, where messages to the Elder were placed, and there had to be some way for the Elder to go inside the tree, but I couldn't see how from where I stood, and I didn't dare investigate.

"Hello, Darcy," the Elder said. Her voice was the one I had heard in the house this afternoon.

The position of Elder, as Ve had told me, was always held by a woman, and there was a good chance I already knew her. That she was a villager. Her identity, however, was top secret. Only a few knew who she was—which was to protect her. As the governess of all Crafts, she had immeasurable power—the rare witch with the abilities of each Craft family. She was Curecrafter, Bakecrafter, Wishcrafter . . . all rolled into one. There were many who sought her wisdom, and her magic.

"Sit, sit," she said.

A tree stump appeared behind me. I sat.

"You wanted to see me?" she said.

I wrung my hands. "I'm here about Michael Healey."

"The spirit imprinted upon you."

"You know about that?"

"Of course I know about that."

Of course.

"Elder?"

"Yes?"

"Were you at my house today, talking with Ve?" I wanted to make sure.

There was a brief silence; then she said, "Yes."

Aha! "I overheard you speaking about Michael. About how you failed him. I'm trying to figure out who killed him, and if you know anything, I'd be very grateful if you shared the information with me."

There was another stretch of silence before she spoke. "Michael came to me a couple of months ago regarding his work at the Elysian Fields. He was upset that Harriette Harkette had claimed his creation as her own, therefore breaking a Floracraft Law. His claims were valid, so Harriette was summoned, and she was told to renounce her claim to the Witching Hour roses and to give credit where credit was due. Harriette refused."

"Uh-oh," I said under my breath.

"I gave her one week to make amends. She did not. Her powers were permanently revoked."

I drew in a sharp breath. Harriette had no Craft powers? That explained why she'd turned over running the greenhouse to Lydia two months ago—and why she was really retiring. Never mind that she couldn't produce black roses—she couldn't create *any* roses. "Does anyone know that Harriette doesn't have her ability anymore?"

"Only Harriette, who shared the news with her fiancé. And now you know. I believed I handled the situation as best I could, but Michael still didn't have his claim to fame, and he also became increasingly concerned regarding thefts of the black roses. He suspected someone inside the compound was stealing them in hopes of harvesting a crop of his or her own black flowers. However, we both knew the thefts were aggravating but pointless. Because of the spell Michael used, the DNA of the plant is unrecognizable. The longevity of the breed has always been an issue. Once the lifespan of the plant is complete, that is it. It is gone. Seeds will not germinate without the help of an Illumicrafter and his spell. The plant is impossible to breed without—"

"The spell."

"Correct. Or a renewal spell at the very least."

"Longevity is moot now that Michael has been killed.

The plants have all died. Except for the few he has resurrected in his ghostly state."

"He is fortunate to have imprinted on you. Your perceptions are especially acute—you recognized he was with you almost immediately. Sometimes it takes years for an imprinter to be noticed."

I supposed "fortunate" was in the eye of the beholder, though, honestly, I hadn't minded a bit that Michael was around. After I overcame my initial heebies about it. "Why isn't he with me all the time? Like right now?"

"Michael will always find his way back to you. I suspect he is also investigating his death in his own way." There was a long silence before she said, "When he and I last spoke, I suggested that he walk away from the situation at the Elysian Fields and cultivate his own business. And he did, working side by side with Dash Khoury. That was two months ago, and I thought the whole matter resolved until Michael was found murdered." Her voice dropped. "I didn't comprehend the danger he was in, and I should have."

I thought she was being a bit hard on herself. "How could you have known?"

"The spell he created is unique, not only for its impact in the mortal world but also the impact in the Craft world. With his spell, his Craft has surpassed both Terracrafters and Floracrafters in terms of floral ingenuity. It has the potential to shake those Crafts to their core. I neglected to consider some of his Flora and Terra rivals might not be too pleased about that. Neglected to foresee that if anyone learned the truth, the danger to him would be immense."

"Put that way, do you think Harriette has been in danger all this time?"

"Undoubtedly."

That notion settled over me like a bucket of cold water.

"I did have the foresight to ask him not to tell anyone of his spell or talk of his Craft to anyone who didn't already know of it until he was ready to launch his new company. My hope in that was to buy time to see if anyone would come forward to reveal that they uncovered the secret about the Witching Hour roses. It never happened. Harriette has kept claiming the roses as hers, and Michael kept his promise to me. I never dreamed someone would take a quest for that spell so far."

"Does his killer realize yet that the spell is useless without an Illumicrafter?" I asked.

"That question has been gnawing at me since Michael's body was found. There is no way to know. Either way, Amy is in danger. You see, Darcy, the killer may believe she knows how the spell works simply because Michael was her brother. Where she is now, she is safe."

"With Fisk and Hot Rod Stiffington, you mean?"

"You've done well with your investigating, Darcy. You must continue. Stay strong. Do not be fooled by what others want you to believe."

"Oh, that's easy," I scoffed.

"I have the faith in you that you do not have in yourself. Yet."

Heat crept up my neck. Her point had been taken.

"You must succeed," she said softly, "where I did not. I am counting on you, Darcy Merriweather. You may go now."

The tree went dark. Reluctantly, I stood up. The tree stump dissolved into colorful sparkles that bloomed into beautiful flowers as soon as they hit the ground.

As I walked back toward home, I realized that I was still no closer to figuring out who killed Michael than when I'd arrived.

Chapter Twenty-three

Kids grinned like one of Starla's jack-o'-lanterns as they glided up and down on the Ghoulousel. Teenagers wandered from ride to ride, game to game. The village green was packed, elbow to elbow. Peppy sounds blasted, assaulting from every direction. Piped music from the carousel, the dinging from a strength game, eerie spooky moans from Boo Manor.

My tough little sister edged a bit closer to me, locking her elbow with mine. I held back a smile and appreciated her body warmth. It was freezing. My breath puffed out in a white cloud as I let out a sigh. I'd given my wool coat a spray of Febreze so I could wear it. Dry cleaning would have to wait. I'd also borrowed one of Ve's knit cloche hats and fuzzy mittens. Winter was knocking on the door, but so far the snow was holding off.

"Do you see any of them?" Harper asked.

Since she was a head shorter than me, she had no hope of seeing above the crowd. As it was, I had to stand on tiptoe. "Nope."

We'd been wandering around the green for half an

hour looking for any of the Wickeds, Lydia, or Dash. I'd walked past the caramel apple booth three times, each time feeling the pull a little bit more. I was still resisting, holding out hope that before the festival packed up for good next Sunday night, Nick would have fulfilled his promise of buying me one.

Cinnamon floated on the wind, and I followed the scent toward the hot apple cider booth. I tugged Harper in that direction, dodging someone dressed up as a goblin. There were a lot of costumes at the festival tonight. Babies dressed as peapods. Toddlers as superheroes. Adults as everything from ghosts to witches (how appropriate) to queens and pirates.

I wondered what Michael was up to. He still hadn't returned. Which was probably a good thing, considering how jittery Harper was already.

"What are you doing?" she asked.

"I'm thirsty. And freezing."

"How can you be so calm? Don't you feel it?"

All I felt was bone-chilling cold and regret at how Nick and I had left things earlier.

I would have loved to compromise with him, but as I told him, I didn't know how. We were both looking into Michael's murder—it was frustrating that he couldn't share what he'd learned with me whereas I was obligated to tell him everything.

Shoving the thoughts aside, I tried to focus on Michael. On figuring out who had killed him. Because that, as I had to keep reminding myself, was the most important thing.

"Feel what?" I asked, playing dumb.

"The bad juju!" She shivered and steered me far away from Boo Manor.

I felt it all right. The danger I sensed earlier had intensified to a point where I had goose bumps that weren't from the cold. "It's strong, but that could be because Glinda Hansel keeps giving me the evil eye."

She stood near the Scarish Wheel, watching. Waiting. I wondered when she slept. I also assumed that because she was here, she hadn't found Amy and Fisk. For now. Amy must have managed to lose Glinda's tail when she stole Fisk's car.

"What's with her, anyway?" Harper asked. "I thought you two were friendly."

"She caught Nick and me cuddling last night."

"Is cuddling a euphemism, because if it is, I'm a big girl now and can hear the proper terminology for s-e-x."

I laughed. "Old enough to hear it, but not say it?"

Her jaw dropped. "For the love! Don't even tell me she caught you and Nick—"

"No! We were cuddling. C-u-d-d-l-i-n-g."

She gave me a hip check. "Smart-ass."

"Oh, you'll say *that*."

She nudged me again. "Thanks."

"For what?"

"Distracting me from the juju. Maybe a hot cider wouldn't be so bad. As long as it's not poisoned."

"I can't make any promises."

She stopped walking and stared at me with her big brown elfish eyes. Suddenly, she looked eight years old.

"I'm kidding," I said.

"Not funny. Will you take a sip of mine first to test it out?" She batted her eyelashes.

Smiling, I said, "No." Though even as I said it, I knew I would. "Hey, when we're done here, can you come home with me? I need your help with something."

"Sounds urgent," she said in an excited voice.

"I need you to hack into a stripper's Web site."

"I'm in," she said without a second thought.

Sometimes I loved my sister more than I could say.

We advanced in the line, and I suddenly heard someone calling my name. I glanced around and was surprised to see Vince Paxton headed toward me.

"Vince?" He looked especially adorable tonight, with his coat, hat, and scarf.

"Sorry to interrupt," he said, not making eye contact with Harper. There was bad blood between them. "But I remembered something else from last night. When Fisk and Michael were fighting."

"Sure," I said. "What is it?"

"It was Fisk. He said something about his grandmother, and he sounded worried. He kept saying, 'Someone was there. Someone heard. Someone knows.'"

"Heard what?" Harper asked.

"I don't know," Vince said.

My heart pounded. I knew. Or at least I thought I did, thanks to Dash. Earlier he had said that Fisk had gone to see Harriette yesterday afternoon and that they had talked about Michael and the spell.

If someone had overheard that conversation . . . someone who wanted the Witching Hour spell . . .

That conversation might just have been Michael's death sentence.

"I thought I'd pass it on." Vince gave us a quick nod. "See you later."

"That was strange," Harper said as he walked away. "Why would Fisk even be talking to his grandmother? Oh, oh! We can ask her. Harriette, ten o'clock."

I swiveled. Sure enough, Harriette stood off to the side, leaning against the fried dough booth. She kept looking at her watch as though she were expecting someone. She was, as usual, dressed in black. Black jeans, black boots, black coat belted at her narrow waist. Black leather gloves, black scarf. Except for her pale

face and her shocking white hair, she blended in with
the night.

The line advanced, and I said, "I should go alone,
since she already knows me."

"You can't leave me here, next to that . . ." She threw
a look at Boo Manor.

"Move closer to the bonfire. I'll be right back."

Harper didn't look too thrilled, but she nodded. However, when I turned toward Harriette, the Floracrafter
was gone. I glanced around. "Where'd she go?"

"I don't know, but there are a couple of Wickeds at
eight o'clock," Harper said, tugging me back into line.
"Are they nuts? Look where they're going!"

I abandoned my search for Harriette and turned in
time to see Hammond Wickham and Ophelia's little boy,
Jacob (dressed as a cowboy), head into the haunted
house. Behind them, Ophelia (dressed as a cowgirl) and
Bertie followed, their heads bent together. I was glad to
see the two of them getting along. I smiled at the wizard
who went in after them, admiring the dazzling hooded
cape, the rope-belted tunic, the crooked walking stick,
and fluffy white beard.

Harper pulled me out of the line. "You have to stop
them. Go after them and get them out of there!"

"Are *you* crazy? They already went inside. They'll be
fine." Even as I said it, though, I felt the shift in the air.
The bad juju.

Harper shivered, a full-body shudder.

She'd felt the juju, too.

We glanced at each other, and I went running toward
Boo Manor. "Ophelia! Bertie!" I tried to push my way to
the front of the line, but I met the protests of many who'd
been waiting quite a while. Many who didn't understand
the urgency.

A hand grabbed my arm. "Is there a problem, Darcy?"

Glinda squeezed a little tighter than necessary, I thought, but I was too grateful to see her to care. "You have to go in there," I said. "Get Bertie and Ophelia."

"What are you talking about?"

I leaned in to her. "Don't you *feel* it?"

"Feel what?" she said, looking at me as if I had lost my mind.

"The danger?"

Naked emotion washed over her face. "It's why I'm here," she said softly.

"Well, what're you waiting for? Bertie and Ophelia are inside Boo Manor. They're in danger."

Suddenly a shot sounded, and a bloodcurdling scream split the air. Glinda shoved me out of the way and went running inside. Everyone around me didn't know how to react. Was this part of the show? Should they be concerned?

I was too shocked to give them guidance, to clear the area. Suddenly, someone tugged on me. Harper had come close enough to the haunted house to grab the edge of my scarf and pull me back.

We huddled as people came running out of Boo Manor, screaming. All the other fairgoers took note and started screaming, too. Within a minute, it was complete bedlam and remained that way until patrol cars started showing up.

Harper and I kept watch on the haunted house. We were keeping track of those who went in. And those who didn't come out. So far, there was no sign of Hammond, Ophelia, little Jacob, or Bertie having exited.

Harper whispered, "I only heard one shot. What did you hear?"

"One shot," I confirmed. My teeth chattered.

Out of the corner of my eye, I saw Nick arrive. He sprinted for Boo Manor, his hand on his gun.

Officers began clearing the area, sending people home. And as soon as the word "shooting" hit the crowd, people ran for their cars.

Harper and I were allowed to linger, probably because everyone on the force knew that Nick and I were in a relationship. We huddled close to the bonfire, trying to keep warm.

At the village's entrance, a line of brake lights headed out, while an ambulance sped toward the green, its siren screaming. It parked in the middle of the street near the bookshop, and two EMTs jumped out.

We watched in silence as they rushed a stretcher toward the haunted house, while in the distance, another siren shrieked the arrival of a second ambulance. My pulse pounded in my ears.

As soon as the EMTs went in, Nick came outside, looked around, and headed our way.

"What the hell happened?" Harper spurted as soon as he was close enough to hear.

Patience really wasn't one of her strongest traits.

Nick dragged a hand down his face and glanced over his shoulder. A stretcher carrying Bertie came out of the haunted house. She looked pale and lifeless.

I gulped. "Is she alive?"

"Hanging on," Nick said. "She was shot in the chest."

The other stretcher came out, carrying Ophelia. Her head was wrapped in gauze, which was already soaked through with blood.

I clutched Harper's arm and looked away, feeling woozy. Blood did that to me. Hammond hurried behind the EMTs, Jacob in his arms. The boy's head was buried in his stepfather's collarbone, and I couldn't even imagine the kind of trauma he'd witnessed.

"But there was only one shot . . . ," Harper said, her eyes wide as she took in the scene.

"Ophelia was clubbed with a stick." Nick shoved his hands in his pockets. "She's awake and lucid, but she's going to need a lot of stitches, and she probably has a concussion."

I didn't poke, prod, or bait him about sharing information with us. I was just glad he was. "What about the shooter?"

"And the clubber?" Harper added.

"Same person, as far as we can tell. Shot Bertie first, then turned the gun on Ophelia, who somehow managed to knock the gun from the shooter's hand. The assailant hit her over the head with a stick, then picked up the gun again and took aim just as Glinda managed to grab the shooter from behind. There was a struggle, and in the ensuing chaos, the shooter escaped."

A stick? My mind flashed back to the wizard in line behind the Wickeds. "Was the shooter dressed like a wizard?"

Nick straightened. "You saw the wizard? Can you give me a description? Man or woman? How tall? Facial features?"

"I—I don't know. Now that you ask specifics, I realize the shooter chose a good costume as a disguise. The wizard was hunched, so I'm not sure how tall. And the face was obscured by a hood and a fake beard, so I'm not even sure whether it was a man or woman. The outfit was beautiful. A cape with beading . . ."

"We found the cape," Nick said. "The shooter shed it on the way out."

Trying to recapture the images of people fleeing from the haunted house, I realized I had been so focused on looking for Ophelia and Bertie that I hadn't taken much note of anyone else. The same thing had apparently happened to Harper.

It was hard to believe that a potential killer had probably glided right past without our realizing it.

"What happened to the gun?" Harper asked.

"Shooter took it." Nick glanced around at the officers securing the area. His eyes were always moving, taking in everything.

"And the stick?" she pressed.

"Dropped it," he said.

"So," she said, excitement bubbling in every word she spoke, "you can probably get DNA from the cape, hair probably, and possibly prints from the stick?"

Nick smiled. "Hopefully. And if we do, then let's also hope there's already a match in the system."

Harper's face was cast in a slightly orange glow from the bonfire. "If you want, I can go around and pluck hairs from everyone in the village for comparison. I don't mind."

The scary thing was, she really didn't.

Nick said, "I'll keep that in mind, Harper."

And he said it with a straight face, too. I was seriously impressed.

Flames flickered and sparks spit as Glinda came out of Boo Manor and walked over to us. A dark bruise had started to form around her eye.

I winced.

"As bad as that?" she said.

Harper nodded. "Though it does make your blue eyes look even bluer. Prettier."

Glinda tipped her head, as if gauging how to take the comment. "Uh, thanks?"

Harper nodded.

Glinda's lips set in a firm line, and the tension between us grew uncomfortable. Finally, she looked at me and said, "If you hadn't sent me in there, Ophelia may have been shot, too. I just, uh, wanted to let you know that you probably saved her life." She spun and walked away.

As I watched her go, I tried to imagine how hard that must have been for her to say, especially in front of Nick.

Nick rocked on his heels. "How did you know something was going to happen, Darcy?"

"It wasn't me. Not really. It was Harper."

He glanced at her.

She shrugged. "I have a sixth sense for bad juju, what can I say?"

Nick's lip twitched, almost curling into a smile. Almost. "You two should go home. I'm going to head to the hospital. I'll let you know how Bertie and Ophelia are doing."

Home sounded wonderful right about now. I nodded. "What about Mimi? I can go and pick her up. . . ."

He shook his head. "It's okay. I don't plan on being out all night, and I hired Colleen to stay with her until I get back. Right now they're doing some kind of pumpkin facial." He made a sour face.

I shuddered. The thought of pumpkin guts on my face made me squirm. "All right then. Call me if the plans change."

"I will."

Great. Even though Glinda had left, the tension remained.

I gave him a little wave, then turned, dragging Harper along with me. I had a feeling she could have stood there all night, watching the comings and goings of the crime-scene techs.

We'd taken only a couple of steps when I heard Nick's voice.

"Darcy?"

I stopped and looked over my shoulder.

He was still standing by the fire, his hands in his pockets, his heart in his eyes. "I haven't forgotten about the caramel apple."

Swallowing a sudden lump in my throat, I gave him a smile. "Me, either."

"I'll call you later," he said softly, kissing my cheek.

"I'll wait up."

I watched him walk away.

Harper tugged on my arm. "It'll work out, Darcy," she said softly. "I think it's meant to be between you two."

I glanced at her. "Another sixth sense?"

"No, I'm just getting soft in my old age. Starting to think that true love might exist." She shuddered.

I nudged her. "Does that have anything to do with Marcus?"

She rolled her eyes but didn't answer.

"By the way, did you ever get anything out of him about Harriette's will?"

"Not yet," she said with a gleam in her eye. "But I'm working on it."

I didn't even want to know.

We had taken only a few more steps before she said, "Is it wrong that I kind of like Glinda?"

It was a tough question. Glinda was turning out to be a hard witch to figure out. "I don't know." It was the truth. She was complex; that was for sure.

Harper nodded as if she understood me perfectly. Again, she linked her elbow through mine. We'd just about made it to the back gate before she said, "Can I say I told you so about that haunted house?"

I smiled. "I'll never doubt you again."

Dashing up the back steps, she said, "I'm writing this day down. I might make it a holiday and everything. Undoubting Darcy Day."

I sighed.

As she went into the house, I lingered, looking back at the deserted festival.

I could no longer feel the magic in the air.

Chapter Twenty-four

"*When the clock strikes the midnight hour, there is revealed the Witching flower.*"

I pried my eyes open, rubbed the sleep out of them, and squinted at the glowing red numbers on the clock. I rubbed my eyes again, thinking the fuzzy numbers I'd seen had to be a mistake.

Looking again, I sat straight up. It was almost nine in the morning, hours past my usual wakeup time.

When the clock strikes the midnight hour, there is revealed the Witching flower.

Missy yawned, her little pink tongue sticking out. I rubbed her ears.

I slipped on my glasses and glanced around, looking for the voice that had spoken to me.

Whump, whump.

"Are you sure you can't talk, Michael?"

Two flickers. *No.*

"You're not sure, or you can't speak?"

No response.

"Let me rephrase. Can you speak?"

No.

"Did you see who spoke to me?"

Yes.

"Was it the Elder?" I asked.

He didn't answer.

"I'm not going to get you to answer me in any way, shape, form, am I?"

No.

"I figured," I mumbled.

Missy crawled into my lap, and I voiced the words that had been whispered to me the last two mornings.

> *"A stem blooms devoid of light,*
> *At the darkest time of night,*
> *When the clock strikes the midnight hour,*
> *There revealed is the Witching flower."*

Whump-whump-whump-whump.

"Is that the Witching Hour spell?" I asked softly.

Yes.

"The whole spell?" Was I going to get another visit tomorrow morning?

Yes.

"Do you know why it was told to me?"

No.

Even though Michael hadn't confirmed it was the Elder in my room this morning, I knew it had to be. Only she and Michael knew the Witching Hour rose spell.

Well, and the killer, but I didn't think it likely that the killer had broken in.

And now I knew the spell, too.

The Elder must have entrusted me with the spell for a reason, but I didn't know why she couldn't have just given it to me in the meadow last night. Sneaking into my room and whispering it to me while I slept was a little creepy.

"You must have to go out," I said to Missy as I fought a yawn.

Her stubby tail waggled.

"Come on, then."

I grabbed my robe from the foot of the bed. I'd finally gone to sleep around two in the morning—leaving Harper downstairs tapping away on my laptop. She'd been obsessed with hacking into Hot Rod's Web site but hadn't had any luck by the time I gave in to my drowsiness. She had insisted she wouldn't stop until she figured it out.

I hadn't heard her leave.

I brushed my teeth, put in my contacts, made a face at myself in the mirror, and pulled my hair into a sloppy topknot.

There were voices in the kitchen as I headed for the back staircase, and I caught the scent of cinnamon rolls in the air. My stomach rumbled as Missy dashed for the stairs, eager to see who our visitors were.

"Well, if it isn't Sleeping Beauty," Harper said as I came down the steps. Missy barked and turned in circles until Harper bent down to give her attention.

Marcus glanced up from my computer screen. "Good morning, Darcy."

Marcus Debrowski was adorably rumpled, with his dark brown hair sticking up all over the place, and his green eyes focused behind a pair of dark-rimmed glasses.

"Morning, Marcus," I said, making sure the doggy door was open so Missy could go out at will. "I'm a little surprised to see you here." Harper, I noticed, was still wearing the same outfit as yesterday and couldn't stop fidgeting.

Missy ran outside, and Harper bounced back onto the stool. Her fingers drummed the counter, and her leg jiggled. I caught her eye. "Have you been here all night?"

Nodding, she held up a mug. "Eighth cup of coffee."

Marcus pried the mug from her hand. "And it's time to cut her off."

She didn't let go.

They eyed each other over the rim of the cup.

Marcus gave up.

Smart man.

"I finally called in some help," Harper said. "I was starting to see double. Maybe triple." She stared at her mug. "This actually might be my tenth cup."

I snatched the mug out of her hand. "Let's switch you to water."

Marcus mouthed an exaggerated "Thank you" as I set the mug in the sink.

Harper elbowed him, and he threw his head back and laughed; then she giggled, too, caught up in his laughter.

I ignored her maniacal overcaffeinated tone and simply enjoyed that she seemed happy. "Where's Ve?" I asked, snagging a cinnamon roll from a tray on the counter.

"Ran to the grocery store," Harper said, still fidgeting.

I figured after ten cups of coffee, the jitters might wear off by next year. "Any luck with the Web site?"

"Hot Rod has so many bells and whistles on this site, it makes me wonder if he's in the witness protection program or something," she said. "I barely dented the security."

"It is above and beyond," Marcus said, tapping away. "He's gone to great lengths to secure his site."

"Is that so unusual in this day of identity theft?" I asked.

"To this degree, yes," Marcus said. "It's going to take me a while to get through his firewalls."

"Want some coffee?" Harper asked him, heading for the coffeepot.

I spun her around and pointed her back at the stool.

"Don't even think about it. Save some for the rest of us." I poured myself a cup. "Marcus?"

He shook his head.

Harper folded her arms on the countertop, then rested her head on them and closed her eyes. Even though she looked exhausted, her body still moved, little twitches of caffeine running freely through her system.

I leaned against the counter and licked sugary glaze from my fingers. "Do you think he's hiding something?"

"Probably," Marcus said.

"Mmm-hmm," Harper murmured, without opening her eyes. "Witness protection."

Marcus reached over and rubbed his hand over her back. It was an unconscious movement, done without even thinking too much about it. It was familiar. Tender.

I smiled behind the rim of my cup, feeling a bit smug since I'd had a hand in setting the two of them up.

"Hiding what?" I asked.

"Probably his identity," Marcus said. "I can't imagine Hot Rod Stiffington is his real name."

I laughed. "Imagine filling that in on your SATs?"

"Maybe he's a preacher or something," Harper mumbled.

"Do you think you can break through and get me an address?" I asked.

"Definitely," Marcus answered. "It might take me a while, though."

Missy came bounding back inside. I filled her bowl with kibble and refilled her water dish. "How long's a while? This is Tilda we're talking about."

"A couple hours at most. Hopefully sooner," he said.

"Not that Tilda cares," Harper mumbled.

It was true. She'd looked happy as a clam in my vision.

A knock sounded from the back door; I shuffled into the mudroom and peeked out the window.

Starla had her face pressed to the glass.

I laughed and let her in. She didn't come alone. In one arm was a big jack-o'-lantern, in the other, Twink, her bichon frise. "Lookie!" she squealed, holding out the pumpkin.

"Another one?" I asked, taking it from her.

She set Twink on the floor. He hopped around, sniffing all around the kitchen. He looked more like a baby bunny than a full-grown dog.

"It was on the front stoop this morning when I woke up," she said, coming into the kitchen. She frowned when she saw Harper, then brushed some hair out of Harper's eyes. "What's wrong?"

"Ugh," Harper moaned.

"Caffeine overdose," I said, setting the pumpkin on the counter. I filled a glass of water for my sister and pushed it in front of her. "She pulled an all-nighter with the help of ten cups of coffee."

Harper lifted her head. "It might have been twelve."

"'Ugh' is right," Starla said in sympathy.

"Was there another note?" I asked, taking the top off the jack-o'-lantern's stem and peeking inside.

Starla bounced up and down. "There was! And a little bag of organic dog biscuits from the Furry Toadstool for Twink."

Ah. This guy knew the way to Starla's heart was through her dog's stomach.

She twisted her hands and searched our faces. Her pale blond hair was styled much like mine—twisted into a loose knot atop her head. On her, it looked slightly glamorous. On me, it looked like a rat's nest on my scalp.

"Which means," she said, "that he knows me well enough to know about Twink. Does that mean he might be a stalker? Or can we rule that out yet?"

I thought about Pepe's reaction to the secret admirer. My little mouse friend would have said if the man was a danger to Starla. "I think we can rule out stalker."

She clapped. "I was hoping you'd say that." Reaching into the pumpkin, she pulled out a small star-shaped note and passed it to me.

I cleared my throat. " 'A date tonight? A future bright.' "

Harper took the note from my hand and examined it closely. "Handwritten, nice printing. If he'd used block letters, then I'd be worried."

"That's it?" Marcus asked, clearly intrigued. "No mention of when or where?"

Starla shook her head. "Maybe there's another jack-o'-lantern coming?"

"That would be my guess," I said.

She rubbed her hands and twirled around. I tried not to be too worried for her. The Beast part of the last clue still had me concerned.

Twink had settled down with Missy in the dog bed by the door. They looked adorable together, and it reminded me that I needed to put some serious thought into getting another dog to keep her company.

"What are you working on?" Starla asked Marcus.

"Finding Tilda," he said.

Starla glanced at me. "Does she have one of those GPS tags so you can track her online?"

I wished. "No." I explained about Ve and Hot Rod, and how Ve had stuffed Tilda in Hot Rod's duffel bag so he'd have to bring the cat back—only he didn't. Starla howled with laughter.

It was rather amusing. But only because Tilda was fine.

She said, "Any word from Nick about what happened in the haunted house last night?"

I shared that he'd called after midnight to let me

know that Bertie had survived surgery and was in ICU. Ophelia had needed more than a hundred stitches and was being kept for observation.

Starla leaned on the counter. "Is anyone else concerned that Harriette might be next?"

I shook my head.

"Why not?" Starla asked.

"Yeah, why?" Harper echoed.

"Because," I said, "I think whoever is doing this wants Harriette to be blamed." I explained about the circumstantial evidence.

"Who'd do that?" Starla asked.

It was the million-dollar question. It was someone who not only wanted Harriette to pay for a crime she didn't commit, but also someone who wanted that Witching Hour spell.

> *A stem blooms devoid of light,*
> *At the darkest time of night,*
> *When the clock strikes the midnight hour,*
> *There revealed is the Witching flower.*

Goose bumps rose on my arms as I thought about someone overhearing Fisk and Harriette's conversation. According to Amy, Fisk had been at the Elysian Fields with his grandmother on Friday, so it had to have been someone connected to the property. Someone who wouldn't be questioned if seen walking around.

Like Lydia or Willard. Imogene, Bertie, Ophelia.

All of them had a desire for the spell. But which one of them would have killed for it? Who had the most to gain?

The thought reminded me of Harriette's will.

I looked at Marcus. "Any chance you can share with us why Harriette wants to change her will? Is she looking to include her fiancé?"

"Ooh," Harper said, jumping up and heading for the coffeepot. I turned her around again. "Because if Lydia was going to lose a big chunk of Harriette's fortune, that might be motive."

Marcus said, "I can't say anything about changes to her will."

Harper glared at me with envy as I refilled my mug and added some milk. "If Harriette is blamed for the death of Michael, who gains control of the Elysian Fields? Of her money?"

We all looked at Marcus. "Her power of attorney," he said.

"And who's that?" I asked.

"Well, right now, no one since she doesn't need one. But if she was facing jail time, it would either be me as her attorney, or more than likely ... it would be Lydia. Harriette signed it over to her once before when Harriette went in for minor surgery. Kind of a just-in-case backup plan."

So Lydia would have control over the Elysian Fields, Harriette's fortune ... everything.

Starla said, "But why hurt the Wickeds? Why try to kill them?"

"I think I can answer that," I said.

They all looked at me. "Lydia told me that Harriette left each of the Wickeds her own greenhouse in her will. If Lydia wanted the Elysian Fields all to herself ... the Wickeds would have to go."

Harper shuddered. "You need to call Nick."

I picked up the kitchen phone and dialed his cell number. It went to voice mail, and I left him a message asking him to call me back as soon as possible. That it was about what was going on at the Elysian Fields.

I hung up and looked at Marcus. "Can you at least confirm that Lew Renault is Harriette's fiancé?"

"Lewis?" Marcus said, looking confused.

"We think he might be Harriette's mysterious fiancé," I said.

Starla gasped. "You're kidding! Her fiancé is real?"

"Her fiancé is *Lew*?" Marcus said in disbelief.

"Maybe. It's not confirmed yet, but it looks that way." I studied Marcus. "You didn't know about Lew?" That didn't make sense if Harriette was changing her will to include him.

He shook his head.

"Then he's not the one Harriette was adding to her will?"

Slowly, he shook his head again, probably breaking some ethics codes in doing so. "What made you think that?"

"Lydia implied that Harriette was adding her fiancé to the will. . . . She overheard a conversation."

Overheard a conversation . . . Hmm. Seemed like Lydia had a history of eavesdropping. Had she been the one listening in on Fisk and Harriette?

"Then who is being added to the will?" Starla asked.

Marcus looked pained. There was no way he could say without compromising confidentiality.

I rubbed my temples, watching the way Harper swung her foot back and forth. It reminded me of Amy . . . and her tattoo of a fish. And how Fisk's car with a fish sticker on it had been seen at Harriette's house. And how Fisk had been part of growing the Witching Hour roses . . . How Fisk had grown close to his grandmother.

My jaw dropped, and I stared at Marcus. He didn't so much as blink.

"What?" Harper asked, looking between us.

I said, "Is it Fisk? Is Harriette changing her will to include Fisk?"

Something flashed in Marcus's eyes—a silent confirmation.

Whoa. It was such big news. And I knew for certain one person who wouldn't like it a bit.

Lydia.

Chapter Twenty-five

Fifteen minutes later, I drove toward the Elysian Fields. I wanted—I needed—to see Harriette. To warn her. To do something to stop the unfolding tragedy.

It had started to snow lightly as I wound my way toward Harriette's. Turning into her driveway, I could sense the bad juju again. Michael could sense it, too, if his increased heart rate was any indication.

Whump-whump-whump-whump.

I kept my cell phone by my side, just in case Nick returned my call. He needed to know what was going on.

As I parked in the gravel lot, I saw one other car there, a silver Mercedes. I glanced from greenhouse to greenhouse and noted movement in two of them—Imogene's and Harriette's.

"Ready?" I asked Michael.

Yes.

As I made my way toward Harriette's greenhouse, I heard a loud *"Psst."* I glanced over and saw Imogene motioning me toward her.

Once I reached her door, she grabbed my arm and pulled me inside. "Thank goodness you're here!" Her out-of-control curly white-blond hair had been subdued today by a black headband. "I've wanted to leave for hours now, but I don't dare leave Harriette alone. Are you staying long?"

"I hadn't planned to. . . ." I glanced toward Harriette's greenhouse. I could see her inside, moving around. "How long has she been in there?"

"All night, I fear. I arrived around five this morning, and she was already inside." Bell sleeves on an oversized cream tunic flapped as she gestured wildly. "She won't let me in. She won't let anyone in."

"Why?"

"She probably fears for her life. Wouldn't you in her shoes?"

I didn't share with Imogene my theory that someone was setting up Harriette. Someone . . . like her own daughter.

I looked closely at Imogene. Despite working with nature her whole life, her skin was a beautiful creamy white, with delicate crow's-feet fanning from the corners of her blue eyes, and deep smile lines creasing her cheeks. Her wrinkled beige linen pants confirmed that she'd been here awhile. Pepe would be horrified she wore linen at this time of year, and Godfrey would prob-ably keel over if he could see her navy blue Birkenstock deck-type shoes. I supposed Imogene would also be con-sidered an eccentric villager with her slightly hippie air. She was a throwback and didn't care a bit.

"Are you feeling okay?" I asked. "That was quite a scare yesterday."

"It was horrible," she said, her eyes glazing over as if she were remembering every horrifying detail. "But I'm doing all right. Fortunately, I had only sipped the poi-soned drink. I'm a sight better than Bertie and Ophelia, I should say. I was the lucky one."

As she spoke, another silver sedan pulled into the lot.

I watched Willard step out, the snowflakes blending into his white hair as he strode up to Harriette's greenhouse door. When he punched in a code on the keypad and turned the handle on the knob, Harriette came at him with a rake, pushing him back out.

"His third time trying to get inside," Imogene said. "He's determined; I'll give him that."

Willard threw his hands in the air, and, next thing I knew, he was stomping prissily up the walkway toward Imogene's door. He burst inside in a whirl of snowflakes and indignation. "She's lost her mind! How am I supposed to sell roses today at the shop if she won't let me cut any?"

He flicked his gaze to me, as if he had no clue who I was—and more than that—as if I were of no importance to him. I'd been dismissed in a blink.

Imogene patted his shoulder. "Don't fret so. Take extra orchids today. And I'll bring some of Bertie's lilies by your shop later on my way home. Maybe by then Harriette will come to her senses, and I'll bring roses, too."

"I hope so," he said, snuffing. "I have dozens of Get Well Soon bouquet orders to fill for Bertie and Ophelia. I'll take as many orchids as you can spare, and please try to work on Harriette. I need those roses. More so than the lilies." He grumbled something about Harriette not already giving him his own greenhouse.

He said "lilies" as if they were a pesky weed to be eradicated, and I recalled the snobbery of Floracrafters. Imogene was a Flora, so of course he'd want her orchids over lilies from a Terracrafter. My stomach turned a bit at the arrogance and pretension.

"I'll do what I can," she said, handing him a pair of snips.

I watched as he walked around, cutting orchids as if they were abundant wildflowers. With each cut, within moments, a new bud immediately appeared. I didn't think I'd ever tire of watching that magical process happen. "Will they always keep growing back like that?"

"Hmm?" Imogene asked.

I motioned to the flowers.

"Oh, well, no. Every couple of months, they need a renewal spell. Without it, the plants would wither and die."

"It's incredible."

Imogene smiled. "I agree."

I glanced back at Harriette's greenhouse. "Where's Lydia today?"

"I'm not sure," she said. "Willard? Where is Lydia? Maybe she can talk Harriette into coming out of that greenhouse."

"She's not feeling well," he said. "I think it's the stress of what's been happening. She's planning to meet me in a little bit at the store."

Again, he flicked a gaze at me as though he resented my presence.

I was beginning to feel the same toward him. To Imogene, I said, "Have there been any leads on what happened to you, Bertie, and Ophelia?"

Willard, I noticed, had slowed his clipping considerably. He was eavesdropping. Perhaps it was a marital trait.

"Sadly, no," Imogene said. "They're hoping to find some DNA or somesuch." She grabbed a broom and swept up some loose soil. "I just cannot imagine who would want to do this to us."

"Jealousy breeds malice," Willard said snidely as he continued to snip beautiful orchids.

Maybe so, but I didn't think jealousy was the root of the malice happening around here. But I kept my mouth shut. If Lydia was involved in the murder of Michael and the attempted murders on the Wickeds, then I didn't want to tip off her husband.

I walked over to the wall closest to Harriette's greenhouse. I could see her sitting on a stool, gazing at something I couldn't see.

Whump, whump.

Michael's presence was next to me, and I could imagine he was watching, too.

Imogene came up behind me and leaned on her broom. "Is she back to staring?"

"What is she looking at?"

"All but one of her Witching Hour roses died recently. She's become obsessed with that one survivor. She's afraid someone's going to break in and steal it."

"Is that a valid concern?"

"Perhaps," Imogene said, "if it's the sole survivor, especially in light of the other plants' perishing."

Whump-whump-whump.

Willard stood rigid on the other side of the worktable. "Whoever poisoned the plants should be shot."

I thought the sentiment a little harsh, especially considering what had happened to Bertie.

"Why would someone poison the plants?" Imogene asked, dismissing Willard's statement with a wave of her hand. "I don't believe that's what happened at all. I think their spell was flawed."

Willard turned a shade of pink that matched the orchids he was holding. "If that's the case, why is one still alive? It was poison. Someone is obviously trying to knock Harriette down a notch."

"Who?" I asked.

His pink blush flushed to a rosy red. "Speculation is pointless."

"Is it?" I asked. "Michael Healey is dead. Imogene, Bertie, and Ophelia were attacked. Whoever wants to knock Harriette down a notch might be responsible for those crimes as well."

Ignoring me, he pointedly looked at Imogene. "I'm leaving now. I will see you later?"

Imogene said, "I'll call you before I leave with the lilies."

He nodded once, sharply, and stormed out.

"Prickly," I said as he gently placed the orchids in the trunk of his car and zoomed off.

Imogene swept her pile of soil into a dustpan and dumped it into a garbage can in the corner. She threw me a sly smile. "You have no idea."

Oh, I had a fairly good idea.

"I'm going to give it a whirl with Harriette now."

"Good luck," Imogene said. "I doubt she'll let you in, so brace yourself for the rejection. I'll be here until she decides to come out. Seeing her like that makes me nervous. Like there's something bad in the air. Does that make sense?"

Bad juju.

"Perfect sense," I said. "I'll do my best to lure her out."

As I stepped outside, snow whirled around me. The taillights of Willard's car faded, and I thought about how he'd reacted a few minutes before. How outraged he'd been. How hard he'd tried to convince us that those plants had been poisoned.

And it suddenly hit me that it wasn't just Lydia who had a lot to gain by taking control of the Elysian Fields.

Her husband did, too.

The walkway was becoming slippery with the falling snow. I carefully made my way to the door of Harriette's greenhouse. She still sat, staring listlessly at the beautiful black rosebush.

I tapped on the glass, and she lethargically turned her

head. If she was surprised to see me, she didn't show it. In fact, she didn't reveal any emotion at all.

She turned back to staring at the flower.

I knocked louder.

She ignored me.

"Harriette," I said loudly, "I need to talk to you."

"Go away," she said, never taking her eyes off the plant.

I glanced to my left. Imogene was watching—she gave me a helpless shrug, and I practically heard her say, "I told you so."

"It's important," I said.

She ignored me.

This wasn't getting me anywhere but frustrated. I was about to give up and just go track down Nick so he could deal with all of this, when I felt Michael touch my hand. The burning sensation crept up my forearm as he lifted it. Unfolding one of my fingers, he jabbed at the electronic keypad next to the door, punching in a code.

The door to the greenhouse popped loose. I pushed on it before it could lock again and went inside. I glanced over to see if Imogene had been watching, and her mouth was hanging open. I gave her a thumbs-up.

Harriette scowled as I came in, and I was grateful she hadn't come after me with a rake. The air inside the greenhouse was warm and humid, the rose scent still as strong as yesterday. Gorgeous roses bloomed all around me in every color of the rainbow. And then there was the black rose. The one plant Michael had resurrected yesterday flourished in a pot on a worktable.

"How did you get in?" she snapped.

I didn't know how to answer that, so I ignored the question. "I need to speak to you, Harriette. It's important."

I noticed she wore the same clothes as yesterday. Her

hair, snow-white, had started to come loose from its twist. Her small eyes bore a sadness I could hardly bear. Unnaturally pallid skin glistened with moisture.

"Are you feeling well?" I asked, suddenly worried about her heart issues.

"Why are you here, Darcy?"

I carefully stepped closer to her. On the worktable in front of her, I noticed discarded packaging. I read the description for the item, and being my nosy self, I couldn't help but pick it up.

Viper-quick, Harriette snatched it out of my hands. "Go home."

I said, "Why do you have a pet-tracking GPS collar?"

All sadness had been erased from her eyes. Now mean snake eyes narrowed on me. "Go. Home."

Hiss.

Whereas her viper countenance would have sent me running for cover two days ago, for some reason I was no longer scared of her. She was only striking out because her whole world was crumbling around her.

Whump, whump.

Michael was nearby, and his presence also gave me some comfort.

I glanced between hands gripping the GPS packaging and the plants, and it hit me what she had done. "You planted the tracking device in the pot of the plant, didn't you?"

She didn't answer.

I went on. "That's brilliant." It really was. If the plant was taken from the immediate area, Harriette would receive an alert either on her phone or on her computer. As her BlackBerry was sitting next to the rosebush, I assumed the former. From there, she could track the plant's location on a map.

She slipped her phone into her pocket and glanced at me. "Please go away."

"I can't. Not yet. I think you're in danger. I think someone's trying to frame you for Michael's murder and possibly for the attacks on the Wickeds."

"I know," she said.

"Do you know who is doing it?"

"No."

I didn't want to bring up my theories about Lydia and Willard. There were some things a mother never needed to hear. As soon as I was done here, however, I would find Nick and make him listen.

For now, I took a stab in the dark. "How many people know that you've lost your powers?"

Slowly, she rose. I saw her eye the rake and took a step back.

"How do you know that?" she hissed.

I laid it all on the line. I figured it was the only way I would be able to get her to trust me. "I'm working with the Elder to solve Michael's murder."

She sank back down, and even though she looked dejected, her spine was still ramrod straight. "Only the Elder, Lewis, and I know. I didn't want to tell anyone else, because then they might figure out . . ."

"That the Witching Hour spell wasn't yours."

Stubbornly, her chin lifted, and she said, "Bertie, Ophelia, and Imogene had begged me to share the spell with them and were aggrieved when I refused. Lydia chastised me for being selfish and unkind. You see, she had motives as well. Willard wanted to get his fussy little hands on the spell, too."

"None of them figured out that you couldn't share the spell because you didn't know it."

"Even if I did know it, I wouldn't have shared it. I couldn't let any of them know the truth."

"Why?"

"Because of exactly what happened, Darcy." Anguish filled her eyes. "Michael is dead."

Whump-whump-whump.

I studied her, and as her words connected in my brain, I inhaled sharply as a stunning realization hit me like a sucker punch. "You . . . You wouldn't renounce your award not because you didn't want to share the prize, but because you were trying to protect Michael. You lost your powers to shield him from harm. You knew what would happen if someone found out he'd cast the spell. You knew someone would kill for that spell—and you were willing to take the hypothetical bullet for him."

I was shocked to see a tear slip from her eye.

Whump-whump-whump.

"I knew as soon as I saw the very first black rose that his spell could be dangerous to him."

"Why use the spell at all then?" All this could have been avoided.

"I was . . . selfish. The flowers were ingenious, gorgeous. A huge achievement. Looking back, I should have just done as you said and urged Michael to discard the spell. This is a cutthroat business. Not many realize that, but I did. It's why I talked him into letting me claim the spell instead. It was foolish of me. So very foolish. If I had known someone would learn he created the spell . . . It is my fault he is dead. No matter how I tried to protect him, he is gone. I will never forgive myself. Not after he lost his life after giving me the greatest gift."

"The black rose?" I asked.

She scoffed. "Not hardly."

I thought for a moment, and pieces clicked into place. My heart ached. "Your grandson."

Another tear fell from her eye. "Fisk would come here sometimes with Michael, at first to help him out around the place, but then ... I think he was curious about me. Over time, a friendship grew. Over time, love grew. I had my grandson back. Thanks to Michael, I had him back."

"You planned to have your will changed to include Fisk, right?"

"His talents are incredible. More than I ever dreamed. He deserves his mother's share of this place—it is rightfully his. Through him I saw how wrong I'd been all these years, labeling others as lesser than I. I lost so much, but through Fisk I saw a way to gain it all back." She wiped her eyes. "I started helping Bertie and Ophelia more and more, to grow their Terra powers. I wanted to mend the error of my ways. And then ..."

"Michael was killed."

"When the first roses disappeared from my greenhouse, I knew that whoever stole them was going to try and breed or clone them, which was something I had tried—and failed—to do myself. These roses are impossible to replicate. Only with the spell could they be created. I knew that placed me in danger, but it was a risk I was willing to shoulder. I never dreamed someone would connect Michael to the roses. No one here even bothered to ask what kind of Craft he had. It was careless of Fisk and me not to make sure we were alone when discussing the roses on Friday. I can only assume the person who heard our conversation is Michael's killer."

I silently begged her to wish to know who'd been eavesdropping.

She didn't. Instead she said, "After I learned Michael had died, the only silver lining I saw was that I could finally let the Witching Hour roses go. I had announced my retirement. The flowers had died. And whoever killed Michael would have realized that the spell was tied to his *life* and was useless now that he was dead—quite the

•

surprise, I imagine. And whoever else wanted the spell would think it was flawed . . . and no longer covet it. The spell could rest in peace—along with Michael."

I wanted to argue the peace part, but I knew there was more. "But?"

"One of the plants recovered, and my nightmare began again."

"Because whoever killed Michael now believes that the plants can somehow be regenerated."

She nodded sharply. "That person is not going to stop until he or she figures out how. How many people more will die in this quest?" Her hands shook as she reached out and touched a rose petal. "I suspect that whoever was desperate enough to kill him will be desperate enough to steal this plant to try and uncover its secrets. I will catch whoever it is, and for Michael justice will be served."

"Why do you think this plant is still alive?" I asked.

For the first time, she smiled. "There's only one way, Darcy. Michael. His spirit must be around here somewhere. Lingering. Do you feel him?"

I nodded.

"I thought you would. Especially since you were the one who found his body. I only hope he can forgive me," she said, "and that he now realizes I was only trying to help him."

"I think he probably realizes that now."

"You think?"

Behind her, he flashed once. *Yes*.

"Absolutely."

She gazed down at the black rose. "This time, I'm ready for someone to take the rose. This time, I'll catch who killed Michael."

"You said you don't know who that person is, but you must have a suspicion."

Her beady eyes narrowed. "All I know, Darcy, is that it's someone who has access to my greenhouse. Someone close to me. Very close." Her gaze wandered over my shoulder, and she wobbled as she quickly stood up. She grabbed onto me for balance, and I held her up.

I glanced over my shoulder and sighed. Four village police cars had pulled into the gravel parking lot, the lights on the top of the cars flashing.

Whump-whump-whump.

Led by Nick, four police officers stormed up the walkway toward the greenhouse door.

"They're here to arrest me," she said.

It looked that way.

"Let them in, Darcy."

"Let me call Marcus first," I said. She needed a lawyer.

"No. Go." She shoved me toward the door, and as I pulled it open, Nick said, "What are you doing here?"

Before I could answer, there was a crash behind me. I spun around and saw Harriette facedown on the ground. I sprinted over to her, and Nick helped me roll her over. To an officer, he said, "Get the EMTs here."

Harriette's eyes were wide with fear. "My chest," she gasped, clutching it.

Nick looked at me. "Heart attack."

Harriette's gaze slid to me. "Tell Lewis. Lewis Renault."

I guessed that confirmed he was her fiancé. "I will," I promised.

Then she closed her eyes and went deathly still.

Chapter Twenty-six

The snow had subsided by the time I made my way to Divinity Ridge. I probably could have called Lew, but this was the sort of news one ought to deliver in person.

By the time the ambulance had arrived, Nick had restarted Harriette's heart with CPR. That was the good news.

The bad news was that it didn't look good for her. Between her age and the stress she was under, a full recovery was unlikely. Imogene, fortunately, had ridden with Harriette to the hospital.

The bad, bad news was that Nick was only waiting for Harriette to pull through before he arrested her. The circumstantial evidence was too much for him to ignore, and though he patiently listened to why I thought she had been framed, he hadn't changed his mind about Harriette's arrest.

However, the slightly good news was that he promised me he would keep investigating, questioning both Lydia and Willard further.

I was a nervous wreck as I pulled into the long drive-

way in front of Lew's quaint snowcapped cottage. I didn't
see any cars in the driveway, but there were tire tracks
coming from a detached garage at the back of the house.
Wispy threads of smoke rose from the chimney, and I
hoped Lew was home.

Shutting off the engine, I reached for the door just as
my cell phone rang. I checked the ID and answered.

"I found him!" Marcus said.

"Hot Rod?"

"The one and only. Sneaky bastard."

I smiled. "That's the best news I've heard all morning." I fumbled for a piece of paper and a pencil. "What's
the address?"

"It's a house, 6680 Divinity Ridge. Do you know
where that is?"

My head snapped up, and I stared at the little cottage.
"I'm parked in its driveway."

"What?" he asked. "How?"

"I'll call you back, Marcus." I snapped the phone
closed and stared at the house; I suddenly noticed movement in the window.

A white and gray Himalayan sat on the sill, flicking
her tail. I could sense her bad attitude through the
glass.

Tilda.

Stunned, I sat there for a moment. Lewis Renault was
Hot Rod Stiffington?

My first thought was that Aunt Ve was going to be
seriously disappointed that he was already taken.

My second was that I needed to hear this explanation.

I jumped out and quickly walked up the front walk.
Before I could even knock, however, the door opened,
and Amy stood there, looking sheepishly at me. "How
did you find me here?"

"Actually, I wasn't looking for you. I was looking for

Lew Renault. And I've been looking for *her* for days." I pointed at Tilda as she sashayed toward me.

"The cat?" Amy said.

Tilda leapt into my arms. I held her close, rubbed her head, and soaked in her purrs. "My cat."

Amy blinked. "I'm so confused."

"Can I come in?"

She nodded.

The house was show-worthy neat, with modern, elegant furniture, dark wood floors, and abstract pictures on the walls.

Tilda kept bumping the top of her head against my chin, and she even gave me a tiny kiss. If I hadn't known better, I would think she had missed me.

I glanced around. "Where's Fisk?"

"Fisk? I don't know what you mean. He's not—"

"Look, Amy. I'm so not in the mood. I know Fisk is hiding out here. I know why he fought with Michael. I know Lewis is Hot Rod Stiffington. And I know Lewis is Harriette's fiancé. I'm not saying I quite understand all those things, but in light of everything that's happened lately with Michael, with the Wickeds, with Harriette, I'd really appreciate if you dropped the act and just started telling the truth."

"I'm right here," Fisk said, coming out from the kitchen area. I almost smiled—he was just as Evan and Starla had described, right down to the puffy lips and droopy pants. He stood next to Amy, putting his arm around her.

Whump, whump.

Well, I was glad Michael was calm, because I was about to snap.

"Where's Lew?" I asked. Was he hiding in the closet?

"Just left for the hospital," Fisk said. "My dad called to let us know what happened to Harriette this morning."

"Your dad knows you're here?"

"He didn't until last night," Fisk said. "I called him after Amy saw you at the house."

I launched into questions. "How did Harriette feel about you and your dad becoming competition? Going into business with Michael?" I asked.

"She doesn't know. I've been trying to figure out how to tell her. I think she hopes I'll take over Elysian Fields one day after she . . ."

Dies.

"And would you?"

He shrugged. "Maybe someday, after Aunt Lydia retires. She works harder than anyone I know, and she deserves to run the place on her own for a while."

"Are you and Lydia close?" I asked.

"Closer than we used to be. She's nice to me. Anyway, Mom and Dad are on the way to the hospital to see Grandma." He sucked in a breath. "I just hope it's not too late."

"You should go, too," I said. There probably wasn't anyone Harriette would rather see more—and now I understood why Harriette had told me to find Lewis. Because she knew he'd tell Fisk as well.

"I wanted to go, but the police . . . ," he said.

"The police think Harriette is Michael's killer. They just want to talk to you. They would let you see your grandmother first, though."

"They think Harriette killed Michael?" Amy said. "That's crazy."

"It's a long story," I said, "but the fact is the real killer is still out there."

I explained to them about the flower Michael had resurrected, and how Harriette was trying to trap the killer. "But we can't be too careful. Whoever the killer is has the Witching Hour spell, but we don't know if that person understands that an Illumicrafter is needed to cast it. That means until the killer is caught, Amy is possibly in danger."

Her eyes went wide, and Fisk tightened his arm around her.

I noticed Tilda had fallen asleep in my arms. "Do you still have the invisibility cloak, Amy?"

She nodded.

"Get it and put it on. Don't take it off until you get the okay from me or the Elder. Go with Fisk to the hospital. The best thing for you right now is to do as Crafters have been doing for centuries: Hide in the open. Fisk, you need to be vigilant. Whoever killed Michael and attacked the Wickeds probably knows that Amy's close to you. Stick to her like glue, and always stay where a lot of people can see you."

He nodded.

Amy dashed upstairs. I glanced at Fisk. "Do you have any idea who could have been eavesdropping on you and your grandmother?"

"None. Just that it had to be someone from the farm." He scrunched up his nose as if he were trying to hold tears at bay. "And even though I wanted Michael to do a renewal spell to help my grandmother, I also tried to warn him that someone might know he created the spell. I hate like hell that our last words to each other were angry ones."

Whump-whump-whump.

I said, "It's never too late to say you're sorry."

"Sometimes it is."

"Not in this case. Is it, Michael?"

He flashed twice. *No.*

"He says no. Two flashes equal no."

The phone rang as Fisk's eyes widened.

"Michael imprinted on me the night he died. He's

with me until his killer is caught. He flashes once for yes, twice for no, three times for I'm sorry, four for thank you. You might want to let Amy know, too."

I heard Amy answer the phone upstairs.

I was filled with frantic energy. "I'm going to go," I said. "Michael, you'll catch up with me later?"

Yes.

Fisk's eyes were filled with tears as I headed for the door.

"Wait, Darcy!" Amy called.

I turned at the sound of footsteps on the stairs, but no one visible on them. A phone, however, was floating through the air—coming closer to me.

"It's for you," Amy said.

"Me?"

"It's Lew. He wants to talk to you."

I took the phone. "Hello?"

"Darcy."

"Hot Rod."

"I need to talk to you," he said. "Can you come to the hospital?"

"What's this about?"

"Harriette has something for you. She said you'd understand."

"Yeah," I said. "I'll be right there."

"I'll meet you out front, under the portico."

I hung up and held the phone out. Amy took it.

"When you go to the hospital, remember what I said," I reminded them. "And don't trust anyone."

Chapter Twenty-seven

I had no choice but to bring Tilda with me to see Hot Rod/Lew at the hospital, which was located just five miles outside village limits. She sat primly in the passenger seat without making any fuss at all over the slippery ride.

She never ceased to amaze me.

Tree branches glistened with fresh snow, but the sun was peeking out, promising that the dusting we'd received wouldn't be around long. I turned into the hospital parking lot, headed toward the front entrance. I waited for a young couple in a crosswalk before I turned into the roundabout in front of the main entrance.

There was no sign of Hot Rod.

I parked and, almost immediately, my phone buzzed. I pulled it from my purse and looked at the screen. Starla had sent me a picture. I clicked the button to open it.

It was another jack-o'-lantern.

The message beneath the picture said, *At six thirty meet me, under the big birch tree.*

My phone buzzed again—another text message coming in. In all caps, Starla wrote: *WHAT DO I WEAR???????*

Smiling, I wrote back.

ME: *Body armor.*

HER: *Not funny.*

ME: *Kind of funny.*

HER: *Not the least little bit.*

ME: *Dark skinny jeans, silk floral tank top, cocoa cashmere cardigan. Boots. Body armor.*

HER: *Thank you. Still not funny.*

I glanced up and spotted Hot Rod headed for my car. He looked like a stereotypical professor in his dark pants and tweed suit coat. He was so unlike the Hot Rod from Friday night that it was hard for my brain to wrap around the change.

Tilda glanced at me, as if asking why we were here. Reaching over, I scooped her up, just as Hot Rod reached for the door handle.

As soon as he sat down, Tilda squirmed out of my arms and dove into his. He held her close, and I felt a little betrayed as her purrs filled the silence.

Finally, Rod looked at me.

"I don't even know where to begin," I said, thinking of all the things I wanted to ask him. "How's Harriette doing?"

His chin jutted stoically. "Not well. They're prepping her for bypass surgery. I need to get back, so I don't have long."

I understood. "Do I call you Rodney or Lew?"

"Lew is fine."

"Okay, Lew." I smiled and said, "Why'd you keep my cat?"

He smiled and shrugged. "I don't know. I knew it was wrong to keep her, but she was so friendly, so happy. I fell in love. Didn't I?" he said, addressing those last words to her.

She twitched a whisker. *Purr, purr, purr.*

The traitor.

"I don't know how she even got into my bag in the first place, but she didn't seem the least bit put out by it. She settled right in with me. It was nice to have another energy around. One that wasn't unhappy or stressed or grieving."

"Like Fisk?"

"He was waiting on my porch steps when I arrived home Friday night. He told me about Michael. I hadn't realized that the body in the parking lot . . ." He shook his head. "He was a good kid. A nice boy. Such a damn shame."

"Are you why Harriette hired a stripper for her birthday party? Did she know that you were going to be the entertainment?"

He smiled. "Oh yes. We had a great laugh about it."

"I can't help but feel manipulated somehow, but I can't figure it out. How did you know I'd choose your company? And how could you two possibly know I'd choose you over the other entertainers?"

"It just went to show that you have good taste," he teased. "And as mine is the only company in town, if I hadn't received a booking, then Harriette would have made a phone call to Ve to recommend the site. It wouldn't have mattered who you chose—I would have showed up saying the other entertainer had fallen ill or some other excuse. Harriette wanted me to meet her friends and family in a somewhat neutral setting. Then she'd spring my identity on them at a later time."

I could only imagine that kind of shock.

"How can you do what you do?" I asked. "I mean, with your type of Craft?"

An Emoticrafter, one that absorbed everyone's emotions around him.

"My Craft is *why* I do what I do. First and foremost,

the company provides a living for me. I can run it from home, with very little interaction with live people."

"But the parties ... They're packed with people."

"Yes, but it's the only time I feel absolute joy and happiness from others. Hardly anyone is ever upset at a party. It keeps me going. It's places like this"—he motioned to the hospital—"that make me want to hide from society. Even now, I can feel your anxiety. Your fear."

My fear was that I wasn't going to be able to figure out Michael's killer before someone else was hurt.

"Maybe you can do a little dance and cheer me up?" I joked.

"Rain check," he said.

"Deal. Can you answer me one more thing?"

"Seems fair."

"Has Harriette been loaning you money?"

"Just once. I needed some roofing repairs, and there had been an error at the bank. . . . I repaid her as soon as I was able to get the mistake sorted out."

"I'm having trouble understanding your relationship. Harriette's known for being so ..." Harsh, critical, snobbish.

"I know," he said. "But as you might have learned today, there's so much more to her than meets the eye. I can feel it, even when others can't see it."

"You love her," I said.   •

"Very much."

"It was Ve who stuffed Tilda in your duffel bag. She hoped you would return the cat that night and stay for a little wine. . . ."

"Ah," he said.

"She's going to be crushed when she finds out you're taken."

He smiled at me. "I am a bit of a heartbreaker."

"I can see that about you."

"I should go back inside. Fisk called to let me know he will be here soon, and I want to be with him in case the police give him any trouble."

"I'm sure he'd appreciate that."

He reached into his coat pocket and pulled out a cell phone. "Harriette wanted me to give this to you. She said that if the alarm on it sounded, you'd know what to do with it."

The alarm would sound only if someone had stolen the last black rosebush. "Tell her not to worry. That I'll take care of it."

Lew put his hand on mine. "Be careful, Darcy." Then he looked Tilda in the eye and said, "Good-bye, sweetheart. Thanks for keeping an old man company."

She continued to purr even as he got out of the car. I watched him go, dodging people as if they had the plague. I set her back on the seat, and she put her paws on the window and stared after him. Then she glanced at me.

A heartbreaker indeed.

"You cannot go live with him," I said.

She flicked an ear and swished her tail. *"Reow,"* she cried.

"Still no."

"Reoooow."

I sighed. "Maybe we can work out some sort of visitation schedule. Maybe."

With that she settled into the passenger seat, looking smug.

As I drove away, I felt as though I'd just been conned by a cat.

I dropped off Tilda at As You Wish and watched with barely disguised merriment as she gave Ve the silent treatment.

I was becoming more and more convinced that Tilda was a familiar. Why she wouldn't speak to me, I had no idea, but I supposed it didn't matter much. I'd come to care for her and her neuroses no matter what.

Archie sat on my shoulder, and Harriette's phone was in my pocket as I walked toward Spellbound to update Harper on all that had happened. Michael was also somewhere nearby.

Whump, whump.

He'd returned to me during the car ride back to As You Wish, and Tilda hadn't reacted even the slightest bit—but I was fairly sure she'd made him sit in the backseat.

Archie said, "I knew all along Fisk was innocent."

"Really now?"

"You do not have to take that tone. I'm quite intelligent, you know."

Because of the police investigation, the festival was closed for the day. It would be open nightly for the rest of this week, and then pack up and move along after next weekend. "Good to know."

"Or that tone, either." He huffed at my sarcasm.

I ignored him. "Have you heard any updates on Ophelia or Bertie?"

"Ophelia is home and resting. Bertie is still in the hospital. She should make a full recovery."

"Good news."

"Indeed."

The sun had melted the snow from the sidewalks, but it still remained on the bushes and branches. Grass tips poked out from beneath a blanket of white. I passed an urn filled with Dash's deep purple flowers, and they still looked healthy as could be even though they were now frosted with delicate flakes.

"And how about Hot Rod?" I asked. "Did you know he and Lew were one and the same?"

"Of course."

I rolled my eyes.

"I saw that," he said.

I said, "Don't make me pluck a feather."

He scoffed. "'Honey, I don't want to hurt you.'"

I said, "You're cranky."

"*Little Murders*."

"I knew that all along."

"Touché, Darcy, touché."

"Why *are* your feathers ruffled this afternoon?"

He glanced at me, and I swore if a macaw could pout, he was doing it. "Did you have to bring her back?"

"Tilda is family. Of course I had to bring her back."

"I was afraid of this scenario."

"Why do I feel like you're plotting?"

He launched off my shoulder and soared high into the sky, laughing like the Wicked Witch of the West in *The Wizard of Oz*. I was going to have to put a tracking collar on Tilda as soon as possible.

Archie swooped back down and flew alongside me. "I must now relieve myself of your abuse and report back to the Elder. She is most anxious for your report."

"Tell her I said hi," I said drily.

He laughed as he flew away. I crossed the street, and as I passed Lotions and Potions, I glanced inside. Vince was at his workstation, scooping the innards out of another pumpkin. I waved and kept on going.

Then, I stopped short as what I'd seen hit me. Slowly, I backed up. Vince looked up again, a quizzical look in his eye. I glanced at him, at the pumpkin, at him again.

Beautiful are you; Beast am I.

I recalled what Pepe had said about how Starla's secret admirer might not be a literal beast. Only someone who considered himself unworthy.

I swallowed hard, afraid to meet Vince's eyes. Afraid to know the truth.

He was a Seeker. A desperate Seeker at that. There were so many reasons why this was wrong. Why it would never work.

My phone buzzed. I pulled it out of my pocket and looked at the screen.

STARLA: *SO NERVOUS*.

A second later, there was another buzz.

STARLA: *But so EXCITED*.

I bit my lip and glanced at Vince. Met his eyes. Felt a chasm form deep in my heart.

There were so many wrongs to this, yes, but from what I could see in Vince's eyes, there might possibly be one right.

He cared for her.

I could see it in his face. His naked emotion, pleading with me, because he realized I'd figured out his secret.

I stood there for a long second, unsure what to do. I wanted to protect my friend, but I wanted her to be happy as well.

Finally, I took a deep breath, gave Vince a half smile, and walked away.

I texted Starla as I walked to the bookshop.

ME: *Stop worrying. I'm sure it'll be fine.*

Fine, fine, fine.

And as I pulled open the door to Harper's store, I wished with all my might that I was right.

Chapter Twenty-eight

Harper drummed her fingers on the edge of her cushy chair.

The caffeine had not yet worn off.

"So, if Harriette is being framed, then this isn't like *Murder on the Orient Express* at all."

There were a few customers in the bookstore, browsing. Angela Curtis, Harper's part-time employee, was back at work, and she said that Harmony was back to relocating articles, bandage and all. Michael's medical records had fortunately come back all clear.

I glanced over at the children's nook, and realized how much I missed Mimi on days I didn't see her. Which, luckily, wasn't often.

I carefully blew into my coffee mug and thought about the little dark-haired boy I'd seen sitting there yesterday. Ophelia's son. I wondered how he was doing today. How deep did emotional scars go? Did the person who attacked Ophelia even stop to think about what the repercussions of witnessing such a crime would do to Jacob?

Of course not. The person committing these crimes was obviously a sociopath. No remorse. No concern.

I sighed as Harper continued to babble on.

"Hmm," she said. "Maybe this is more like *And Then There Were None*."

"How so?" I asked, more to keep her talking than anything. Honestly, I was a little tired and didn't want to hold up my end of the conversation.

Undoubtedly, I would not win the Sister of the Year award.

"Do you remember the story?" she asked, her eyes alight with enthusiasm and the remnants of twelve cups of coffee.

"Vaguely."

"Well, there was this island, right?"

I nodded, trying not to smile.

"And all these criminals that were never convicted of their crimes, for one reason or another."

"Are you saying Michael and the Wickeds are criminals?" I couldn't help but ask.

"Hush," she said. "So, they're all sent this mysterious invitation to the island. There might be money involved in luring them—I can't quite remember. Anyway, there are ten of them. And one by one each of them dies."

"Mmm-hmm," I said.

"But there are only ten on the island, right? So who killed all of them?"

The story was vaguely coming back to me. "One of them wasn't really dead, right?"

She snapped her fingers. "Right. He killed everyone; then he died of some terminal illness in the end."

Maybe it was because I'd had a long day, but I wasn't getting the connection to Michael and the Wickeds. "Maybe this case has nothing to do with an Agatha Christie book at all."

She frowned. "Don't you see that it possibly has *everything* to do with this story?"

"Not rea—" I was cut off by a loud bleating sound. It startled me so much, I spilled coffee on my pants.

Harper nearly fell out of her chair. She looked all around. "What is that sound?"

I quickly set my mug on the table and pulled Harriette's phone from my pocket. I figured out how to silence it and jumped up. "The bait has been taken."

Whump-whump-whump.

Harper glanced around, feeling the disturbance in her force. She wasn't distracted long—she grabbed the phone out of my hand. "How does the GPS thing work?"

I grabbed it back. "Look at the map. See the blip? The bush must be in a car—it's moving at a good clip."

"What do we do?" Harper asked, jiggling foot to foot. "We need a car. We have to give chase. Can I drive? Which way is it going?"

"First, you really need to switch to decaf, and second, this isn't *The Italian Job.* Besides, you need to stay here."

"What? Says who? I'm the boss. I can do what I want."

"Says me. It's too dangerous."

"But not for you?"

"For me, too, but I'll be careful. However, if you're with me, then I can't be careful about me if I'm too busy worrying about how careful you're being."

She lifted an eyebrow. "Huh. I can't believe that made sense to me."

"You need to stay here." The phone blipped.

Harper leaned over my shoulder for the update. The car had turned onto the village square.

We ran to the front window and looked left. Nothing. Not a darn thing. No car in sight.

The phone blipped again. We looked at the map. The car had stopped.

"Where is that?" Harper asked.

The car was in the service alley behind several shops. Lotions and Potions, the Trimmed Wick, Bewitching Boutique, the Black Thorn florist.

My heart thumped against my ribs. The Black Thorn. It had to be.

Harper had put it together, too. "Looks like I might have been wrong about the *And Then There Were None* theory, and you were right about Lydia."

"Or Willard," I added.

"Or both," she said.

I shuddered, not sure what to do.

"Go, go!" Harper said, pushing me out the door. "Stay hidden, keep low, get a visual. Do not make contact. I'll call the police. Go!"

"Decaf!" I shouted as I stumbled onto the sidewalk.

I smiled at a couple walking by, trying to pass myself off as a sane person. It was a tough sell if judged by the way they kept a wide berth.

My heart hammered as I headed down the sidewalk. I took a sharp left down the wide passage between buildings. When I reached the service alley, I pressed my back to the wall of Lotions and Potions and peeked around the corner, making a quick assessment.

Several Dumpsters stood near a tall fence separating the alley from the neighborhood homes on the other side. A silver sedan was parked at the far end of the alley. I saw Willard exit the back of the Black Thorn and walk over to the car. He took something out of the backseat and carried it into the shop.

I glanced at the phone for an update, but it didn't beep. The black rosebush was apparently still in the car.

Quickly, I darted across the alleyway and hid behind a Dumpster. I followed the fence line, keeping low.

Whump-whump-whump.

"See what happens when you hang around with me?

It's a glamorous life, being up close and personal to dirt and trash," I said to him. "Next time you might want to imprint on someone else."

He flashed twice. *No.*

"Aww," I whispered. And suddenly, I teared up. Right there in the alley, behind the Dumpsters, and it wasn't from the horrible sour smell. Suddenly, I realized I was going to miss Michael when he finally moved on.

Letting out a breath, I sat on my haunches. Tried to catch my breath. Control the tears. Keep in check the grief that I'd been holding in since seeing a bloody sock on a path two nights ago.

I felt a hot nudge on my arm.

"I'm okay," I said, trying to keep it together.

No.

"Are you calling me a liar?" I teased.

Yes.

"I just . . . I just realized that I've kind of grown used to your being with me, that's all. And that when you're gone . . . you're really gone. No more seeing you at the bakery. No more extra cake pops. No more big smile." My eyes stung and welled with tears. "I'm . . . sad."

Yes.

"You, too?" I asked.

Yes.

"You'll be happier when you move on," I said. "And when you're not hanging around with me."

He didn't answer.

"You will," I reassured him. I flicked a pebble. "Are you scared?"

Yes.

"Do you think you'll become a familiar?"

He didn't answer.

I translated his lack of response as uncertainty. "I wish I could give you a hug."

Suddenly, I felt warmth drape over the back of my neck and felt a tug. After a minute, he let go.

I supposed it was time I did, too.

"Thank you," I said softly. I sniffled and pulled myself together. "Are you ready to find out who did this to you?"

Yes.

"Okay, then. Try to stay quiet, will you?" I said with a sad smile as I crept along the fence line. "You're so darn loud. Sheesh."

He gave me a playful push.

I didn't even mind.

I let out a deep breath and dashed to the next Dumpster, ducking behind it. As I neared the back door to the Black Thorn, I watched as Willard once again came outside, went to the backseat of the car, and carried something back into the shop.

"I can't see what he's carrying. Can you?" I whispered. Amy's invisibility cloak would be really handy right now.

No.

"I'm going closer."

No.

"I have to."

I didn't wait for him to argue. I duck-walked as quickly as my thighs could tolerate to the side of the car. I pressed my back against the passenger door panel and slowly rose up. I whipped around to peek into the car.

There was nothing amiss in the front seats—no black rosebush buckled in place or anything that incriminating. Except . . . I squinted. Something was sticking out from beneath the front seat. I threw a glance at the back door of the shop. It was closed.

My heart beat in my throat as I lifted the door handle. I felt it give and let out a breath of relief. I gently eased it open—just far enough for me to reach a hand inside.

Whump-whump-whump.

I was already nervous enough without his anxiety added in. I finally grasped what I'd been looking for and pulled it out. I carefully closed the car door, so the map light would go out. Then I stared at what was in my hand, and my adrenaline kicked up a notch.

It was a fake beard, the kind Santa might wear. Or a homicidal wizard. I realized I was holding a big clue—evidence that Willard had been the wizard who shot Bertie and tried to kill Ophelia.

I heard the door to the shop swing open, and I froze, barely daring to breathe. He still had a gun. He hadn't thought twice about shooting Bertie, and if he found me here, he wouldn't think twice about shooting me. Especially not after this morning, when I seemed to get on his last nerve.

The driver's side back door of the car opened, and I could hear Willard grunt. The door then slammed shut, and I heard footsteps shuffle away.

I let out a breath. I tucked the fake beard into my shirt and lifted myself up again to peer in the backseat. What I saw threw me for a loop.

Roses. Dozens of them. A few lilies, too, but not many. My mind spun.

It was still spinning when the back door of the shop opened and Willard came back out. He stopped short, taking in my deer-in-the-headlights expression. "Darcy?" he said.

I slowly stood, felt my knees wobble, and leaned on the car. "Hi," I said.

"What are you doing here? Explain yourself right this instant."

Chapter Twenty-nine

What *was* I doing here? I was freaking out, that was what. "I—uh . . ."

I could barely focus. My mind churned.

I thought about what Harper had said earlier: *Maybe this is more like* And Then There Were None.

She'd been right. She'd been so right. Because all I kept hearing in my head, as if it were stuck on repeat, was a snippet of conversation from earlier today.

I'll bring some of Bertie's lilies by your shop later on my way home. Maybe by then Harriette will come to her senses, and I'll bring roses, too.

Surely Harper would gloat when she found out.

"This isn't your car, is it?" I said to Willard.

"No." He gave me an odd look. "Are you feeling well?"

"Pop the trunk."

"Pardon?" he said.

"Quick! Pop open the trunk."

He hesitated.

"Do it!" I said in a harsh whisper.

My tone snapped him into action. He pulled open the

driver's door and released the latch for the trunk. He met me there as I lifted it up.

In the trunk, nestled in a box, was a black rosebush.

Willard gasped. "Is that . . ."

"Yes," I said. "It is."

I pulled out my phone and dialed 9-1-1. I'd just pushed the last digit when the back door of the shop opened. Imogene came strolling out, chatting with Lydia. I quickly slipped my phone back into my pocket, leaving it on.

Both women stopped short when they saw us.

"Darcy!" Lydia said. "I didn't know you were here."

I swallowed hard. "I'm, ah, surprised to see you as well. I thought you'd be at the hospital."

Lydia tipped her head. "Hospital? Why?"

"You don't know?" I said.

"Know what?"

"Your mother had a heart attack about two hours ago. She's in surgery right now."

Lydia's eyes nearly popped out of her head. "What? You're joking. Clearly, you're joking."

"No one called you?" I asked. "Imogene rode with her to the hospital. . . ."

Lydia's gaze snapped to Imogene. "I don't have my cell phone with me, and the shop's phone goes to voice mail when we're not open. . . . Is it true, Imogene?"

"Yes," she said drolly.

"Oh my God!" Lydia cried. "We have to go. Is she okay? Willard! Come on. Imogene, will you drive us?"

Imogene narrowed her eyes on me. "You couldn't leave well enough alone."

Lydia looked among the three of us. "What is going on? We need to get to the hospital."

Willard reached into the trunk, pulled out the Witching Hour rose, and set the pot on the roof of the car. "What's this doing in your trunk, Imogene?"

Imogene glared. In a quick movement, she pulled a small gun from her coat pocket and waved it at the three of us. "No one's going anywhere but back inside. Come on, all of you. I have to figure out what to do with you."

Whump-whump-whump.

"Now!" she demanded as she grabbed the rosebush and tucked it into the crook of her arm.

I followed Willard, who grabbed hold of Lydia on our way in. Imogene followed behind us, and she kept jabbing the gun into my back.

Whump-whump-whump-whump.

The back hallway led into a large workroom. A wide table took up most of the space, and on it were a couple of dozen roses that Willard had already brought inside.

Imogene set the black rose on the tabletop. "First," she said, "give me your cell phones."

Lydia said, "Mine's at home. I don't usually carry it with me on Sundays."

Willard said, "I don't own one."

Imogene looked at me. I pulled a phone from my pocket and handed it over. Imogene dropped it on the floor and smashed it with her Birkenstock sneaker.

Harriette probably wouldn't appreciate the loss of her BlackBerry.

But I was quite happy my own phone was still in my pocket, dialed into the police.

"What's in your other pocket, Darcy?"

Crap. I pulled out my cell and handed it over. She stomped on that one, too. There went my link to the police, but I hoped between Harper's and my calls that the police were on their way.

Imogene paced back and forth, as the three of us huddled together against the worktable. Behind her was a wall filled with colorful ribbons. The picture it created didn't jibe in my mind; the happy colors didn't fit the mood.

I had to say something, do something. Buy us some time. "You should go, Imogene. Hop in your car and drive. By the time we call the police, you'll be long gone."

"I'll say, since you'll all be dead," she snapped.

"Oh," Willard moaned. He swayed, his eyes rolled into the back of his head, and he fainted dead away.

"Why am I not surprised?" Imogene murmured.

Lydia dropped down to slap Willard's cheeks. "Will! Honey!"

"Leave him," Imogene snapped. "Stand up."

Willard lay in an unprissy heap on the floor. He would have been so embarrassed if he could have seen himself.

Lydia stood back up. "Imogene? It was you? You killed Michael? Attacked Bertie and Ophelia?"

"Oh, shut up, Lydia. I'm so sick of you."

It looked like Imogene was getting an itchy finger. I tried to distract her. "If Harriette's in the hospital, who are you going to blame for our murders?" I asked. *Keep her talking; keep her mind occupied....*

"Oh, it'll be easy enough to blame either Lydia or Willard," Imogene said. "One of them snapped over the stress of Harriette's being charged with murder and commits a double murder and a suicide. Sorry, Darcy, but your death will be explained as being an unfortunate case of wrong place, wrong time."

Huh. She didn't seem the least bit contrite to me.

Whump-whump-whump.

"Why?" Lydia pleaded.

"Shut. Up," Imogene said.

"Really, Imogene," I said, pushing my luck. "You could at least give an explanation."

She aimed the gun at me. "Well, you seem to have it all figured out. Why don't you tell us?"

I had enough of a theory to bluff my way through it. "Fine," I said. *Keep talking. Buy time.* "Long story long,

Imogene wanted the Witching Hour spell. Maybe she wanted to make millions—"

Redness bloomed on Imogene's neck and cheeks as she cut me off. "I don't need millions. I have millions."

"Then why?" Lydia cried. Tears streamed down her cheeks.

Imogene welled up as well, and I realized her motive might run a lot deeper than money.

"Harriette had you!" she shouted. "And Trista. Bertie had her son. Ophelia has Jacob. All I have is my damn orchids! If I could have created a black orchid, it could have been *my* legacy."

I recalled what she'd said about her regret at never having kids. I hadn't suspected it wasn't just regret but a . . . wound.

"But no, Harriette wouldn't share the damn spell," Imogene seethed. "I was so angry. Who does she think she is, anyway? Miss High-and-Mighty Floracrafter. I can see her keeping it from Bertie and Ophelia, but me? I'm a Floracrafter, too. She should have shared without a second thought."

Putting the pieces together, I said to Lydia, "Imogene started stealing roses to try and extract the DNA from the plant, see if she could replicate the spell somehow. But nothing worked, did it, Imogene?"

"Damn things kept dying."

"What Imogene didn't realize then was that it wasn't Harriette's spell to share," I said to Lydia as if we were having a regular old conversation. "Harriette didn't even know the spell."

"What do you mean?" Lydia sniffled. "Of course it was Mother's spell."

"No," I said softly. "It was Michael Healey's spell. Something Imogene found out on Friday after she overheard a conversation your mother had with Fisk."

More tears flowed down Lydia's face. "That can't possibly be true."

"It is," I said simply.

"Imagine my surprise," Imogene said, "when I came across them whispering in the woods behind the greenhouses. Ironically, I'd just stolen two of the plants from Harriette's greenhouse when I heard Fisk telling Harriette that Michael refused to come back to cast a renewal spell on the Witching Hour roses. I realized then that it was Michael's spell."

"And that was when she decided to get the spell from him." A lump formed in my throat. "And when he told it to her, to spare his life, she killed him anyway."

Whump-whump-whump.

"And his death wasn't spur of the moment, a snap decision after hearing the conversation," I said. "It had been planned, quickly planned, yes, but still. Somewhere in Imogene's twisted mind, she decided that she wanted revenge on the Wickeds. Mostly on Harriette. She plotted Michael's murder to look like all the Wickeds might have had a hand in it, but the one person she really wanted to frame was Harriette."

Imogene shrugged. "I don't have much faith in the ability of the police department."

"Meanwhile," I said, "in order to carry out her plan to frame Harriette, Imogene poisoned herself yesterday at the festival. Just enough to cause discomfort but not really harm her. A diversionary tactic to throw suspicion off herself." Just like Aunt Ve had done with Tilda, and how the killer in *And Then There Were None* had gotten away with it. "Then last night, dressed as a wizard, she followed Bertie and Ophelia into the haunted house at the festival."

"You tried to kill them!" Lydia cried. "How could you?"

"Easily. I hate them. I hate Harriette. I hate you. I hate him," she said, pointing the gun at Willard. "None of you ever appreciated the important things in life. Bertie fights with Ophelia. Harriette hasn't spoken to Trista in years and treats you like a servant. They don't deserve the things they have. Not to mention that I should be the one in control of the Elysian Fields. But Harriette, she was so *selfish*. It was always her way or no way. And we were supposed to be grateful for what little she gave us. Ophelia and Bertie were always kissing up, and then recently, Harriette started showing a softer side to them. Sharing more with them. Giving more. It made me sick. You all make me sick!"

I rolled my eyes and went fishing to figure out how much Imogene knew about the spell. "And the sad fact is that Imogene killed Michael for nothing. Because his spell won't work for anyone other than himself. I'm sure she's had no luck with it at all. Have you, Imogene?"

Fury tightened the lines of her face. "I will figure it out, unlock the spell's secrets. I am, and always have been, a superior Floracrafter. I plan to take this last plant and dissect it top to bottom. It's just a matter of time before I have the ability to turn my orchids black."

Hope bubbled that she had no clue how the spell actually worked. She couldn't possibly know about the new moon angle . . . especially if she still thought she could get clues from the plant itself. Now I just needed to figure out if she knew Michael had been an Illumicrafter—and how that played into the spell. "No, you won't. The spell is ineffective now that Michael is dead. It's why all the black roses died when he did, including the ones you stole."

Whump-whump-whump-whump.

Surprise filled her eyes; then she narrowed them in suspicion. "Then why is there still one black rosebush alive?"

I let out the breath I was holding. She had no clue about Michael's glow being a key to the spell. She was so wrapped up in her sense of superiority that she didn't believe another Craft could have anything to do with how the spell worked.

Behind her, on the worktable, I saw a flash of movement. A long tail.

Reinforcements, I realized.

I almost let out a cry of relief when I saw Pepe peek out from behind a roll of floral tape. He made a circle motion above his head and pointed outside. Then, using two fingers, he made a walking motion. And then he made the universal charade for a gun.

I was apparently fluent in mouse sign language. The police were outside, surrounding the building, guns drawn.

I'd never been more grateful in all my life.

I bluffed. "It's a fake. It's dyed. It was planted in the greenhouse by the police to see if the killer would try to steal it. And . . . you did. It has a tracking device in it. The police are probably outside right now."

She swung the gun in my direction. "You're lying."

"Check for yourself."

Carefully, she removed the rosebush from its pot and slowly lifted out the GPS tracker. Her eyes were wide as she studied it.

At that moment, someone shouted, "Police! Come out with your hands up."

I thought it might have been Nick, but I wasn't sure. "Told you so."

Lydia whimpered in relief.

Hatred filled Imogene's eyes. Her arm came up and leveled the gun on me. And as if in slow motion, I saw her finger pull the trigger of the gun.

A blast of heat enveloped me, and it felt as though I had plunged into quicksand. I couldn't move; I couldn't breathe. I saw the bullet meant for me suddenly stop moving forward. It was suspended in midair. Hanging, motionless.

It, too, had been mired.

But it wasn't quicksand.

It was *Michael*.

Imogene's mouth dropped open. I was burning up as I watched Pepe launch himself at her, digging his teeth into her rear end. It would have been funny if I could laugh. If I could take a breath. Spots swam before my eyes at the loss of oxygen.

Imogene screamed and wiggled, trying to shake Pepe loose, and Lydia dove for the gun, wresting it out of Imogene's hands. The gun went off in the struggle, and Imogene slumped to the ground. Blood spread from a wound in her chest. Suddenly, the room flooded with police officers, who quickly took control.

And just as abruptly, the morass I was stuck in released me. I fell to the floor, gasping for breath. My chest heaved. I felt as if I had a third-degree sunburn.

Nick dropped down next to me and cupped my face, then pulled his hands back and stared at them. He leaned close, panic flaring in his eyes, desperation in the gold flecks. "You're burning."

But I wasn't. Not anymore.

"Michael," I whispered, partly wanting to explain, partly calling to him. "He saved me."

I tried so hard to feel the *whump*ing. I was desperate to feel his presence.

To thank him.

But he was already gone.

Chapter Thirty

It had been a terribly long week since Imogene had died from what was determined to be a self-inflicted gun-shot wound inside the Black Thorn. These past seven days had been filled with more downs than ups, but to-night . . . Tonight I was going to try and put it all behind me and enjoy myself. Indian summer was here, it was a beautiful night, warm and breezy. Stars twinkled, but there was no moon visible. It was a new moon.

"You have that look again," Nick said, putting his arm around me.

The Ghoulousel's perky music filled the air, and the line for the ride stretched all the way to the Scarish Wheel. It was Halloween, and the last night of the festival. Almost every little kid was wearing a costume.

Two of the riders on the carousel had their heads thrown back in laughter. Starla and Vince. I watched them carefully and tried to feel happy for my friend. I wasn't there yet. I was still too leery of Vince. But he was definitely growing on me.

I breathed in, trying to ease the anxiety that had been

threatening to swallow me whole for a week now. It was time to let it go. It was time to look ahead.

"Just thinking about stuff," I said.

Nick and I were in line for the caramel apple booth. Finally.

"I know," he said softly, pressing his lips to my temple.

I was glad he didn't say that time would make me feel better. He just let me *feel*. And he let me lean on him. Which meant more to me than I could ever say.

Michael had been buried on Tuesday. I spent the whole day crying, and even now I couldn't think of that day without welling up. It had been a painful, yet beautiful good-bye.

On Wednesday, Nick agreed to let Mimi go to lunch with Glinda so Mimi could hear stories of her mom. On the surface, it seemed like a really sweet gesture, but I couldn't help but feel that Glinda, under the facade, was using Mimi—and using Melina—to get to Nick.

"Will you walk into my parlor?" said the spider to the fly.

Glinda was playing some sort of game with Nick, I was sure of it. And I didn't like it. What she underestimated was *me*. I was ready to fight for him, so I dared her to bring it on.

On Thursday, Harriette passed away due to complications from her heart surgery.

Her funeral had been yesterday, and every time I thought of it since, my throat swelled and tears flowed. Even now. I blinked them away and tried to focus on the good.

The good of how Trista and her mother had reconciled before she died. Of how Lydia and Trista had put the past behind them and were ready to start fresh. Of how Lydia suggested to Dash that they join forces to create a new family-based flower business. One they created together, bringing Floras and Terras to work together. Bertie and Ophelia would keep their greenhouses, and Dash and Fisk would take over Imogene's. And of how Fisk had given the most eloquent eulogy for his grandmother. Of how Fisk had been strong for Amy early in the week, then how she had been strong for him yesterday. If they could make it through this, then I believed they could get through anything, no matter how young they were. Of Lewis, who weathered the turbulent emotions of the day to say good-bye to his beloved. He'd been devastated.

I'd debated all week whether to share with Amy the Witching Hour spell. Time was of the essence, especially with the new moon tonight. In the end, I finally decided that the Elder wouldn't have shared the spell with me unless she had wanted me to pass it on.

> *A stem blooms devoid of light,*
> *At the darkest time of night,*
> *When the clock strikes the midnight hour,*
> *There revealed is the Witching flower.*

What Amy did with the spell was her choice, and when I left her last night, she still hadn't decided. Although she recognized and admired Michael's ingenuity in creating the spell, she had also seen the dangers associated with it. A job at the new Elysian Fields with Dash and Fisk using her inherent Illumicrafter skills was always an option, but she wouldn't need the job for the money.

Before she died, Harriette had gone ahead and changed her will. It now included not only Fisk, but also Amy, who now had the funds to keep her apartment (which she planned to do) and continue her schooling. As far as anyone else knew, the spell had died with Michael. The flowers Michael had resurrected—that were now housed in Dash's greenhouse—would soon start to wilt unless Amy kept them alive using a renewal spell. My guess was that she would do that, because by keeping those plants alive, a little bit of Michael stayed alive, too.

I looked across the green, to a spot where Mimi stood next to Glinda as they played a squirt gun game that sent witches on brooms rising on a stream of water. I felt a tug of jealousy at the way Mimi laughed so easily with her new friend. Missy sat at their feet, watching them closely.

Nick and I still hadn't resolved our problem about sharing information on cases, but with Michael's murder behind us, it was easier to simply let the issue go. I had no plans to get wrapped up in another murder case ever again.

"Pepe showed me the honorary badge you gave him," I said. "He's quite proud."

"I should really give him a position on the force."

"He'd love to make himself a uniform," I joked, "but Godfrey might get jealous."

Nick laughed. "I can see that fight now."

Pepe and his butt biting had become something of a legend in only a week's time. Outwardly, he pretended to be embarrassed by the fuss, but I knew he secretly loved the attention.

Nick nudged me playfully. "Maybe Mimi was right, and I should hire you, too."

"How much do you pay?" I asked with a teasing lilt.

"It's a very good wage, plus there are fringe benefits."

"Such as?"

He leaned in and kissed me. Full on the mouth, right there in front of all the kids—and Starla and Vince—on the Ghoulousel. "All the caramel apples you want."

"Well," I said, "that's an offer I can't refuse, but at this point, I'll take just *one* caramel apple."

The line had barely budged.

"We're getting there," he said. "Patience."

Frankly, I thought I'd been patient enough. We were talking caramel. Caramel!

"What do you think of those terms?" he asked.

He had a joking tone to his voice, but I heard a note of seriousness, too. He was fishing to see if I was really interested in a job. I had to squash that notion fast.

"Hmm," I said. "For some reason I think I can get the fringe benefits without having to work with Glinda."

Was she a nice but complex person? Or was she manipulative and conniving?

Not knowing made me nervous.

Ve and Terry walked by, holding hands, and I laughed at the reactions from other people, congratulating Terry on his Elvis "costume." This was probably the one night a year that he could get away with walking around without a disguise. He posed for pictures and signed autographs as well.

Talk about eccentric.

Ve's heartbreak over Hot Rod hadn't lasted long, and she'd picked up her relationship with Terry where she'd left it off—deciding that a bird in the hand was better than nothing. He, of course, had taken her back without a second thought. Tilda, however, was still giving Ve the cold shoulder.

I smiled, thinking about Tilda. This morning, Lew and I had worked out a visitation agreement regarding the fussy feline. I thought that especially now he needed Tilda's happy energy around him, and he'd had tears of gratitude in his eyes when I left her there to spend the day with him. From here on out, it would be a regular occurrence—she would spend every other weekend with him.

I'd yet to break the news to Ve.

The line advanced, and finally—*finally!*—we reached the counter. Nick bought me the biggest apple there.

Was there a more perfect food on earth than caramel? I didn't think so. The apple was merely a vessel in which to transport the sweetness to my mouth. In heaven, I smiled.

Nick gazed at me. "I've missed that."

"What, me a sticky mess?" Sadly, it was a common occurrence, too.

"Your smile."

I nudged him with my elbow. "Tell me, Nick Sawyer, how do you feel about Ferris wheels?"

"Depends on who I'm riding with."

"Well," I said, "I have a proposition for you. A ride with me, and maybe, if we're lucky we'll get stopped at the top."

"Luck? There's no luck about it. I've already paid off the operator. He's been waiting for us for half an hour now."

"I knew there was a reason I liked you so much," I said.

"And here I thought you were just using me for my body." He laughed, pulling me as close to him as he possibly could.

As we walked toward the ride hip to hip, I took another deep breath, and I smiled wide. It was there. I could smell it.

The scent of magic was back in the air.

And suddenly, a weight lifted from my chest, and I knew everything was going to be fine.

Fine, fine, fine.

Epilogue

A few nights later, Melina Sawyer was not as sure things were going to be fine.

First off, she was becoming altogether too comfortable living as a dog. Heaven help her, ear rubs made her the happiest familiar around, and doggy treats made her jump for joy. On top of that, there were some days she forgot her real name was Melina and not Missy.

Secondly, she wasn't thrilled about the recent rift between Darcy and Nick. Her plan was for them to live happily ever after. She couldn't let them mess it up with squabbles over police cases.

The back door opened, and Ve stepped out. Moonlight fell across her face as she sat next to Mel on the porch step.

"You've been sitting out here a long time," Ve said.

To an ordinary observer, the scene would simply look like a woman talking to her pet. What was unusual about this conversation was that the pet could talk back.

"Just thinking," Mel said.

"About Nick and Darcy?"

Ve knew her well.

Mel said, "On one hand I'm happy for Nick. On the

other . . . it is bittersweet seeing him fall in love with another woman."

"It's what you wanted, no?" Ve asked. "And Darcy is wonderful with Mimi. . . ."

"I know," Mel said. The picture Darcy had drawn of her had melted her heart and at the same time cemented that she'd made the right decision to play matchmaker between Nick and Darcy. "It's just . . . hard." Much harder than she ever dreamed when she asked the Elder to be put into this form.

Ve stretched her legs. "I can only imagine. Do you think it might be time to let Darcy in on your secret? She already suspects there's a familiar in the house."

A familiar, yes, but she probably had no idea it was her boyfriend's former wife. That was bound to come as quite a shock.

"Not yet," Mel said. "Losing my anonymity means losing my ability to keep tabs on people without their realizing it."

Wise Ve knew right away whom she referred to. "Ah. Glinda."

The situation with Nick and Darcy was difficult to observe, yes, but what bothered her most was this new development with Glinda. Mel wanted to believe that her old friend's kindness toward Mimi was genuine, but she just . . . didn't.

"There's trouble in the air," Mel said.

"Bad juju, as Darcy and Harper would say. I feel it, too. You think it involves Glinda?"

"I'm not sure. I need to keep a close eye on the situation."

She wanted to believe with all her heart that things were going to be fine.

But she didn't.

Not at all.

Read on for a sneak peek at the first book in
Heather Blake's new Magic Potion series,

A Potion to Die For

Coming in November from Obsidian

If there were a Wanted poster for witches, I was sure my freckled face would be on it.

Ducking behind a tree to catch my breath, I sucked in a deep lungful of humid air as I listened to the cries of the search party.

I didn't have much time before the frenzied mob turned the corner and spotted me, but I needed to take a rest or risk keeling over in the street.

It was times like these that I wished I was the kind of witch who had a broomstick. Then I could just fly off, safe and sound, and wouldn't be hiding behind a live oak, my hair sticking to its bark while my lungs were on fire.

But *noooo*. I had to be a healing witch from a long line of hoodoo practitioners (and one rogue voodoo-er, but no need to go into that this very moment). I was a love potion expert, matchmaker, all-around relationship guru, and an unlikely medicine woman.

Fat lot of good all that did me right now.

In fact, my magic potions were why I was in this predicament in the first place.

I'd bet my life savings (which, admittedly, weren't

much) that my archnemesis, Delia Bell Barrows, had a broomstick. And though I had never before been envious of the black witch, I was feeling a stab of jealousy now.

Quickly glancing around, I suddenly hoped Delia lurked somewhere nearby—something she had been doing a lot of lately. I'd been trying my best to avoid a confrontation with her, but if she had a broomstick handy—and was willing to loan it to me—I would be more than willing to talk.

There were some things worth compromising principles for, obviously. Like a rabid mob.

But the brick-paved road, lined on both sides with tall shade trees, was deserted. If Delia was around, she had a good hiding spot. Smart, because there was a witch hunt going on in the streets of Hitching Post, Alabama.

And I, Carly Hartwell, was the hunted witch.

Again.

This really had to stop.

Pushing off from the tree, I spared a glance behind me before running at a dead sprint through the center of town toward my shop, Potion Potables, with the mob hot on my heels. The storefront was painted a dark purple with lavender trim, and the name of the shop was written in bold curlicue letters on the large picture window. Underneath was the shop's tagline: MIND, BODY, HEART, AND SOUL. Behind the glass, several vignettes featuring antique glass jars, mortar and pestles, apothecary scales and weights I'd collected over the years filled the big display space.

At this point I should have felt nothing but utter relief. I was almost there. So . . . close.

But instead of relief, a new panic arose.

Because standing in front of my door was none other than Delia.

I could hardly believe it. *Now* she shows up.

I grabbed the store key and held it at the ready. "Out of the way, Delia!"

Delia stood firm, neck to toe in black—from her cape to her toenails, which stuck out from a pair of black patent flip-flops that had a skull-and-crossbones decoration. A little black dog, tucked into a basket like Toto, barked.

The dog was new. The cape, all the black, and the skull-and-crossbones fascination was not.

"I need to talk to you, Carly," Delia said. "Right now."

I hip checked Delia out of the way, and the dog yapped. Sticking the key into the lock, I said, "You're going to have to wait. Like everyone else." I threw a nod over my shoulder.

The crowd, at least forty strong, bore down.

Delia let out a gasp. "Did Mr. Dunwoody give a forecast this morning?"

"Yes." The lock tumbled, and I pushed open the door and scooted inside. Much to my dismay, Delia snuck in behind me.

I had two options: to kick the black witch out—which would then let the crowd in . . . or keep Delia in—and the crowd out.

Delia won.

Slamming the door, I threw the lock.

Just in time. Fists pounded the wood frame and dozens of eyes peered through the window.

I yelled through the leaded glass panel, "I'll be open in half an hour!" but the eager crowd kept banging on the door.

Trying to catch my breath, I walked over to the cash register counter, an old twelve-drawer chestnut filing cabinet. I opened one of the drawers and grabbed a small roll of numbered paper tickets. Walking back to the door, I shoved them through the wide mail slot.

"Take numbers," I shouted at the eager faces. "You know the drill!"

Because, unfortunately, this wasn't the first time this had happened.

Turning my back to the crowd, I leaned against the door, and then slid down its frame to the floor. For a second I rested against the wood, breathing in the comforting scents of my shop. The lavender, lemon balm, mint. The hint of peach leaf, sage, cinnamon. All brought back memories of my grandma Adelaide Hartwell, who'd opened the shop more than fifty years before.

"You should probably exercise more," Delia said. Her little dog barked.

My chest felt so tight I thought any minute it might explode. "I think I just ran a 5K. Second time this month."

"What exactly did Mr. Dunwoody's forecast say?"

"Sunny with a chance of divorce."

Delia peeked out the window. "That explains why there are so many of them. I wonder whose marriage is on the chopping block."

The matrimonial predictions of Mr. Dunwoody, my septuagenarian neighbor, were never wrong. His occasional "forecasts" foretold of residential current affairs, so to speak. On a beautiful spring Friday in Hitching Post, the wedding capital of the South, one might think a wedding ceremony—or a few dozen—was on tap. But it had been known, a time or two, for a couple to have a sudden change of heart over their recent nuptials (usually after the alcohol wore off the next morning) and set out to get the marriage immediately annulled or file for a quickie, uncontested divorce.

And even though Mr. Dunwoody was never wrong, I often wished he'd keep his forecasts to himself.

Being the owner of Potion Potables, a shop that specialized in love potions, was a bit like being a mystical bartender. People talked to me. A lot. About everything. Especially about falling in love and getting married, which was the height of irony considering everyone on my mother's side of the family were confirmed matrimonial cynics. Luckily, the hopeless romanticism on my father's side balanced things out for me. Mostly.

Somehow over the years I had become the town's unofficial relationship expert. It was at times rewarding . . . and a bit exasperating. The weight of responsibility was overwhelming, and I didn't always have the answers, magic potions or not.

Because Southerners embraced crazy like a warm blanket on a chilly night, not many here cared much that I called myself a witch, or that I practiced magic using a touch of hoodoo. But the town thought I did have all the answers—and expected me to find solutions.

My customers cared only about whether I could make their lives better. Be it an upset stomach or a relationship falling apart, they wanted healing.

And when there was a divorce forecast, they were relentless until I made them a love potion ensuring their marriage would be secure. I had a lot of work to get done. Work I'd rather not have done with Delia around.

"Why are you here?" I asked her.

"I had a dream," Delia said, fussing with her dog's basket.

"A Martin Luther King, Jr., kind? Or an REM-drool-on-the-pillow kind?" I asked, looking up at her.

"REM. But I don't drool."

"Noted," I said, but I didn't believe it for a minute. I shifted on the floor—my rear was going numb. "What was it about? The dream."

Delia said, "You."

"Me? Why?"

Delia closed her eyes and shook her head. After a dramatic pause, she looked at me straight on. "Don't ask me. It's not like I have any control over what I dream. Trust me. Otherwise, I'd be dreaming of David Beckham, not you."

I could understand that. "Why are you telling me this?"

We weren't exactly on friendly terms.

Delia bit her thumbnail. All of her black-painted nails had been nibbled to the quick. "I don't like you. I've never liked you, and I daresay the feeling is mutual."

I didn't feel the need to agree aloud. I had *some* manners after all. "But?" I knew there was one coming.

"I felt I had to warn you. Because even though I don't like you, I don't particularly want to see anything bad happen to you."

Now I was really worried. "Warn me about what?"

Caution filled Delia's ice blue eyes. "You're in danger."

Danger of losing my sanity, maybe. This whole day had been more than a little surreal and it wasn't even nine a.m. I laughed. "You know this from a dream?"

"It's not funny, Carly. At all. I . . . see things in dreams. Things that come true. You're in very real danger."

She said it so calmly, so easily, that I immediately believed her. I'd learned from a very early age not to dismiss things that weren't easily understood or explainable.

"What kind of danger?" I asked. I'd finally caught my breath and needed a glass of water. I hauled myself off the floor and headed for the small break room in the back of the shop. I wasn't the least bit surprised when Delia followed.

"I don't know," she admitted.

I flipped on a light. And froze. Delia bumped into my back.

We stood staring at the sight before us.

Delia said breathlessly, "It might have something to do with him."

"Him" being the dead man lying facedown on the floor, blood dried under his head, his stiff hands clutching a potion bottle.

Also available from

Heather Blake

IT TAKES A WITCH
A Wishcraft Mystery

Darcy Merriweather has just discovered she hails from a long line of Wishcrafters—witches with the power to cast spells by making a wish. She's come to Enchanted Village to learn her trade—but instead finds herself in the middle of a murder investigation...

"Magic and murder...what could be better? It's exactly the book you've been wishing for!"
—National bestselling author Casey Daniels

Available wherever books are sold or at
penguin.com

facebook.com/TheCrimeSceneBooks